"M[...]**dy**
half hanging out of the train car.

He swung himself up, his other sleeve snagging on the ladder. "Get inside before you fall off. I know what I'm doing."

"But you're stuck!"

He ignored his exasperation, only slightly convinced falling out of the train would make the damn woman believe that she was in danger, and climbed the ladder to the top of the car. The trap door he hoped for greeted him and he jimmied open the top, then slid through and into the car.

The face that greeted him was as welcome as it was irate.

"How'd you know to do that?"

"I played a hunch."

"What if you'd been stuck there?"

"I wasn't."

"But what if—"

Max dragged her forward, crushing his mouth to hers. He spread his legs against the swaying of the train and pulled her even closer, flush against his body.

It wasn't the time or the situation for romance, but he'd be damned if he let another moment go without touching her.

* * *

Be sure to check out the next books in the
Dangerous in Dallas series.
Danger and desire fill the hot Texas nights. . .

THE PROFESSIONAL

BY
ADDISON FOX

All rights reserved including the right of reproduction in whole or in part in any form. This edition is published by arrangement with Harlequin Books S.A.

This is a work of fiction. Names, characters, places, locations and incidents are purely fictional and bear no relationship to any real life individuals, living or dead, or to any actual places, business establishments, locations, events or incidents. Any resemblance is entirely coincidental.

This book is sold subject to the condition that it shall not, by way of trade or otherwise, be lent, resold, hired out or otherwise circulated without the prior consent of the publisher in any form of binding or cover other than that in which it is published and without a similar condition including this condition being imposed on the subsequent purchaser.

® and ™ are trademarks owned and used by the trademark owner and/or its licensee. Trademarks marked with ® are registered with the United Kingdom Patent Office and/or the Office for Harmonisation in the Internal Market and in other countries.

Published in Great Britain 2015
by Mills & Boon, an imprint of Harlequin (UK) Limited,
Eton House, 18-24 Paradise Road, Richmond, Surrey, TW9 1SR

© 2015 Frances Karkosak

ISBN: 978-0-263-91801-4

18-1015

Harlequin (UK) Limited's policy is to use papers that are natural, renewable and recyclable products and made from wood grown in sustainable forests. The logging and manufacturing processes conform to the legal environmental regulations of the country of origin.

Printed and bound in Spain
by CPI, Barcelona

Texas transplant **Addison Fox** is a lifelong romance reader, addicted to happy-ever-after. There's nothing she enjoys more than penning novels about two strong-willed, exciting people on that magical fall into love. When she's not writing, she can be found spending time with family and friends, reading or enjoying a glass of wine.

Contact Addison at her website—www.addisonfox.com—or catch up with her on Facebook (addisonfoxauthor) and Twitter (@addisonfox).

For April

Keeper of details, a ready supply of hand sanitizer and cautionary tales about too-warm sushi.

You have a warmth and smile that is infectious and a heart that is unfailingly kind.
I'm so blessed by our friendship.

Chapter 1

Violet Richardson removed herself from striking distance of the bouquet and took her usual spot on the wall. That place—halfway between the kitchen and the entrance—provided a comfortable perch to oversee the lavish ballroom.

It also gave her eyes on anyone coming and going.

In the past, she'd believed it was a necessity to ensure any wedding she coordinated ran well. Not well, she mentally corrected herself. *Perfectly.*

But since the previous week, she'd accepted that having eyes on the ballroom would ensure the threat stalking her and her business partners wouldn't spill over to their wedding clients.

The Kelley-Gardner nuptials had been a long project, full of all the things she loved about her job. A manic mother of the bride, a guest list that could fell a celebrity chef, and a bride and groom who practically glowed with their love for each other.

The wedding had also put Elegance and Lace firmly on the map as one of the city's premier event providers.

She and her partners, Cassidy and Lilah, had worked tirelessly to make their business into one of Dallas's best. Despite the recent rash of danger in their lives, she couldn't hide her satisfaction at what they'd created.

"Lilah's wheeling out the cake and all's on schedule." Gabriella Sanchez took a spot beside her, her unobtrusive black suit doing nothing to hide the saucy curves beneath. Gabby had started out as a caterer they partnered with on events and had quickly become a friend.

The clock that perpetually ticked in Violet's mind counted off the required time to cross the ballroom to the cake and gave Lilah a few extra minutes to fuss. "She's been working on this one for almost a week."

"It's a good thing she started early after—" Gabriella broke off, her soft brown eyes marred with the memories of the prior week. Lilah and her new fiancé, Reed, had faced off with the threat that had stalked their business, only to discover the name that went with the threat was Reed's stepfather, Tripp Lange.

Shaking off the rush of anger and sadness at what her friend had experienced, Violet gripped Gabriella's hand, desperate to hang on to something solid. "She and Reed found each other and Cassidy and Tucker did as well. It *is* a good thing."

Gabby squeezed back before she offered up a small moue of disgust. "As beautiful as this place is, the catering needs a serious overhaul."

Her friend's dig had Violet refocusing on the event. The hotel was doing the formal catering, but they'd brought Gabby along as extra arms and legs. "Please don't tell me you snuck into the kitchen."

"It wasn't sneaking."

Violet ignored the delicate sniff and only pressed harder. "Gab—"

"My cousin's best friend works here, and I wanted to say hi."

Violet knew Gabby was a walking connection to half of Dallas, either as family or as friends of family. But none of it hid the fact that she wanted eyes on the kitchen. Her own catering business had been on the rise, but the competition between the local caterers and the large hotels had gotten fiercer in the last few years.

"They put a swimming pool of sauce on the beef entrées," Gabby hissed. "You know as well as I do there's only one reason a kitchen does that."

"To hide the quality of the meat."

"Exactly!"

"Who made you mad, Sexy Sanchez? I see that lovely Latin temper spiking."

Violet's back went as straight as the surface of Lilah's fondant, as that dark, husky drawl interrupted Gabby's moment of triumph. For a large man, Max Baldwin's ability to materialize out of nowhere was unsettling.

And damned annoying.

"The kitchen's subpar." Violet's voice was as prim as a nun's habit, and she was oddly gratified at the corresponding spike of annoyance in Max's vivid blue gaze.

"Like that's a secret." He pulled Gabby close in a side hug. "Besides, if we're comparing other food to Gabby's, the White House would lose out in a cooking contest."

"Max!" Gabby hugged him back, her natural ease with people evident in the soft lines of her smile. "That's so sweet."

"He's—"

Max interrupted her before Violet could finish the

thought. "And I'm not buttering her up for a week of left-overs after she finishes tomorrow's cooking."

Violet snapped her lips closed as Max guessed her next jab. Over the past few months, Gabby had begun bringing any of her catering leftovers to the businesses around the Design District. She'd claimed it was a loss leader—she was only going to throw the food out anyway—and this gave the local businesses exposure to her work and more opportunities to keep her in mind.

As a business strategist, she was brilliant.

But it was her spirit of generosity that made Gabby truly stand out. Quite unexpectedly, the weekly food offering had begun to make their little neighborhood a community. A small, close-knit group of business owners who looked out for each other and depended on each other.

It had been humbling to realize how much that sense of family mattered.

"I wasn't suggesting you were." Violet cursed herself for the prim attitude—hell, why did she even feel the need to answer?—and avoided looking directly at Max.

"It doesn't change the fact I want in on those leftovers. Especially if you have those little beef Wellington pastries."

"I do, and you're first on my list because of them." Gabby giggled before she patted Max on the arm. "And since I just saw one of the servers attempt to put a few cookies back on a plate that fell on the floor, I'm going to go make a nuisance of myself."

"Where?" Violet's gaze swung in the same direction as Gabby's. "I can do it."

"Nah. I feel the need to whip up a fuss. It'll make me feel better about the beef."

Before Violet could insist, Gabby was off, her long

strides through the ballroom drawing more than a few appreciative stares from the wedding's guests.

"It's a good event. You, Cassidy and Lilah have done an amazing job." That husky voice slid over her like a warm bath.

"Thank you."

"Since it's running smoothly, maybe you can give me more than a cold shoulder."

Violet held the sigh and shifted her stance so she could see Max yet still keep an eye on the ballroom. "I'm just doing my job."

"Reed's on watch over Lilah, and Cassidy and Tucker have the ballroom entrance. You can take a moment and talk to me."

Violet did sigh this time, more for herself than because of his request.

Why was she so prickly around him?

Although she knew she was leery of opening up to others save close friends, she was a fundamentally kind person. And she *liked* other people. Heck, her business was about working with a wide variety of individuals, and she was good at it.

So why did Max Baldwin put her back up?

The man was an annoyance. That was all.

He was too big. Too loud. And far too grumpy for her taste.

He also had broad shoulders that tempted her to touch him whenever he got within fifty feet. Her fingers practically itched every time she took in the sandy-blondish hair that got darker as her gaze followed the short cut to the crown of his head.

Since her gaze did just that, a heated, appreciative rush swamped the pit of her stomach.

Damn hormones.

"I do appreciate you and the guys being here."

"Tucker and I wouldn't miss it, and Reed's still struggling with the news. I think the sense of purpose and activity helps."

Violet nodded, the reality of what Detective Reed Graystone had endured still a raw wound for all of them. Assigned to their case by someone inside the Dallas PD, Reed had only just uncovered that that connection—and corresponding corruption—had its roots in his powerful stepfather, Tripp Lange.

"Lilah's been keeping a close eye. She said he's holding up."

"Graystone's tough. He'll hold up because he has no choice. None of it changes the fact that with what he's exposed, the danger's still out there. Still lurking."

"But Tripp's in jail."

"For how long?" Max turned toward her, his eyes alight with fire and a mix of—concern? anguish?—before he pressed on. "The man's got connections layered beneath connections. You think he's going to sit in a cell for very long?"

"I think this case is too big and too strange not to catch the eye of someone who will ensure it gets solved."

"Then you're more naive than I ever gave you credit for."

Satisfaction filled his chest as the barb struck Violet square in hers. She actually sputtered before she caught herself. "I'm far from naive."

"Then start acting like it. Tripp Lange will be out of jail before any of us can blink. I'm surprised he's still there."

"He's been exposed as a major criminal. He's got to be under tight supervision."

Max fought the urge to gently shake some sense into

her, the concerns he'd harbored since discovering the cache of jewels in the floor of Violet's business only getting stronger and more forceful by the day. Violet was the practical one of the women who ran Elegance and Lace, and even with that pragmatism, she clearly had no idea what they were up against.

"Come on, Max. I'm serious. Lange's in jail and Reed's requested any and all updates on his case. The danger has passed."

Max shrugged, his gaze drifting to where the object of their discussion stood. The good detective hovered over Lilah while his new fiancée hovered over her masterpiece of a wedding cake. "Reed's stepfather has a lot of people in his pocket. People he's paid good money for. What's their incentive to start cooperating now?"

Graystone was a good man. A more than solid cop and, from what he'd seen of the man's interactions with Lilah, as well as their broader group, an honorable soul who believed in the badge.

What did it do to a man to see those beliefs destroyed in a hard sweep of money and corruption?

He knew what it was like to have your faith in something destroyed. Your knees cut out from underneath you, even as you sank in a pool of quicksand.

Graystone would hold up, but he'd pay a price. Thankfully he had the love of a good woman—a woman he saw as his equal—to help see him through.

At the thought of having a woman, Max's gaze swung back toward Violet.

Damn, but she was a looker. Every time he got within a mile of her, a strange sort of awareness settled itself at the base of his spine, drumming on his nerves with hard spikes. He wanted to chalk it up to simple attraction, nothing more. But as easy as that would be—and nothing about Violet Richardson was easy, in the biblical sense or otherwise—he knew it was something else.

Something fierce and needy that gripped a man in a hard fever and refused to let go.

Despite knowing her for well over a year, since they were first introduced at their local business owners' meetings, and then getting to know her far better after the break-in at her shop, he still found the woman to be a mystery.

Her business partners were easygoing and friendly, and both had welcomed him into their social circle with open arms. Violet, on the other hand, had railroaded him at every opportunity. Her green eyes tempted, even as the cool set of her shoulders and that pure-as-vodka voice shut him down at every turn.

"You ever think about it?" he asked.

"About what?"

The change of topic added a hint of confusion to her question, but it also went a long way toward cooling the ire sparking at the suggestion she was naive.

He waved a hand toward the ballroom, filled to the brim with laughing people, drinking people, dancing people, many doing all three. "This. Getting hitched. Doing forever with someone."

"No."

"Because you don't want to?"

"Because I've never even come close."

He had figured her for having a swath of old boyfriends, several of whom had made it close to the fiancé stage, so the acknowledgment that she'd been no closer than he to taking a walk toward the altar was a surprise.

He brushed a finger down her cheek, the soft skin

more tempting than anything he could have imagined, and he fought to keep his hand steady through the trembling that suddenly gripped him. "That's a surprise."

Her breath caught as she stared up at him, and he took it as the smallest sign of victory that she was affected. But when she spoke, it was pure Violet.

Brisk and practical.

"It shouldn't be. I'm difficult on the best of days. Something you remind me of on a regular basis."

"I've never said that."

"You don't have to."

She stepped back, her eyes wide with awareness and the wariness of cornered prey. "I need to see to a few things."

He moved into her space again, deliberately blocking her view of the ballroom. "It won't stop running without you."

"Let's not wait to find out."

He stood still for one moment longer, not sure why he was baiting her and even less sure why he'd chosen this moment. She did have a job to do and was smack in the middle of a major event.

Still, he pressed on.

"I'd like an answer to my question."

"What question is that? Why I'm so naive or why I keep ignoring you?"

"Neither. I'd like to know what you have against this." He flung a hand out in the direction of the merry revelers. "Forever."

The green eyes that usually glittered at him like hard emeralds softened for the briefest moment as she shifted her gaze toward the ballroom. But it was the light, wistful whisper that gripped him by the throat and hung on. Hard.

"You know, Max, I try to be hopeful. But most days I just think happy-ever-afters are for suckers."

* * *

Violet fought the shaking of her limbs as she strode across the ballroom. Damn Max Baldwin and his all-seeing blue eyes and his freaking questions that cut far too close.

Damn him.

A hard knot of tears thickened her throat, and she swallowed around it. She would not cry here. Goodness, what had happened to her? She was a professional. She owned a business and she was responsible for the event going on around her.

She could cry later.

On a hard breath, she gave herself a moment to collect her thoughts. She'd been doing it for years. Pressing down on the hurt and pain to ensure no one saw the wreck that lived inside. And she'd be damned if she showed that sorry face to the assembled crowd at the Kelley-Gardner nuptials. Over four hundred of Dallas's elite and she was considering a breakdown.

No freaking way.

Instead, she'd use the anger and the frustration and just work that much harder. Max Baldwin didn't know anything, and his leading questions were designed to throw her off guard.

"Violet!"

Kimberly Kelley, now Kimberly Gardner, bounced over to her on light feet. The silk creation that wrapped her tall, slender body was as traditional as it was modern. Another Cassidy Tate creation.

Her friend had managed to capture all the gravitas and elegance of a wedding while ensuring the bride still looked fully twenty-first century. Violet made a mental note to have the photographer snap some extra photos for their portfolio with the bride in motion.

"Kimberly. It's a beautiful day."

"It's wonderful and amazing, just like you promised. Jordan and I truly can't thank you and Cassidy and Lilah enough. It's the perfect day." Kimberly smiled as she took in the assembled crowd. "Perfect."

Although she only had a few years in age on the bride, Violet couldn't help thinking that bright-eyed, wondrous smile had never been hers. She'd never looked that young. And she'd certainly never been that carefree.

But she'd given that gift to another, and that had to be enough. It had to *mean* something. Didn't it?

"I'm so glad you're enjoying the day. You look amazing."

"I did want to thank you, and we *will* be going out to lunch, my treat, after Jordan and I are back from Aruba. But I also stopped you for another reason. The security team wanted to talk to you."

"Of course." Violet had already begun moving when a slender hand gripped her wrist. "They can wait a minute. Come here."

Before she could take another step, Violet was wrapped in a tight hug. "Thank you."

Those damnable tears threatened again, and Violet held them back. Instead, she hung on an extra moment before stepping away. "Go enjoy the day. Find Jordan and dance until dawn. That's all the thanks I need."

Kimberly nodded before rushing toward her new husband. Violet watched for a moment before she turned on her heel and headed for the lobby area outside the ballroom.

What could security possibly need?

The chaos that greeted her had Violet reconsidering a four-hundred-person guest list.

Individuals in various states of drunken enjoyment lit-

tered the reception area outside the ballroom. Two men—
obviously some of the more heavily intoxicated of the
bunch—had stripped out of their tuxedo jackets and bow
ties and were circling each other like prize fighters.

"What is this?" Violet deliberately kept her voice calm,
pushing as much authority as she could into her words,
and used their quiet force to gain everyone's attention.

She should have used a roar.

The two men leaped on each other. She barely missed
being a part of the fray as the hard smack of fists on flesh
echoed off the two men, who grunted and groaned as
they locked into battle.

"Stop it!" The words were as ineffective as she knew
they'd be, but it was the cheering of the crowd that had
her seeing red. "Stop it *now!*"

The Kelley and Gardner families came from money,
including a political dynasty on the groom's side. The
added security was meant to ensure the family was safe.
Instead, they were out here dealing with a group of guests
acting like ill-behaved gorillas.

On a hard exhalation, Violet had to admit that was an
insult to gorillas.

Two of the security team members she'd met earlier
were on opposite sides of the brawl, trying to find ways
to pull the two grappling guests apart, but neither seemed
to get a good grip on the duo. If she was honest, she suspected they were ill prepared for dealing with a scuffle
between two wealthy guests.

Which was still no excuse for inaction.

"Gentlemen!" She pushed another layer of authority
into her tone and added a nice veneer of bitchiness as she
eyed where she could get a good foot into the middle,
toppling the two men. Before she could strike a handy
shin, the two men were suddenly pushed apart.

"What the hell's the matter with you?" Max stood between them, holding each at arm's length, his gaze dark and his shoulders straining hard against the thick material of his suit jacket.

Blood dripped from one of the men and the other spit a mouthful onto the carpet, nearly wrenching a scream from Violet that even their fight hadn't managed to do. This was a nice venue. One of the most prime venues in the city, truth be told, and they'd behaved like this?

She moved up close to the hard body of the one who'd spat his displeasure, her finger already drilling a hole in his chest. "What's the matter with you? This is Kimberly and Jordan's special day—"

"Get out of my face, lady." The man nearly shoved her, and it was only Max's hard press on the guy's chest that held him still.

"What's your—" Violet broke off as she caught the hazy dimness in the man's gaze, his pupils blown wide even in the bright light of the room. "This man needs help."

"Violet." Max's voice was urgent even as he maintained a firm, restraining hold.

Violet laid a hand on Max's arm to steady him before she turned to one of the security guards. "Go get John. He's on detail in the ballroom. Tell him we have someone out here who needs help."

Her words were still echoing off the now-quiet crowd when the tuxedo-clad fighter fell flat on his back.

Chapter 2

Max had watched the man fall as if in slow motion. He'd fumbled to get a firm grip, but the guy was already laid out cold before he could get any sort of hold.

What the hell?

Violet dropped to her knees beside the man, feeling for a pulse as she shouted orders to those assembled around the ballroom. Several of the guys who'd drunkenly cheered on the fight rapidly sobered as they realized the situation had gone from a good-natured fight to something far more serious.

Max scanned the room, looking for someone who could help him wrangle the other guy until they got to the bottom of what was going on. He caught sight of a man seated calmly on a couch. Who watched a fight that passively? The man only lifted his eyebrows and offered a small shrug as if to say "young men and their ways," but Max ignored it as he turned.

Was the jerk really that callous?

Hell, there was a woman stuck in the middle of this who could have been struck by flying fists, and at least one of the fighters was high on who knew what.

At the realization that Violet could have been hurt, thoughts of the uninterested bystander vanished, and his gaze lasered in on the object of his increasing attention. As he expected, she'd inserted herself smack in the middle of it all, shouting orders like a drill sergeant from her position beside the downed man.

"The ambulance is on its way. In the meantime, get him comfortable and covered and get something under his head."

With a quick leap to her feet, she focused on the other half of the fight. "What happened here?"

"Nothing."

"You were brawling in the middle of a wedding."

"Nate started it." The immediate chest puff beneath the studs of the man's tuxedo shirt had Max moving to stand next to the second fighter.

"What did he start? You're at a party."

"Trash talk. Weird stuff." The guy stopped and scratched at his temple. "Really weird stuff."

"Like what?"

"We were talking about the wedding and how Jordan's now handcuffed to Kim. In a good way, ya know?" The guy scratched his forehead again, the adrenaline fading from his voice as the heat of the moment faded into the aftermath. "And then he breaks off and starts talking about handcuffs and how he's going to find a woman of his own to handcuff. And then he—" A wash of red filled the man's face. "He said a few things about my sister that I don't want to repeat."

Max let the man process, the unreality of the moment

giving way to his increasing ability to think through what happened. "You know him?"

"Sure I know him. Since we were kids. Nate's a good guy."

"And the two of you usually don't brawl like your lives depend on it?"

"No. Heck no."

Because Nate's a good guy, Max thought.

"All we were doing was having a few drinks. Over there." With the excitement fading, people had moved back to the bar set up for the Gardners' guests. Open bars had a way of bringing out the party animal in everyone, but Max couldn't help thinking there was something else at play.

Max glanced down at the felled Nate, his eyes still closed and his breathing coming in rapid pants. The security team surrounded him and the lead Violet had called for was on his knees, assessing the man's situation. "Does Nate like to add anything to liven up his party?"

"You mean drugs?" The guy's eyes widened. "No, man. Nothing."

Violet had stayed quiet, but she chose that moment to speak up. "Is it possible someone slipped him something?"

"We were—" The fading buzz and postadrenaline low had dulled the man's eyes, but they flashed with a shot of fire. "There was a guy. Over there. Older guy. He talked us up for a few minutes. Said how much he was enjoying the party. Asked if we were friends with the bride or the groom."

The man's gaze flew around the reception area before he shook his head. "He's gone."

"What did he look like?"

"Unremarkable. I don't know. He just sort of blended in. It's a party, ya know."

Yeah. He did know. For all the security in place, the hotel was large and no one had perceived there was much danger, especially once the groom's grandmother—a three-decade congresswoman—was ensconced in the ballroom, protection detail nearby.

Max took a view of the room through fresh eyes, his surprise at the man who'd sat unmoving on the couch flashing in his memory.

Had the guy dropped something in Nate's drink?

Although he followed a steady progression around the room, reading each quadrant for anything suspicious, Max knew what he'd find.

Everything was back to normal, and there wasn't a stranger in sight.

Violet waited until the ambulance had come and gone before finding Kimberly and Jordan in the ballroom. She hated telling them anything, but they had a right to know about their guest, and she'd rather they heard it from her so she could spin the story, minimizing its impact on the event.

Nate had been checked out, and while the paramedics had shared precious little information, she did get out of one of them where they were taking him. Brad, the guy Nate had fought with, joined his friend in the ambulance and promised to report back with any updates.

"Where's the ambulance?" Cassidy's breathless voice grabbed her just as Violet got the bride and groom in her sights.

"On its way to the hospital."

"What happened?"

Violet wanted to get it over with, but she also knew

Cassidy would be a good sounding board for how casual she could make the story. "Heated words followed by a fight in the lobby."

Cassidy's tone only ratcheted up as Violet finished the last notes of the retelling. "And that required an ambulance?"

Reconsidering, Violet couldn't quite stop the wry grin. "I was hoping the fight would divert attention from the whole ambulance part."

"Try again." Cassidy's soft blue gaze was serious as she moved them both toward the wall. "In the meantime, calm down for a few minutes. Another dance or two isn't going to make a difference, and it will give you some time to settle."

Violet knew her friend was right, and she used the short walk to unruffle her feathers. There was something at every wedding that was unplanned and often unpleasant, but she got through.

For some reason, she couldn't find any hint of that quiet calm today.

"Now spill. What really happened?"

"That's what's so odd. The two guys fighting were best friends. But the one in an ambulance headed for Baylor's emergency room right now is clearly high on something. He collapsed after Max broke up the fight."

"Max broke it up?"

"He was considerably more effective than security."

Violet inwardly winced at her dry tone. Max *had* helped, and she was grateful.

"He's been keeping a watchful eye," Cassidy said.

"Too watchful."

Cassidy's gaze was equally watchful, but her tone was full of the censure only old friends could manage. "You need to get over this annoyance with him. We have the rubies because he made a judgment call on his feet. Being mad isn't going to change that."

"I know. Damn it." Violet tapped a toe, the nervous movement something to focus on. "I know."

And she did know.

The discovery of a cache of jewels underneath the floor of their shop wasn't Max's fault. The fact that their landlady had hidden fakes of the British Crown Jewels and three very real—and very precious—rubies wasn't Max's fault, either. He'd just had the misfortune to snag the rubies off the top of the heap before Cassidy's ex-fiancé, Robert, stole the rest of the find.

"In fact, if I'm not mistaken, Max would like to find any number of ways to make it up to you."

A flash of heat cratered in her stomach before spreading outward like a warm flow of lava as Violet imagined all those ways Max could make it up to her. Then she locked the erotic images away. She wasn't interested in pursuing anything—casual or otherwise—with such an overbearing man. The attraction might be out of her control, but what she did about it wasn't. "You're subtle, Cupid."

"I'm only saying what we've all seen from the beginning. The man's got eyes for you, and I know you well enough to know you return the sentiment."

"I don't—"

Cassidy's hand came up in a stop gesture with all the speed of a Supreme. "Don't insult me or yourself by lying."

Violet hesitated before she pressed on. She did feel something for Max, but it didn't matter, and no amount of breath had made her friends see reason. Just because Cassidy and Lilah had found happy-ever-afters with the men who'd descended into the middle of their lives like a hurricane didn't mean she'd find the same.

In fact, her history suggested the exact opposite.

She wasn't cut out for romantic love. And thanks to her parents' loveless marriage and subsequent poor decisions in that realm, she had no basis for it. Instead, Violet had the deep, abiding love of friends, and she knew that was enough.

She'd decided long ago it had to be.

"Please think about it."

"I don't see why I need to. You and Lilah have done enough thinking about it for three of me."

"Vi—"

She grabbed her friend's hands in a tight grip, her voice firm but kind. "I appreciate it. You know I do. But this really isn't the place for it. I just sent a man out of here in an ambulance."

The rapid change in subject had its desired effect, even if Violet regretted the slight manipulation. She had put a man in an ambulance and finishing the wedding needed to be their focus right now. Cassidy glanced around the ballroom, her voice hesitant when she finally spoke. "Do you think the brawl has anything to do with us?"

"I don't see how. We've monitored everyone who's entered and exited. Reed's stepfather is in jail. I don't see a connection."

"You're right. Of course you are." Cassidy shook her head. "I don't know why I can't believe it's over. Reed watched them cart the man off in a police cruiser."

The urge to share Max's point of view—that they were all naive to think Tripp Lange wouldn't find a way to work this entire situation to his advantage—was nearly out of her mouth when she pulled it back.

Just because Max speculated didn't mean he was right.

And despite the fact that they'd collectively spent the last two weeks on high alert over the discovery in their shop didn't mean it wasn't time for things to go back to normal.

The culprit was behind bars, and anyone who'd worked with him was dead.

It was time to relax.

Alex Ebner, assistant to the man whispered about only as The Duke, settled himself in the front seat of the black limousine. "The women are all there, just as you suggested they would be."

"And the men?"

"Stuck to them, as you also suspected."

"You speak of my stepson as well?"

Alex thought about his casual stroll through the ballroom. "He hasn't left the baker's side."

"Excellent."

Alex waited, as he always did. He was deeply loyal, and he was more than willing to wait as The Duke determined whatever came next. He'd been raised in the old ways, and he took pride in that. Authority. Leadership. Power.

They had value—they *still* had value—and he was content to follow his leader.

Those traits he prized also came with a price. He understood that—had been raised to understand it—and it was his job to stay in the background and ensure the toll never became too taxing.

In exchange, he was paid handsomely. He had time off. And, most important, his family was cared for in the lap of luxury back in the homeland.

"What about the coordinator? The sleek one who gives orders?"

"Hard at work. She just dealt with the little matter in the lobby."

"Is she followed?"

"Baldwin's grandson stays close to her, but she keeps shaking him off. It's humorous to watch."

"Then she's the one. Violet Richardson."

Alex nodded. "She's got the least restrictions and moves about as she pleases."

He'd gotten close several times and had nearly snagged the woman, but each time she'd managed a swift turn to elude him. Her apartment had proven equally challenging, the elegant home in one of Dallas's newest high-rise buildings sporting state-of-the-art security and surveillance.

They'd moved fully underground at this point, and it was no use risking that. His boss had planned well, though. Alex considered the ease with which they were released from jail and the speed with which they'd gone to ground at The Duke's hidden property.

The Duke had another name—one well-known in Dallas circles. Tripp Lange was one of the city's wealthiest men, his riches earned through a combination of hard work and maniacal focus that had moved him from poor immigrant to success.

But that success had come with a price.

They'd still not managed to uncover the location of Tripp's wife, Diana, despite extensive digging. Her son had whisked her away as he closed in on Lange, and no amount of prodding and poking any of Lange's contacts in the Dallas PD had managed to uncover her whereabouts.

Tripp wanted the rubies and he wanted his wife back. Violet Richardson and her relationships with the rest of her little wedding troupe were the key to securing both.

"You've checked the egress points. You know where you want to take her."

"It's all prepared."

"Then move ahead."

Max couldn't shake the sense that something was out of his reach. He knew that sense—and trusted it to the very depths of his being—which was why he kept up a continuous walk of the perimeter of the ballroom.

The wedding had technically entered its last hour, and he was counting down the minutes to getting them all out of there. He didn't care if Violet fought him like a she-cat. He was dragging her out the moment they kicked the last guest toward the hotel elevators, or what would likely be a drunken, snaking taxi line. She could come back in the morning and manage any required follow-up.

Things always looked better in daylight.

Which was a fallacy, he well knew. He'd spent many an op during his time in the Army Corps of Engineers in broad daylight and an equal number in those silent hours after midnight. Both could do irreparable damage.

He passed the open ballroom doors, his gaze alighting on the bar, still two and three deep with wedding guests. The image of the guy on the couch nagged at him, and Max headed for the harried row of bartenders still mixing drinks.

A manager he'd noted earlier had added to his duties by bar-backing, and he'd just arrived with two fresh bottles of liquid courage. Max waited until the man logged the liquor before waving him over.

"Hey man, I know you're busy. I need to ask you something."

"You're with the planners, right?" The guy offered a tired smile before he stuck out his hand. "Zach Turner.

We do a heck of a lot of events with Elegance and Lace, and they run a smooth party."

"A rather wild one, if the fact your bartenders haven't stopped serving is any indication."

Zach tossed a smile over his shoulder. "Wild, yes. Great tips, an even bigger yes."

"Did you notice the man out here earlier? Older than the frat boys in the wedding party but not an old relative, if you know what I mean?"

"Elegant guy? Sort of blended in if you didn't look too hard." Zach snapped his fingers. "Saw him on the couch over there just before that brawl lit up."

"That's the one."

Max waited another few beats, curious to see if the man made the same connections he had before he inadvertently led the witness.

"Odd guy. He mingled for a bit, talking up the wedding party. I kept an eye on him for a while, not sure if he was hitting on the crowd or trying to pick a few pockets."

At what Max could only assume was a wash of shock and surprise on his face, Zach continued. "Oh yeah, it happens way more often than you think. People come to a nice event and no one thinks too much about their wallets and purses. But old Uncle Nicky or crazy Aunt Sally sure as hell do."

Max shook his head, the shock fading into that strange sort of acceptance that came with seeing far too much. "People are an endless surprise."

"Always. But I've been doing this for nearly thirty years. I can usually pick out Cousin Sticky Fingers at twenty paces. Guy gave me an odd vibe, but not a sticky one."

"What sort of vibe did he give you?"

Zach's dark gaze narrowed before awareness lit him

up like a lightning strike. "You concerned the fight had some chemical enhancement?"

"Yep. No doubt about it. The paramedics didn't say much, but it was all over the guy's blown pupils and dead faint to the floor."

"Well, hell." Zach gestured toward the long hallway that extended off the ballroom lobby. "Let me hook you up with house security."

Violet drifted through her various roles as the wedding wound down. She confirmed with Lilah the top layer of cake was already preserved for the couple's first anniversary, while the rest of the cake was sliced and individually packaged and waiting for guests to take as they departed. She smiled as the DJ counted off the number of songs left until the big finale, a slow, torchy number that would send the happy couple off on their week-long honeymoon. And she got a full update from the caterer on where they stood on a count of the bar bill.

And silently credited the family's foresight to go with a flat price per head.

While she appreciated the hearty flow of liquor would no doubt leave a horde of satisfied partygoers in its wake, she immediately shifted her direction to confirm the taxi line was in place and the staff had all eyes on anyone who shouldn't have keys in hand.

A good number of guests had also reserved rooms at the hotel, which went a long way toward assuaging her concern, but there was still margin for error. Many guests had driven, and they needed a sober driver to make it home.

"This one was a humdinger, Miss Richardson," the hotel's doorman boomed at her when she passed, his smile as bright as when she'd walked in at noon.

"That it was, Carl. You keeping an eye on the departures for me?"

"Always. Boss added two extra pairs of eyes on valet, too."

"Good."

She kept on toward the exit, the taxi stand housing only two waiting guests who'd obviously decided to skip the rush.

"It was a wonderful evening," a tottering woman gushed. "I want my son and his fiancée to call you. Do you have a card?"

With a rueful smile for the woman's husband, Violet pulled a card out of her suit jacket pocket. More than half their business came from satisfied guests who wanted a similar event for themselves, and Violet couldn't stop the spear of pride at a job well done, despite the craziness that had descended on their lives in the past few weeks. "We'd be delighted to discuss your son's event."

The woman's husband deposited her in a cab as she still hollered about booking an appointment, and Violet could give herself only a moment to watch the proceedings as she waved them off.

Damn, she loved her job.

It was crazy and nuts and often stressful, but she loved it. And she knew she'd found a purpose for her life.

Giggles echoed off the concave ceiling of the porte cochere, and she stepped back to let a tumble of two bridesmaids and three groomsmen hit the taxi line.

"Fun time, Violet." One of the bridesmaids, named Macy, tossed a pointed look at a groomsman she'd had her eye on all day before pulling Violet in for a big hug. "Fun time."

"Where are you off to?"

"Uptown for a nightcap."

Violet suspected she knew what would come after the nightcap and simply waved them on, pleased they were still smart enough to keep the night going in taxis. The lack of a car now meant they'd need another cab for their return trip, which meant she could relax another notch.

"Have fun."

Macy giggled in her ear, her whisper louder than the woman likely planned. "I mean to."

They all piled into a minivan cab and off to whatever came next, and Violet gave herself another moment, surprised at the hard clench that tightened her rib cage. The same melancholy that had come over her inside the wedding while hugging the bride hit her once more, the jab swift.

Where had those days gone? The carefree ones that didn't have an overarching tinge of disappointment or the fear time was marching on without her?

When had thirty begun to feel ancient?

Shaking off the melancholy, she moved out of the way of another couple as they approached the valet station. One glance at the wife—keys in hand—and Violet knew the woman had played the evening's designated driver, so she kept moving, determined to leave the policing to the hotel staff. They had as vested an interest as she did in ensuring people left their establishment safely, and she'd leave them to it.

An empty lobby stared back at her, indicating no one else was yet ready to depart, and she glanced at her watch before mentally calculating the time left until she needed to find the bride and groom and help see them off.

Figuring she had a good five minutes, she stopped and gave herself one of them.

Why was she so out of sorts?

On a hard exhale, she drifted toward the end of the

sidewalk that fronted the hotel before it dropped off toward the driveway to the service entrance. She was close enough to help out in a crisis but far enough away to avoid recognition.

The moment of anonymity was all she needed to get her equilibrium back. Why it had chosen to abandon her during one of the largest events Elegance and Lace had ever put on was a mystery, but she'd worry about that later. For now, she was going to clear her mind, then march back inside and give Kimberly and Jordan an amazing send-off.

In just a minute.

The hot August night wrapped around her in a tight stranglehold, and she was tempted to remove her suit jacket. The cool air from the lobby had diffused some of the heat at the taxi line, but this far away from the door it was absolutely stifling.

A minute was only a minute, though, and she'd already used up half of hers. Stripping was a waste of the time she had left.

"Ever responsible and practical," she muttered to herself before compromising and unbuttoning the top button of her blouse.

The hot air coated her skin and with it, an image of Max filled her thoughts. A place he'd occupied far too often these last weeks.

Heck, the past year, if she was truly being honest.

She'd noticed him at the first community business meeting he'd attended in the Design District after opening his architectural firm, Dragon Designs. Since getting to know Max and Tucker better, she'd learned that Tucker had abdicated any interest in playing their firm's business lead and had been more than willing to hand the role over to Max.

Which had put Max and Violet firmly in each other's orbit.

Even without the pressure of Cassidy and Lilah's on-going interest in seeing the two of them get together, Violet could admit that Max did manage to push all her buttons. He was strong and solid. And if she were honest with herself, she liked that he was a bit surly. The man wasn't a pushover, and it was a trait she admired.

Maybe if they hadn't gotten involved in the mystery of the jewels under the floor, and maybe if her best friend wasn't marrying his best friend, things could be different.

A fling, maybe?

Thirty, remember? That small voice that kept her constant company rose up. *Call it what it is. An affair.*

Violet turned the thought over in her mind. Like sophisticated women had been doing since the dawn of time, she could manage her life and this crazy attraction through a discreet affair in which both knew the score. No pressure for a happy-ever-after or expectations neither had any interest in fulfilling.

She'd scratch the itch and move on.

It would be perfect if it weren't for the fact that her two best friends were also her daily colleagues. To say each of them missed nothing about the other two was an understatement. Lilah and Cassidy saw *everything*.

As she did with them.

Which took her right back to square one. Nothing could come of this odd little spark for Max.

The heavy tread of feet interrupted her musings and she shifted her attention, mentally sighing that her minute was gone. It was time to get back to the wedding.

Her gaze caught on a man moving with swift determination up the sidewalk. An odd spark of recognition lit in her gut. Was he a wedding guest?

Or had she seen him somewhere else?

It was only as he closed in on her, his large hands wrapping around her shoulders, that she registered the depth of the threat.

And as a sharp prick hit her neck, she watched the bright lights of Dallas blur before the black took her over.

Chapter 3

Max scanned the various screens inside the security center before settling in with the computer operator, Jake. The man had seemed to light up with the unexpected excitement as he asked, "Do you know the rough time and what part of the hotel?"

"The lobby cameras pointed around the bar. Around ten o'clock."

The man made quick work of the request, his fingers flying over the keyboard at his station before he pointed toward an even larger screen in his sight line. "I'll put the footage up here."

Max saw the lobby still filled with revelers getting drinks and zeroed in on the couch. "There. He was on that couch for some time."

Jake scrolled several frames forward, the clock ticking off the time in the lower right-hand corner, before Max stopped him. "That's him."

The screen expanded as Jake enlarged the image. Max

nodded as the strange man's face came into view. "Now we need to see if he was mingling with the guests who were fighting."

Jake nodded, his focus absolute as he scrolled through earlier footage, the clack of the keys the only noise in the room. Max watched him work before his own focus shifted, his normal inability to sit still taking over.

He paced the wall of screens, taking in various views. Two of the wedding guests were getting amorous in one of the hotel elevators, while another couple in a different elevator was clearly in the midst of a heated—and likely liquor-fueled—fight. Since both couples deserved their privacy, he continued to scan the wall, the image of the bride and groom and their assembled guests filling several more screens, displayed from different angles.

Before the notion even fully registered, Max found himself searching for Violet.

Where was she? He'd have assumed she'd be smack in the middle of whatever was happening with the bride and groom, but another glance through all the ballroom screens showed no sign of her. Cassidy and Lilah both stood on point, and he saw Tucker and Reed not far behind them, but Violet was nowhere.

"Jake—" He broke off as he caught sight of the exterior cameras. Panic washed like icy needles over his skin.

"What?"

The man's eyes widened as Max moved toward his chair, his large form hovering over the tech. "Pull it up. The driveway camera. Now."

Jake did as he was told, his hands flying, and in moments the driveway camera footage came into full view.

Along with an image of Violet being dragged toward a waiting car.

"Call the police!" Max shouted the order as he ran hell-for-leather toward the front door.

Tripp Lange stared at the heap of very attractive woman deposited on the bench seat opposite him as they put Dallas in their rearview mirror. They'd already stopped at his private home on the outskirts of town and changed into the waiting car Alex had prepared in advance. So now, barely twenty minutes after snatching the woman, they were headed for the Hill Country.

Alex had done well, as always. He'd waited for the perfect moment, then leaped.

The fact Violet Richardson had made the snatch-and-grab relatively easy with her late-night stroll was beside the point. They had her.

And through her, he'd get the rubies and his wife back.

"What did you use, Alex?"

The man's voice was crisp and clear from the front seat. "That sedative I've been working on. I've changed the ratio of sedative to paralytic, and I think it's the right one. She'll come to, but it will take her longer to get her bearings."

"Good."

They had a two-hour drive ahead of them, and Tripp wanted to make sure Violet stayed out.

"And her cell phone?"

Alex waved the device through the window partition. "Already off."

Tripp studied the woman, her slender body relaxed in sleep. A black suit covered her in prim lines, but the hint of skin at her throat and chest suggested there was something of a tiger beneath the gloss. She was on the taller side—at least five-six—and another four inches added with the heels.

All in all, an incredibly attractive package.

But one that hid, for the most part, behind severe suits and an all-business attitude.

She was a calculated risk, no doubt. Alex had spent a fair amount of time observing her, and she was no one's pushover. The previous week, his man of business had witnessed her dealing with a hotel manager who'd thought to change the terms of their agreement. Alex had been more than impressed with her handling of the situation.

Which also meant she'd be a challenge to break on the path to securing what he wanted.

It was a good thing he knew not only how to break people but also exactly what made Violet Richardson vulnerable.

Max shoved a hand through his still military-short hair and fought the urge to scream at the team of police parked at the hotel's service entrance. Per the manager's request, they'd moved out of sight of the departing guests, and it still chapped Max's ass. Violet was one of theirs, and they were acting as if her disappearance from their grounds needed to be covered up.

Instead, all it meant was they were wasting precious time.

Reed laid a hand on his shoulder and gestured him a few feet away from the cruiser.

"My stepfather was released from jail late this afternoon."

The news hit with the force of an atomic bomb, and for one of the rare moments of his life, Max was speechless. Quickly gathering himself, he let out a roar. "What the hell, Reed?"

"I'm trying to find out on whose, orders but you know as well as I do his connections run deep."

Max did know. Since discovering the rubies in the floor of Violet's shop, he'd come to understand just how devious and corrupt some people could be.

And how deeply buried they could keep those facets of their personality.

"The man's been paying off the whole freaking city. I have no idea who I can trust," Reed said.

The haze of worry for Violet broke for a moment as Max caught sight of the craggy lines of anxiety that painted Reed's face. He knew what the man had been through over the past week, first finding out his life was a lie both personally and professionally, and then having to put his mother into hiding from his stepfather. "Is there anyone you can ask?"

"I've got a few contacts, but I need to see them directly. Get a feel for them as I ask questions. Lilah's going to stay with Tucker and Cassidy while I do."

Fear for Violet and the increasing distance her kidnappers put between them rose back up to swamp him in another nasty wave. "They haven't found any trace of her? Nothing on traffic cams?"

"No." Reed glanced toward the assembled police. "They lost them after a few lights here downtown. No one's picked up a trail yet."

"Where could he be taking her?"

"How the hell should I know? He's got warrens hidden everywhere from what I've been able to uncover privately. Places buried so deep it would take an honest team at the PD days to find them."

Reed's words echoed in his ear, the reference to an honest team rolling over and over in Max's mind. From his time in the corps he knew how important it was to trust your comrades—your backup—and the anguish

Reed was feeling was tangible. "Wait. Look, you've been with the Dallas PD for how long?"

"Almost fifteen years."

"And in all that time, nothing's jangled? No one's seemed off?"

A small light filtered through the man's grim gaze. "Hell, yeah. There are those folks people whisper about. The jackasses who always seem to keep their jobs despite the screw-ups. Or who always manage to fade under the radar every time something goes sideways. Why?"

"Because the entire force isn't dirty. It can't be. What you likely have is a small group who need to keep their own counsel and secrets. Rout them out and you find the problem."

Max watched Reed weigh his words and continued to work through the problem in his mind. Every way he turned it, the truth seemed more and more clear. Dallas was a huge city, and the majority of its citizens were good, law-abiding people. For Tripp Lange to have as much power and influence as he did—and for no one to know about it—the cancer in the department had to be relatively contained.

"Come on. Think through the people you trust. We'll start there and work it through."

"There's a guy I went through the academy with. He's one of our lead detectives on digital forensics. He's a good guy. A family man with strong ethics."

"Let's go."

The first thing she noticed was the absence of noise. Where had all the guests gone? The loud buzz of the wedding had faded, and the only sound she heard was the light, gentle hum of an air conditioner.

Where was everyone?

The thought hit hard and fast, and Violet's eyes popped open at the realization she needed to send Kimberly and Jordan off on their honeymoon. The guests. Where were—?

The fear at missing the rest of the wedding quickly morphed into something far worse as she realized she hadn't moved. She was still flat on her back, the room around her full of shadows. She tried again, willing herself into a sitting position, but her body never moved.

Panic filled her chest in a hard press, and she struggled to catch her breath as her gaze rabbited around the room.

Where was she?

As the question rolled over and over, desperately seeking some purchase inside the terror, another question, this one louder than the first, took root.

How had Reed's stepfather found her?

With the legendary focus she was known for—and teased about by Cassidy and Lilah—Violet slowed her gaze along with her breathing and took stock of the room. The thought of her two best friends went a long way toward calming her, and she kept them both close to her heart. They were okay.

They had to be okay.

Neither had been out of Reed's or Tucker's sight the entire wedding. Which had to be why she was the one who was taken. Her friends were safe.

Safe.

She'd focus on that and believe it. Because anything else was unacceptable.

Violet kept that image in her mind—her two best friends unharmed—and continued to take stock of the room. She was in what looked like a guest room. Although she couldn't move her head, she knew she was on a bed, the expansive king visible in her peripheral vision. A small light was plugged into the far wall, the soft glow illuminating the room. The cord was visible where it went into the plug, and she considered how she might use it.

Assuming, of course, she could find a way to move her arms and legs.

Stilling her breath and the horrifying thought that her captors might have done something permanent to her, she tried once more to move. When a seated position proved impossible, she took another deep breath and focused on smaller motions. Envisioning her hand, she willed movement into her fingers.

And was rewarded with the light sound of her fingertips scratching over the soft cotton of the bedspread.

It's temporary. Just temporary.

A breath she hadn't even realized she'd been holding released in a rush before she added her condition to her arsenal of tools. How long could she play the paralyzed card? Whatever drug she'd been given obviously just needed time to wear off. Her captors likely knew approximately how long, but if she could find a way to use uncertainty to her advantage, she might have surprise on her side.

With the same quiet focus she'd used on her fingers, Violet settled herself with a few deep breaths and took stock of the rest of her body. She tried wiggling her toes, satisfied when she heard some movement against the mattress, even if she couldn't move her head to see the progress. And her fingers seemed to gain increasing momentum as she worked on her right hand, then her left.

A hard jiggle against the door lock drew her attention, and she briefly toyed with playing possum before settling on a new approach. She didn't run and she didn't cower. She'd hit this head-on.

The same man who'd taken her came to stand in front of the bed. "You're awake."

Despite her bravado and the inability to feel much physically, a disturbing sense of menace raced through her body in cold chills.

"No thanks to you and your boss."

The man cocked his head. "So we can dispense with the formalities, then?"

"What does Lange want?"

"The rubies."

"He's already got one."

"But there are three." The man's gaze roamed over her with calculated speculation. "Unless there were more in the cache beneath your floor."

"There are three. There have only ever been three. They're the Renaissance stones of legend."

Violet knew she had precious little to trade, but there was no use giving false information over their fantastical find. The Queen of England—wife to King Edward—had wanted the rubies secreted out of England after the Second World War, and their landlady's father had been the one to do it.

The fact Mrs. Beauregard thought burying the legendary stones beneath a layer of concrete in an old Dallas warehouse was a good idea was an entirely different matter.

"How'd you know the stones were even in the warehouse? My partners and I have been there for three years and never even looked beneath the carpet."

Although she had a pretty good idea of how Tripp Lange knew—his connections with Cassidy's late brother-in-law were the start of a terrible chain of contacts—she was curious to see what his rent-a-thug knew.

"The stones aren't a secret for those precious few who make it their business to know about these things. Mr. Lange is one of those individuals. He has patience and the will to see every acquisition through." The man moved in, as quiet and lethal as a snake, and Violet wished like hell she could move to the corner of the bed.

"He will have the Renaissance Stones. All of them."

Max fought the need to slam his fists against the front door of the modest north Dallas home and instead waited while Reed rang the bell. He glanced out over the thick, well-manicured lawn, visible in the small pathway lights that led from the driveway to the front door, and took several deep, calming breaths. As he settled, his gaze roamed over the large pots of flowers that flanked the porch. The bright blooms nestled in a weed-free bed of dirt offered a sizable suggestion about the family who lived there.

They took pride in their home and in what was theirs. The effect was welcoming and homey, and Max knew he'd have been more fascinated with it if his thoughts didn't drip with oily fear for Violet.

Home.

Did he even know what that was?

He'd thought Dallas could be his home, but now, more than two years after moving back and starting his business, he still wasn't sure. The innate sense of being a nomad had pushed him into the Army Corps of Engineers, and it was humbling to realize a decade and a half later he'd still not lost the itch to roam.

The door swung open and Reed stepped up, his hand outstretched. "Thanks for seeing us, Ryan."

Reed made quick introductions before Ryan Masterson waved them forward, surprisingly unruffled by the late-night visit. "Come on in."

Max stepped into the neat foyer and took in the warm vibe. He'd never had anything like this at home. Even his time with Pops had been caring, but not exactly something straight out of Donna Reed.

Kicking away the strange, abstract thought, he focused on the matter at hand and hoped like hell Reed's friend could supply some answers.

"I'm sorry to bother you so late, but I need help," Reed said.

Max had seen the laser focus the moment Ryan opened the door, but at Reed's plea, the man's tall, lean stance turned hard, his eyes all-cop. "What's going on?"

"What do you know about the Lange case?"

Max didn't miss the immediate awareness in Ryan's demeanor as his gaze remained steady on Reed. Clearly the department knew one of their own had been duped by a man he trusted. "I'm aware of it."

"Then you know he was released this afternoon."

The subtle veneer of pity fell along with Ryan's jaw. "What? No."

"Late afternoon, somewhere between four and five, best I can tell. He then took the opportunity to kidnap my fiancée's best friend and business partner."

The word *kidnap* hung in Max's thoughts with all the finality of a gunshot, and he waited, watching to see Ryan's reaction. He knew Reed did the same and had to trust they could both smell a rat if the cop was dirty or at all under the influence of Tripp Lange's money.

"What can I do?"

A breath he didn't even realize he was holding exhaled on a hard rush as Max leaned forward. "She and her partners run a wedding business, and they had a huge event tonight at the Windhaven. Best we can tell, she stepped outside for a bit of fresh air and was snatched there."

"By Lange?"

Max nodded. "He wasn't visible in the video feeds, but it's his henchman."

"I've seen the footage and identified him as a known associate," Reed said. "Alex Ebner, also released this afternoon."

"You check the traffic cams?"

"We've got them for the first few lights outside the hotel. Then the uniforms on scene lose the trail."

The grim expression that covered Ryan's face broke, revealing a hard, gritty smile. "Then you came to the right place."

Max fought the hope that leaped beneath his ribs—the first since that horrible moment of watching Violet snatched off the video feed—and kept his focus steady on Ryan. "Why's that?"

"Because I'm not going to lose the trail."

Chapter 4

Violet wiggled her fingers, the novelty of being able to do so not having yet worn off. She'd lost all sense of time—and the heavy curtains at the window further prevented any sense of the hour—but the slow, steady progression of life into her limbs had remained her sole focus.

Her legs were still weak. She'd tried swinging them off the bed and barely made it to the edge, so a peek out the curtains would have to wait. In the meantime, she'd stared at the walls, reflecting on what she knew—or thought she knew—about the men holding her captive.

Reed had been shocked to discover his stepfather, Tripp Lange, was the man behind the heinous crimes that had been committed thus far in the name of greed and avarice. Since their showdown two—no, three?—days ago, the detective had spent every free hour attempting to track down the depth of his stepfather's secret empire.

He'd been woefully underprepared for the small pieces

he had uncovered, including Lange's reputation as The Duke, whispered in Dallas's underworld. The man was purported to be a brutal adversary, and the few who had dealings with him were focused only on satisfying whatever bargain they'd struck with the devil.

What had concerned Reed most was Lange's possible connections within the Dallas PD. During their tussle, Tripp had admitted he'd had Reed assigned to the break-in at Elegance and Lace. And he'd obviously managed to spring himself free of jail in no time.

What other maneuvers had he orchestrated?

The heavy tread of feet outside the door pulled her from her thoughts as the thick wood door swung open. As if she'd conjured him, Tripp Lange walked through, followed by what she could only assume was his bodyguard and man-of-all-business.

The man who'd stared her down earlier.

"Hello, Miss Richardson."

"Mr. Lange." She nodded before struggling to a sitting position. The struggle chafed, but not nearly as much as lying prone beneath their twin stares.

She took in the two men, quickly cataloging the odd pair. Tripp's man was all muscle. He was roughly the same size as Max's six-foot-one but not quite as broad. And where Max had a sense of solidness to his form that was in his genes, Lange's man clearly worked at his. The corded muscles in his neck suggested a fair amount of gym time, as did his almost ridiculously stiff posture.

Lange, on the other hand… Violet fought the shudder and again forced herself to look objectively, much as she did when attempting to reason with an angry bridesmaid over a chosen dress. There were things that could be learned if you looked and listened.

The man was small and trim, his harsh demeanor more

evident in his features and the stoic set of his body. A hard jawline that held about as much sympathy as a python for its victim and a pair of pale green eyes to finish off the reptilian look.

What had Reed's mother seen in the man?

By all accounts, they had a happy marriage. One in which Diana Graystone Lange been loved and doted on, happy in the illusion he'd woven around her.

Yet another illusion of love, shattered to bits.

"Ah, excellent. The paralytic is wearing off." Lange turned to the man next to him. "Just as you suggested, Alex. About six to eight hours of potency."

Violet noted the name while mentally adding the time and guessed it was nearing seven or eight o'clock in the morning. The wedding had been winding down when she went out for a breath at nearly midnight.

Which meant she'd been missing all night.

Unwilling to show any weakness, she tamped down on the fear that she'd been gone too long for anyone to find a trail and focused on whatever she could possibly learn now.

"Way to stack the deck in your favor." She pushed every bit of Dallas socialite into her tone and prayed she didn't get a smack for her efforts.

What she received instead was far more alarming than she ever could have imagined. Tripp leaned forward, those snake eyes telegraphing menace and a cocky sort of assurance. "I always stack the deck in my favor, Miss Richardson. Gambling is for the weak-minded. Those who understand that remain in control."

A horrible sickness curled in her belly—a physical reminder that she wasn't in control—yet she pressed on. "Clearly the strategy is working for you. You're in hiding, kidnapping innocent women, while your wife refuses to see you. Good plan."

Tripp moved even closer, so close she could see the pores of his face and the black lines that rimmed his eerie irises. "The bravado is amusing, but taunting me won't help. Nor will jabs about my wife. I will have the rubies. I will have my wife. And then I'll be rid of you and your friends. Is that understood?"

She said nothing, even as she refused to break eye contact. As Tripp lifted his head from hers, he tossed his final salvo. "You can at least take heart that I don't play with my prey."

Alex dropped a wrapped bagel and a bottle of water on the end table before turning to follow his boss. It was only at the last minute, as the man turned from the door, that something dark and violent struck through the roiling fear already swimming in her stomach.

Lange might not want to play with his prey, but Alex looked like he lived for it.

Max shoveled in his third biscuit as he paced Masterson's small home office. The man's wife had been sweet and understanding, dropping off a bakery box of goodies around six. It was now two hours later, and the butter-laden foods had done nothing to assuage the increasing concern they wouldn't find Violet in time.

"Let's track it back, Ryan." Reed flipped through a small notepad he'd pulled from his pocket earlier. "Can we trace Lange's movements from when he was released? We've got him and his partner, Alex, for about three miles, but the trail goes cold after they get out of downtown."

"We found them the other night in Fair Park at the warehouse Tripp owns." Max stepped forward to point at one of the large computer monitors that currently show-cased the view from eight different Dallas traffic cameras. "Did they go back?"

"The warehouse is blocked off, and there's round-the-clock protection on it." A dark look passed over Reed's face, his mouth turned down in a hard frown. "Of course, there are supposed to be guards on it. Let me make a quick call and confirm that order didn't get lost as neatly as Lange's paperwork."

Ryan stopped him. "Let me. I can pull the records from here. It's a standard query."

Within moments, Ryan let out a sigh. "Nope. Two officers have been there since the arrests last Thursday. No break in protocol and CSI is expected to sweep it fully on Monday."

At the image of forensic detectives working through the warehouse for any clues, Max had a different thought. "What if we're going about this wrong?"

"How so?" Ryan reached for his coffee, his ability to pass over the bakery box an impressive feat.

"Lange's got to have dummy corporations layered under dummy corporations. What work's been done to find the companies he owns?"

Reed flipped through his notebook once more. "We've been working on that. My partner, Jessie, spent all day yesterday combing real estate files. She couldn't find a thing about the Fair Park property."

"Which means the records have been wiped." Ryan reached for a donut at that point, his excitement palpable. "Which is something I can do a heck of a lot with."

Max gestured Reed toward the door. "Let's give him a minute to work. I want to check in with Tucker, and I'm sure you want to call Lilah."

Tucker had holed up with Lilah, Cassidy and his boxer,

Bailey, at Lilah's town house, and they owed them all a check-in. Reed followed him into the hall, and at the sound of cartoons echoing from the living room, they moved as far as they could in the opposite direction, their voices low.

"Wherever they are, sooner or later they're coming back for the other two rubies. Violet's alive until then." Max balled his fists. She had to be.

Of course, if he knew Violet, there was no way she was giving up the location of her ruby. Nor would she even hint she didn't know the location of its twin, hidden by Cassidy in a separate bank. Violet was a pro at assessing every situation and would no doubt battle Lange to the bitter end of whatever game the man was playing. As strategy went, he admired the hell out of her. But as someone who cared for her, one thought trumped all others in his mind.

What might happen to her in the meantime?

"Max?" Reed's shoulders stiffened with awareness. "We can get to where Cassidy hid her ruby. What about Violet?"

Max pushed through the pain, forcing a calm he didn't feel. "She's been silent on which bank she used. No one's gotten it out of her, and believe me, I've tried."

"Do you think she told Lilah or Cassidy?"

"Tucker already told me Cassidy doesn't know."

"Damn it." Reed paced a few steps down the quiet hallway before turning back. "She wanted to protect them. Which means she's also going to try to bluff her way through the negotiation with my stepfather."

The trio of biscuits in his stomach balled like lead at the image of Violet attempting to negotiate with Tripp Lange. "Would we expect anything less?"

A shout from the office had them both running, and

Max stopped at the set of screens, a real estate document blown up on one of the monitors. "Here it is," Ryan said. "It's under Alex's name, not Tripp's. But if you trace the financial backing, you can find Lange all over it."

"Where are they?"

"About an hour outside the city. Twenty miles due east of Waxahachie. The property's about two hundred acres."

Max punched the details into his phone, his mind already whirling with next steps. "Thanks, Ryan. I owe you for this."

Reed followed him into the hall, his long strides barely keeping pace as Max barreled toward the driveway. "Slow down, Baldwin."

Max spun at the words, his mind already picturing the op, a list of supplies he needed keeping pace with his tactical plans.

"You can't go after her alone."

"Like hell I can't."

Reed moved into his space. "This is police business."

"And you can see how well the police have done so far."

Max regretted the words the moment they were out, but he didn't have time to argue with Reed. Tripp Lange had proven himself far outside the law, and the time and red tape to drag him back through it could cost Violet her life.

He'd be damned if he waited.

"I need to get to her."

"I get it, but you can't go in there blind. Tucker and I will go with you."

"Nope." Additional memories assaulted him—each and every op he'd run while in the military like a film loop in his mind. Even the missions that still tormented him with bitter regret had prepared him for what was to come. "It's what I do."

"You're not going alone."

"Like Violet Richardson would ever let me live it down if I dragged her friends' fiancés into battle."

Violet stretched her legs once more, the lingering pain in her limbs stinging like needles. She ignored the discomfort—she had mobility again—and kept up the steady pacing through the room. She'd already checked every corner, mentally cataloging what she'd found.

A toddler could have been left alone in the damn room for all the danger it posed.

Even the en suite bathroom was free of anything useful unless she could figure out a MacGyver-like weapon made solely from toilet paper.

Despite several days locked up in jail, Tripp Lange and his flunky had prepared well. She already suspected this room had been specially designed for the purpose of holding someone, and her deliberate search had only proven her correct.

Absolutely no piece of furniture, lamp cord or even bedding had been overlooked. And unless she was planning on making a noose for her captors out of a thick, well-stitched quilt, she was out of options.

The bigger question, to her mind, was what they expected. The rubies, yes, but Lange had to know she'd placed hers in a safe-deposit box. No bank was open on Sunday, yet he'd still gambled and taken her anyway.

Which then brought her back to a question: Where *were* they?

The hours she'd spent knocked out, courtesy of God knew what drug, had ensured she could be down the block from the hotel or clear in another country by now.

Her bet was on something local because he'd want convenient access to the ruby, but still...

A sly, oily panic filled her stomach as a new thought struck.

Was she simply the first taken?

Lange had Lilah's ruby, but that wouldn't mean anything if he felt he could use her friend as a means to his goal. And Cassidy's was hidden, with the same security as the one she'd stowed a week ago. But that didn't mean her friends—the sisters of her heart—weren't vulnerable.

On a hard breath, she fought to keep herself calm. The scenarios she'd already raced through had her pulse rabbiting in response, and she needed to stay in control.

Always in control.

Calming herself, she ticked off the proof points in her mind. Lilah and Cassidy were under watch. They were protected. Tucker and Reed had practically glued themselves to her friends, and she was more grateful than she could ever say for that fact.

Of course, if she were being fair, Max had attempted the same with her, and she'd given him the coldest of shoulders. Which she now knew was not only petty but also the height of stupidity.

Tears Violet hadn't even realized she held back balled in her throat, spilling over in a hot wave down her cheeks. Had she really been so stupid?

Here she was, the professional epitome of responsibility and thoughtfulness. She put together elaborate events—for a living—yet she'd managed to disregard her own life in a wash of pride and arrogance.

So why had she pushed Max Baldwin away?

Strong, stubborn, *capable* Max.

As the man's solid form took shape in her mind, she scrubbed at her cheeks, brushing away the tears. She'd done this—put herself in a place of extreme vulnerability. Over the past two weeks she'd understood the threat but made no effort to understand its roots.

And she'd naively assumed justice would run its course when the man at the heart of the crimes had been captured.

The door swung open on a hard slam, Tripp Lange in its frame like a physical reinforcement to her thoughts. Alex hovered behind him, an obvious deterrent to any attempt at running.

"It's time we discussed the location of your ruby."

Alex closed the door and flipped the lock at his back. As he turned toward her, a paring knife glinted in his hand along with a small sap, no bigger than a sock, in the other.

Violet backed away, the violence inherent in those two items telegraphing itself across the stifling expanse of room.

"Miss Richardson."

Violet said nothing, even as she fought the unsteady pounding of her heart in her throat. These men didn't make idle threats. She and her partners had already seen their handiwork firsthand, initially in the form of Cassidy's ex-brother-in-law, Charlie, dumped at their back entrance. Then, just days ago, Lilah's ex-husband, Steven, had outlived his usefulness to Lange. The man had crawled, bloody and broken, to their shop, dying in Lilah's lap.

"I trust you've rested?" Lange never moved from his position inside the door, but she flinched all the same at his words.

"What do you think?"

"I think you've been deluding yourself."

"How so?" She fought to keep a quaver from her voice,

but the thickness of her vocal cords had the question coming out on a hard croak.

"You have quite the reputation, Miss Richardson. Good family. Impeccable breeding. And a business that's become quite the envy of society."

"I've worked hard. As have my partners."

"Yes, yes." He nodded, his mouth drawn up in a small frown. "And yet, look where it's gotten you."

"Kidnapped?"

"Misguided, more like."

The fear hadn't abated, but even Violet couldn't hide her confusion. "I'm sorry?"

"You've somehow assumed you're above reproach. Invincible. It's a difficult lesson to learn until one is taken down a peg or two." Lange nodded, his face holding the serious expression of a professor leading his class or a respected judge handing down a sentence.

"Was that the purpose of kidnapping me?"

Lange did laugh at that, a small, cold welling of sound that lacked any evidence of humor or warmth. "Goodness no, Miss Richardson. The purpose of kidnapping you was to get the jewels. The advice, however, is offered freely."

"And what advice is that?"

"Never stand in the way of a determined man. It will never end well."

The retort formed but the words lodged in her throat as Lange gestured Alex forward with a quick flick of his fingers. The small bag of who knew what slammed into her stomach with the force of a battering ram, and Violet doubled over, her breath rushing out as pain radiated through her midsection. Before she could catch her breath or even stand, Alex had the sap in motion once more, swinging it down over her hunched shoulders with swift efficiency.

She screamed, the sound barely echoing off the thick furnishings in the room as pain—sharp and dark—rolled through the upper part of her shoulder and down her rib cage.

Tears welled, choking off her air as she fell to her knees. Trembling, she lay on the ground, only to be dragged forward with a hard snap on her wrist. Another layer of pain met the first, and it was only when she lifted her head and registered the thin blade of Alex's paring knife slicing her forearm that she nearly gave in to the black that swam behind her eyes.

Through sheer force of will, she dragged her bleeding arm away while swinging out with her free fist, slamming hard into the only area she could find purchase— Alex's shin. The move was enough to push the man off balance, even as another layer of agonizing pain ran the width of her bruised shoulder.

Alex righted his footing and leaped toward her once more, but Lange held out a hand, stopping the man's progress. "Enough."

"Hardly." The menace layered in that single word was sharper than his blade, and Violet refused to stay on her knees. Rising to her full height, she shot Lange a dark look. "I thought you didn't play with your prey."

"Persuasion isn't play." Those reptilian eyes stayed flat, even as they skipped around the room. "And since you've had quite a bit of alone time in here, I'm sure you've been planning and plotting. So Alex's demonstration was a firm reminder to stop."

Words were on the tip of her tongue—something, *anything*—to give herself the upper hand she was so used to holding, but she held them in.

"Excellent. Since we understand each other, I will be back in the morning with a fresh set of clothing. Then we'll go to whatever bank you've secured your ruby in, and we will retrieve it."

Whether it was her lack of retort or a simple need to punctuate his point, she didn't know, but the hand that swung out and connected with her cheek was swift and immediate.

And had Violet dropping once more to her knees.

"Are we clear, Miss Richardson?"

Although it pained her to utter even that small acquiescence, Violet knew some battles weren't won via a direct attack. "Yes."

The long cut on her forearm still bled, and Violet had finally given in and ripped off the sleeve of her suit jacket, using the thin silk lining as a bandage. Wads of toilet paper made an appropriate layer of protection over the wound, and she avoided thinking about the sting as she continued to settle and resettle herself on the bed.

She knew Lange was ruthless, and she now had several large bruises as an indication of just how far he would go.

And how soulless he really was.

It had been only after long hours of painful pacing that she realized the injuries might work in her favor. She'd run that idea through several lenses, wondering how she might make the appropriate plea with bank personnel.

Or convince them she needed help without putting any additional people in danger.

A casual shrug of her sleeve before revealing the wound Alex had inflicted? A rush of the counter, begging the employees to call the police? There were many ways to create a diversion, but when she imagined the bank lobby of the branch she'd used, she continued to discard each and every one.

Although the bank maintained a shielded teller line,

the outer offices were all unprotected. Add on any civilians in the bank and she was putting a lot of people in danger for a gem she had no interest in keeping. Even if the thought of giving Reed's stepfather what he wanted violated every ounce of decency and goodness she possessed.

Tripp Lange had killed for stones. Repeatedly. They were nothing more than rocks, mined from the earth and given some ridiculous layer of significance by small-minded individuals.

Lilah had discovered the legend of the Renaissance Stones as she came to understand the gems better, and Violet had filled in the gaps with some quick online research.

The stones were originally one stone, mined by the Dutch East India Company in the late seventeenth century and reputed for both its size and exquisite, flawless beauty. It was subsequently cut into the current trio, three rubies of near-perfect quality, all designed to rest in the crown of a king or queen. After its discovery, the stone was brought to a jeweler in Antwerp for cutting. The man was then murdered barely a week after the stones left his possession.

She'd read the history from there, the quiet battle between the Dutch and the English for rightful ownership of the pieces. The wave of misery the stones left in the wake of all who came in contact with them. It hadn't taken long for whispers of a curse to accompany the legend of the stones, and although she'd originally shrugged off the silliness of that line of thinking, a glance down at her arm had Violet reconsidering.

They'd had nothing but trouble since the stones were recovered. Three men—that she knew of—had been murdered at Lange's hand, and his other assistant was killed during the showdown with Reed.

While she was more likely to believe human greed and avarice were at the heart of the stones' mythic power, she couldn't fully disregard the depth of what had already happened.

Or the fact that Tripp's behavior had escalated as he continued to get closer and closer to the jewels.

Pain was a steady accompaniment as she struggled to a sitting position once more. The man already had one stone. He likely had it on him, somewhere in the house. If she could convince him to bring it along to the bank, she could use that to her benefit.

The idea tumbled around in her thoughts and she twisted it, turning each facet as she tried to determine what to do. The stones were large for jewels but relatively small as individual items. Lilah had hidden hers inside her shoe, so the relative size was modest.

Everything she'd understood so far about Lange indicated he was enamored of the pieces, so much so that he'd be likely not to leave the stone behind. Would he carry it in his pocket? Or inside his suit jacket?

With the first real glimmer of hope since she'd awoken in the dim room, Violet realized she could use that knowledge. He had to get her out in the open if he wanted her stone. And when he did, she'd observe his movements and get a read on any area of his body that he focused on with surreptitious pats or subtle favoring.

And then she'd strike.

All she needed was enough motion to get the gem off his person, and she could put it through the window of the bank's teller line. The bulletproof glass had small openings across the line so people could slide their transactions to the teller.

She needed to be sure of her motions and she had to move quickly but she could use that small window. And once she got that stone behind glass, she had a bargaining chip. The others in the bank would be safe because he wasn't leaving the stone behind, and she would refuse to get the second stone if he hurt anyone.

Violet resettled herself against the pillows, the pain fading slightly in the rush of adrenaline and satisfaction. The idea wasn't perfect, and she'd have to deal with the Alex factor as well, but it had merit. And for the first time since she'd woken up, her limbs unmoving, she felt some small sense of control.

She closed her eyes, regulating her breathing as she visualized the layout of the bank. The area where she could make her move. The best spot to overpower Lange. The holes built into the teller line where she could push through the pilfered ruby.

Her small smile of satisfaction was short-lived as a large boom with all the force of a jet engine echoed around her. The bed began to shake and she scrambled to sit up, shocked as the opposite wall vanished before her eyes, crumbling to dust.

Chapter 5

Max ripped off the night-vision goggles as soft light filtered through the space in front of him. The heat signature his equipment had observed through the wall was spot-on, and his heart nearly burst as he caught sight of Violet.

Mentally tallying the time, he waved her forward, the lingering dust clogging the air between them.

"Max!"

The dust was the only reason he could name when his breath caught in his throat, the heavy beat of his heart thudding in his chest.

She was alive.

He'd spent the entire drive convincing himself she was still alive, but it was only at the moment he'd secured the heat signature on his equipment that he finally believed.

Dragging her against his chest, he took one moment to satisfy himself that she was whole before he nodded toward the still-smoldering rubble. "We need to go."

"But the ruby."

"Now!" He glanced down, momentarily puzzled. "Where are your shoes?"

"I haven't had them since I got here. Apparently high heels are weapons."

He nodded, the countdown clock of how quickly Lange would come running still ticking in his head. "The ones you wear certainly are."

The heavy shouts and pounding of feet outside the door registered through the still-settling dust, and he reached for her waist, pulling her up into his arms. Her scream of protest was a surprise, but he ignored it as he maneuvered through the rubble in his thick boots. "I'll set you down outside."

Max moved over the detritus in the room—pieces of bricks, sheetrock and the broken ceramic of a large lamp— before the warm Texas summer night wrapped around them. He set Violet on her feet and grabbed her hand. "Let's go."

Her long legs kept pace with him as they wove over the vast stretch of property that bordered the house. He'd spent the early evening doing full recon of the property and knew this was the most dangerous part of the rescue. The piece of land Lange owned was several acres of wide-open field, rimmed by a thick copse of trees at the property's western perimeter. The trees might provide a measure of safety, but until they reached them, he and Violet were easy targets.

Lange's age worked against him when it came to speed and an ability to keep up, but Max knew they wouldn't be so lucky with Lange's assistant, Alex. Reed had already given Max details on the assistant. He wasn't a U.S. citizen, and digging into international records took time, but what they'd gleaned so far was that he was ex-military.

From his own dealings, Max took the knowledge a step further.

The man was young enough and determined enough to be a massive threat, and the only thing working in their favor right now was the dark.

"He's behind us!" Violet screamed but kept pace beside him, despite her lack of shoes over the hard, dry ground.

A loud shot went wide, whizzing past Max. Although the shot was a bad one, its trajectory gave Max all the intel he needed.

He was the target.

Alex obviously wanted to take him down to gain quicker access to Violet.

"Car's stowed just down the road at the edge of the field. It's my grandfather's car instead of my truck because it was easier to hide. I've cut a hole in the fence for you to wiggle through. Keep on going. It's unlocked and the keys are under the driver's seat."

"What!"

Her words evaporated behind him like smoke as Max flipped his night-vision goggles over his eyes, then stopped and dropped to his knee, gun in his hand. Without hesitation, he found the moving target in his sights and fired. Dirt spewed up at the man's feet, a missed body shot but enough to piss him off. The man slowed briefly to lift his gun, and that gave Max the opportunity he needed.

Hands steady, he lined up his own shot and aimed for the knee. And heard a surprisingly satisfying howl of pain as he hit his target.

The gun was still hot from its recent firing. Max could see where it was flung to the ground, its heat signature imprinted on his goggles. He debated taking one more shot at the doubled-over figure but knew Violet's safety was more important than vengeance.

There'd be time for that later.

Regaining his feet, he followed the imprint of Violet's body, now about a hundred yards away, closing in on the fence that rimmed the property. Max kept his gaze on her bobbing figure and dropped his goggles so she was visible in the moonlight.

She was safe.

That thought kept him company as he raced over the remaining ground. He reached her as she was climbing through the fence, and he couldn't help his quick appreciation for the delectable backside that winked up at him like a beautiful upside-down heart.

"Stop looking at my ass."

Max crawled through, then grinned at her as he cleared the fence. "Ah. There's my girl."

"I'm not—" Her words vanished into the Texas countryside as the unmistakable squeal of tires lit up the night air. Burning rubber assailed his nose as a black SUV came barreling toward them.

"Violet!"

Max had her in hand, dragging her back under the fence and toward a small copse of trees she'd seen at the far end of the property. The sheer menace of the SUV bore down on the car Max had parked down the way. The horrific shriek of metal on metal lit up the air around them, followed by a wash of sparks where the two vehicles struck each other.

Violet found herself briefly mesmerized by the display before the driver shifted, backed up and headed determinedly toward them on the other side of the barbed-wire fence.

Was this it?

Had she really been rescued by Max only to die like this? On the side of the road in the middle of who knew where?

"Come on!" Max's large hand was firm around hers as he dragged her farther into the trees.

As escape routes went, it wasn't ideal, but the trees were enough of a deterrent that the driver would either lose them or have to get out on foot. Max maintained a determined pace, his steps sure and steady as he navigated through the increasingly wooded area.

The SUV crashed through the fence, and the gunning of the engine bore down on them with all the menace of a hellhound. Again, Violet couldn't quite shake the idea that she'd made it this far only to risk death at the hands of a maniac bent on destruction.

The vision of both of them lying flattened in the Texas countryside vanished as she stepped on something sharp, an involuntary cry escaping her lips before she hopped toward Max on one foot.

"What is it?"

"My foot."

Max barely broke his stride. He simply reached for her, slinging her over his shoulder. She wanted to protest but knew the move was meant to protect instead of conquer, so she kept quiet as he headed farther into the trees. Her stomach still stung from Alex's earlier beating, but she held back the cry of pain as her body bounced on Max's broad shoulder.

The man was carrying her, for heaven's sake. She could toughen up and add as little distraction as possible. The SUV's engine faded as they got deeper into the trees, and after another hundred yards, Max stopped.

He set her down, his breathing thick with adrenaline and the additional weight she'd added to the walk. "Bastard can't reach us here in that vanity monstrosity he's driving. Now he's got to follow on foot."

His even white teeth glinted in the moonlight on a hard smile. "And I'd love nothing more than to get him out in the open."

A small thought—albeit brief—flitted through her mind that she should be concerned about Max's obvious relish for violence. Yet the pain that still lingered in her body as well as the memory of waking earlier with absolute lack of movement in her limbs dulled any sense of concern.

She wanted violence, too. And with that realization came another. The firm, steady hunger for vengeance.

The feeling was foreign—she'd felt it only once before—but this time it settled much more easily about her frame.

He fumbled through a large pocket on the side of his pants. "I'd give you my shoes, but their size will only slow you down. Put these on."

She glanced down at a thin set of gloves. The material was flexible but oddly solid. "I've never seen anything like these."

"They're a high-tech fiber designed to give maximum flexibility to the wearer but protect the skin. Sort of like neoprene but better. They weren't designed for feet, but we'll improvise."

The fingers hung off the tips of her toes, but the palms of the gloves were large enough to cover her feet. They weren't ideal, but they were better than what she had— nothing—and Violet nodded after confirming they were snug. "I'm good."

He kept his voice low. "There's a small creek that flows through here. I looked at it during my recon earlier. The creek bed is dry from the summer heat, and we can follow it."

"Where will it take us?"

"I saw a small barn about two properties down. It's a bit of a hike, but we need a place to regroup."

"Where are Tucker and Reed?"

"Dallas. They stayed with Cassidy and Lilah."

Violet nearly stopped, but they'd already wasted enough time, and she had no doubt Tripp wasn't far off.

"Why'd they leave you on your own?"

"I left them."

Moonlight filtered through the trees, and Max only increased the pace as they tromped over brush and fallen logs.

Violet sensed something beneath his words—a hesitation to speak that was very unlike the Max Baldwin she knew.

"Why'd you leave them?"

"I know how to run an op."

"Quite well. Obviously. But I know Tucker has the same training you do, and Reed's a cop. So why the Lone Ranger act?"

Violet knew this was the last moment she should be pushing for answers, but it was suddenly deeply important she understand why he'd come for her. Without backup. At absolute risk to himself.

"Tucker and Reed needed to stay with Cassidy and Lilah. There was no way I wanted them left unprotected."

"They're tougher than they look."

"Tell me about it. Both of them were chomping at the bit to come along."

"So answer my question. Why'd you put yourself at risk?"

"Because—" He broke off, anguish stamped as clearly in that word as if he'd been struck.

"Why, Max?"

He never broke stride—never slowed down—but his

gaze never left hers as they pressed on. "I had to get to you. And if you were dead, I needed to deal with it in my own time. In my own way."

Air whooshed out of her lungs in one hard exhale.

She'd expected either an edgy retort or some smart-ass remark, since that was all she and Max seemed capable of when they were together.

Which made his revelation that much more of a surprise.

The damnable tears that had thickened her throat off and on for the last twenty-four hours welled once more. She'd struggled with self-pity at the wedding and fear for Cassidy and Lilah while in Lange's clutches. These tears were for something else.

Max had come for her.

Despite their constant war of words and her usual ice-cold demeanor, he'd come.

The large shoulders that seemed capable of carrying the world hunched in front of her, his unyielding pace moving them ever onward. He looked invincible and acted as if nothing affected him.

Yet she'd misjudged him. Terribly so.

"Thank you. I—"

The hard crack of a bullet broke the night air, piercing the bark of a nearby tree. A second followed in rapid succession, and Max pressed hard on her back.

"Down! Now!"

With movements born from years of training and practice, he had his gun in hand and fired through the trees.

"Where is he?" Lilah asked. "Shouldn't he have her by now?"

Reed fought the twin demons of anger and fear that had kept him steady company since the previous week's showdown with his stepfather, and he pulled Lilah close.

A sense of awe crept in—as it always did when he was with her—helping to assuage the anger even as the fear grew with each passing hour.

He had to protect her. Had to keep her safe. "These things take time."

"Max has been gone since noon. And that's after packing an arsenal in the trunk. He should have gotten to her and called us to let us know she's okay."

"Max knows what he's doing." Or Reed hoped like hell the man knew. He'd sensed all the things that had been left unspoken as Max had driven away, including the man's own anger and fear.

The vigilante approach never sat well with Reed—he'd had too many years of police training for the idea to ever sit well—but he also knew his contacts were unreliable at best and flat-out dangerous at worse.

Tripp Lange was in bed with some high-ranking members of the Dallas PD, and Reed needed to keep his focus there, even if playing the rogue cop was liable to get him kicked off the force. "I should have gone with him."

"We all should have gone with him."

"You and Cassidy are his bargaining chips. There's no way I'm putting either of you within a thousand miles of him if I can help it." He and Lilah had gone a few rounds on the subject, and he knew damn well Cassidy and Tucker had done the same. And in the end, they'd all come back to the same answer. Max would recon the area and he'd rescue Violet. If he needed help, he'd call.

Only the last time Max had called, he was about to step foot on the property and scout the area. And they'd not heard from him since.

"You could have gone, you know. You and Tucker. Cassidy and I would have been fine. We'd have been afraid for you both, but we'd have been fine."

"We're not leaving—" His words were cut off by a rush of air and an armful of woman. Lilah's mouth latched onto his, desperate and urgent. The kiss was a mirror for his own turmoil and the fear that he'd lose her after only just finding her.

The moments wove around them, light as air and strong as the tides, and he reveled in the love of his mate.

His partner.

They'd found each other under the most extraordinary of circumstances, and he knew no matter what happened, he'd take that gift with him always.

Lilah pulled back, a wry smile painting her lips despite the fear that still lingered in her expressive brown eyes. "Sometimes I can't help myself."

"Do you see me arguing?"

"No." She wrapped her arms around his chest and laid her cheek against his heartbeat. "But I wish there had been another way to get her back. I know why you stayed, and selfishly, I'm glad. But I want my friend back."

Reed rubbed the narrow space between her delicate shoulder blades, large, slow circles, as the comfort to be found in another overtook them both. It was his family that was responsible for what had happened. The man might not be blood, but the guilt was rapier-sharp and as tangible as if Tripp had been his own father.

Tripp Lange had practically raised him. He'd been his mother's husband for nearly twenty years. And they'd all been oblivious to the evil mastermind in their midst.

"I want that, too, Lilah. More than I can ever say."

Damn it to hell.

The words played over and over in Max's mind, a harsh reminder that he couldn't lose focus. Couldn't get himself caught up in the what-ifs that had nearly drowned him on the drive.

The air around them settled and Lange remained quiet, the cease-fire in the woods undoubtedly temporary. Max dug in one of his pockets for a bomb of tear gas. He didn't want to waste the opportunity and knew the air would disperse the effects quickly if he didn't hit Lange just right.

Dropping his goggles back into place, he watched and waited for the heat signature of Lange's body to register, satisfied when a dim area about twenty yards away lit up.

Gotcha!

He lobbed the bomb toward his quarry before laying down a round of fire. The man fell to his knees, his hard shout quickly absorbed by the thick foliage. The form in his sights lay unmoving, but Max waited a moment. He placed a hand on Violet's arm, holding her steady, and uttered a quiet "Shhh." He got a subtle nod in response.

He watched Lange's form through his goggles and saw the man get to his feet before he bent over again at the waist, the tear gas obviously doing its work. Max aimed, prepared to take one more shot, before the figure turned and ran, moving in the opposite direction.

The urge to follow was strong. No, Max amended to himself. The urge to *hunt*.

But Violet's safety came first.

The barn was still a fair walk away, and they had to cross wide-open field once more before getting to safety. Although Lange had turned tail, Max had no illusion the situation was anything resembling permanent.

The man would regroup and try again.

And there was no way in hell Max was letting him get away.

"Do you see anything?" Violet's whisper floated up to him, even as she stayed down as he'd instructed.

"He turned away. Headed back for reinforcements, no doubt."

"Did you—" Her sharp breath hissed in the dark before she continued. "Did you kill Alex?"

"I got his knee."

"Was that intentional?" Violet struggled to her feet, her movements stiff.

"Let's just say it wasn't unintentional."

"Whatever that means," she muttered as she rose from her bent position at the waist.

Violet had two speeds—still and crazy—so the gingerly movements were an immediate red flag. "Are you okay?"

"Fine."

"You're moving slow."

"I've been lying on hard ground." Her gaze was averted, her focus fully on brushing off her skirt. Since the suit was beyond ruin, the move was a clear evasion.

He didn't know Violet Richardson as well as he'd like, but he did know the woman didn't back down. And her voice was always full of absolute certainty.

So the hesitation he heard there was a massive clue.

"Did they hurt you?"

"Does it matter?"

Max gazed once more in the direction where Lange had lain before pulling off the goggles and turning toward Violet. He hugged her close, the sudden need to touch her overwhelming any sense of distance he usually created on an op.

She wasn't simply an object to be saved. And he wasn't going to keep pretending he had any objectivity.

At all.

He wrapped her tight in his arms. She stood stock still for the briefest moment before he felt her relax, her arms moving around his waist.

They needed to keep moving and put as much distance as possible between Lange and her.

But for the briefest pause, he wanted to touch her.

If he touched her, he wouldn't go stalking off through the brush, laying down round after round of fire that would kill Tripp Lange before anyone had a chance to question him. Before they understood just how deep the corruption went and how far Lange's influence extended.

Before Reed has his fair shot at his stepfather.

He hadn't known Graystone long, but the detective was a good man, and he deserved a chance to look his stepfather in the eye and demand answers.

So he held on to Violet and willed himself to stay in the moment.

The gentle rise and fall of her chest against his calmed like no words could. For now, he'd focus on the fact that she was safe and whole. And once he got her settled in the barn, he would head back to the car. It might be ruined, but he could retrieve his cell phone and the items Cassidy and Lilah had packed for Violet that were in the trunk.

Max had hated leaving the phone behind—along with access to the people waiting for them back in Dallas— but he hadn't wanted it on his person in the event things went sideways in the compound. Once he'd retrieved it, he would call the guys and give them Violet's location.

And then he'd go hunting.

He'd never considered himself above the law, but he'd also never had a reason to take it into his own hands. That had all changed the moment he'd seen Violet slump against Lange's man on the video feed at the hotel.

They'd laid hands on her.

And there was no way they weren't paying for that choice.

Chapter 6

Violet peeled the gloves off her feet, surprised they'd worked so well. The scratches she'd suffered early on still hurt, but she'd sustained no further injuries since Max had given her the gloves.

The gentle whicker of horses drifted up to her, and she took some small comfort in the soft noises. There were two equine occupants of the barn, and they'd been relatively uninterested in their new roommates when she and Max had crept inside. He'd already staked out the area, leaving a window unlocked. She nearly had a leg over the sill before he stilled her, slipping through the window, then coming back around to let her in through the barn's rear door.

Now here she was, ensconced in the barn loft. Although deeply grateful for the rescue, she'd grown increasingly aware of the outfit she'd put on the previous morning and which had now seen its fair share of dirt, grass stains and sweat.

Scrumptious.

"Our supplies are in the car, so we're S-O-L there, but I did sneak a box of granola bars from the office downstairs. Snagged a few waters from the office fridge, too."

An odd sense of reality stole over Violet as she tried to process Max's words. During the time in Lange's clutches, she'd vacillated between sheer terror and crafty calculations. Although on opposite ends of the spectrum of emotion, each was accompanied by steep adrenaline spikes that kept her alert and on edge.

The sight of Max sitting beside her, the air around them quiet, his hand full of the same brand of granola bars she snacked on during the days she missed lunch, pierced the bubble of unreality.

Voice unnaturally sharp, she wagged a finger. "We can't steal these."

Max shrugged. "I left a twenty in the desk drawer. It more than pays for a few granola bars and bottles of water."

"Still. We—"

"Eat it, Violet. There's no sin in taking what you need at the moment you need it."

Again, that damnable compulsion to argue rose up, but she tamped it down, instead taking a bite of the bar he'd already unwrapped for her. Seemingly satisfied, Max unscrewed the cap on one of the waters and handed it over. "Hydrate a bit. I can't imagine you had much at Lange's, and you need more water to help dispel whatever it was they drugged you with."

"The side effects have faded."

"Humor me and drink it anyway."

Violet did as he asked and took a sip, the oh-so-familiar urge to do battle with Max simmering in her veins.

"How'd you know where to find me?"

"We knew you were kidnapped almost from the moment it happened." Before she could ask, he added, "I was in the security office at the hotel and saw you taken on the screen. We were on it immediately. I'm just sorry it took as long as it did to get to you."

"But you were so fast. How could you know where they'd taken me?"

"Reed summoned a few officers he trusted, and we tracked the traffic cameras. Lost you after several turns downtown, and then it was Reed's colleague in digital forensics who did the digging to find Lange's investments. That's what got us the lead on the property."

"And then you came alone to get me."

"I know what I'm doing."

They sat in silence. She had a million more questions, yet none seemed able to form. Instead, a series of abstract thoughts flooded her mind, as shapeless as air.

Did Kimberly and Jordan get off on time for their honeymoon?

How had she never noticed just how broad Max's shoulders were?

Who closed out the event with the hotel?

Was it her imagination, or did the blue of his eyes hold secrets?

And underneath it all, the lone thought that had kept her company on their jaunt through the properties that rimmed Lange's place.

He'd come for her.

"Did Kimberly and Jordan get off to their honeymoon?" As the question came out, another, more alarming thought hit her. "Do they know what happened to me?"

"Gabriella stepped in and finalized the last few details for the guests so Cassidy and Lilah could join Tucker,

Reed and me in the security suite, and then Cassidy closed out the bill before we left." Max downed the rest of his water and crushed the plastic in his hands. "The bride and groom knew nothing."

"Good."

"Good?"

"Of course. They were my responsibility. I'd hate to think this incident ruined their wedding."

"You'd think you'd take yourself as seriously."

The words were low and barely audible as they faded into the straw that surrounded them in the loft, but they were as powerful as an atomic bomb. Violet set her shoulders, even as the tight movement ran a layer of pain down the back of her rib cage. "Kimberly, Jordan and their guests were my responsibility."

"*You're* your responsibility. And yet here you were, traipsing outside the hotel without a damn care in the world." Max moved closer, his gaze ruthless on hers.

"We moved into the last hour without any issues so I did a sweep outside. I made sure several couples got into taxis because they'd been drinking, and then I just needed some air. Just a minute or two to myself."

"You got your freaking minute, all right." The veneer of judgment walled up between them with surprising efficiency, as unmovable as bricks mortared together. But before she could say anything, Max leaned in even closer, his eyes awash in blue flame. "And for the record, darlin', this was more than an incident."

"You know what I meant."

"Do I? Because to anyone listening, all it sounds like is that you chipped your fresh new manicure."

"I—"

Violet fought to find the right words, Max's anger and disdain like a living, breathing, *writhing* thing between them. Which made his next move even more surprising than she could have imagined.

The man dragged her forward onto his lap and slammed his lips down on hers. Her skin prickled with awareness and she dug her fingers into those strong, re-assuring, *safe*, broad shoulders, able to do nothing but hold on.

With a soft cry in the back of her throat, Violet parted her lips. Their tongues met, slightly hesitant before their verbal battle of wills morphed into something far more elemental and needy.

Desire flamed to life between them, so hot she thought her clothes might incinerate at the touch of his fingers. With a need born of endless, lonely nights and fueled by the recent reality that she might never see him again, Violet took what she'd secretly wanted for so long.

Heady satisfaction whipped through Max, a desperate urgency counterbalanced with a fierce need to both pro-tect and pleasure. He'd never experienced anything like it in his entire life, including the wild frustration that she wasn't taking her situation seriously enough.

Damn but the woman was infuriating.

And delicious.

And everything he never knew he wanted, wrapped up in layers of haughty disdain and shocking vulnerability.

He wasn't one for games—had actively spent his adult life avoiding them—so it came as no small surprise the strange push-pull that had kept him dancing to her tune for the past year was as strong as ever.

The freaking Pied Piper's song, beating like jungle drums in his blood.

The odd thoughts played a steady counterpoint to the frantic, reckless need to imprint himself on the woman in his arms. From the softness of her skin, to the warmth of her mouth, to the active play of her hands over his shoulders, chest and stomach, Violet was responsive and—in that moment—his.

His hands danced over her skin, following a journey of their own design. Across the soft skin at the V of her blouse, down over the silken material to cup one firm breast, then on to the curve of her hip.

The gentle hum of the barn surrounded them, the soft breaths of the horses. Louder noises drifted from outside, the sounds of August. The rapid, high-pitched whine of cicadas moved through the air, a subtle melody full of life and energy.

Violet was *alive*.

He'd scarcely allowed himself to think otherwise on the entire drive to the compound, even as the raw, aching fear he wouldn't arrive soon enough haunted him through each and every mile.

Pushing the thoughts away, he focused on Violet—on life—and eased her down onto a blanket he'd found in a corner of the loft. She hadn't stopped kissing him, her own movements growing more and more frantic.

Max stilled and lifted his mouth from hers. His fingers were at the buttons of her shirt, and he hesitated for the briefest moment before her hands came over his. Her smile was bewitching in the moonlight. "Please."

He needed no further encouragement but was surprised to realize how his hands trembled as he worked the small pearl buttons. The material floated over his wrists as he pushed it aside, then pressed his lips on the soft curve of her breast. Her heart beat beneath his lips, sure and true, and Max cupped her breast before moving lower.

The hard cry that escaped her lips shocked him, and Max went still.

"Violet?"

"I'm sorry. I'm—"

An image of her slowly regaining her feet earlier came back in a rush, and Max scrambled to a sitting position. "Where does it hurt?"

"Nowhere."

"Where?"

Her gaze narrowed but she didn't close her blouse. "Here." She pointed toward her stomach before tapping the back of her shoulder, then her forearm. "And here and here."

Max ran his hands over her stomach, his touch gentle as his fingertips grazed the bruised area. Now that he was looking for the injury, his gaze clinical instead of heated, it was easy to see the purple bruising over her diaphragm in the dim light of the barn. Rage erupted in his veins, hotter than lava, but he held all notes of anger from his tone. "What did they use?"

"It's over, Max. It's done."

He lifted his eyes from the bruising, his suspicions already racing toward her captors' likely brutal methods. "What was it?"

She blew out a breath. "Alex had a small sap. I don't know what was in it, but—" She hesitated, then reached for the edges of her blouse, drawing the material together. "It doesn't matter what was in it. The damn thing hurt."

"An old choice but highly effective."

Violet sat up, her slight wince dragging at the corners of her mouth before she spoke. Her head was down, her voice muffled into her chest as she focused on redoing her buttons. "Lange said he doesn't play with his prey. His lackey clearly feels differently."

"All evidence to the contrary on Lange. Hiding behind someone else doesn't change the intention." Once again, pure white-hot rage tinged the edges of his vision red. If he weren't so concerned for her protection, he'd have already left the barn.

Prey my ass, Max thought to himself. Lange had no idea what that really meant.

Or what it truly meant to be hunted.

"That's why they call it dirty work." Violet shook her head. She opened her mouth to speak, then shut it once more. Finally, after what was an obvious internal battle with herself, she spoke.

"It's his eyes. They're soulless. How does that happen?"

As a woman known for her calm efficiency, he sensed how much it cost her to try to maintain that illusion. Her voice quavered, and her hands fluttered at her stomach, smoothing the material lightly over the now hidden bruise.

"How does what happen?"

"Reed's mother lived with the man for decades. He's well respected in the community. And he's got a lot of good, active business interests. How does a person hide who he really is that way?"

Since he'd wondered the same, he could only agree. How did a person live such a dual life? And although the question would haunt Reed for the rest of his life, Max knew they'd all carry the scars.

"Lilah bore some of that with her abusive ex-husband," Violet said. "One face in public and another in private. But this is something else entirely. Painful as it was, Lilah at least knew the monster she lived with. Reed's stepfather has lived two lives for years and years."

"And he dragged you into the wrong one." Max extended a hand to cup her cheek. "Oh, Violet, I'm so sorry."

He was a soldier. He'd trained with the full understanding that orders were orders, oftentimes fraught with difficult actions. He knew how to do the job. How to handle the decisions others didn't want to make or weren't capable of handling.

Yet he'd have taken any op and gone up against any enemy rather than face the tears that glistened in her eyes.

"It's okay. Shhh now."

Max had created a small private area when he'd scouted out the barn earlier, using several boxes and bales of hay to carve out what minimal protection he could. He leaned back against the edge of a bale, already covered in an old blanket, and opened his arms.

Violet moved into them without hesitation.

The tears subsided almost as fast as they'd begun, but Violet's grip remained tight about his waist long after her breathing slowed. Max gave her the space to process what had happened, all while tracing warm, smooth circles on her back. He'd felt her wince when he hit a particularly sensitive spot and took care to avoid what was no doubt a nasty bruise.

And each time he avoided it, he counted yet another way he was going to rip Tripp Lange limb from limb.

"I never cry." Her soft statement floated up toward him, a quiet interruption of his violent thoughts.

"Everyone's entitled to a few tears now and then."

"But I don't cry. It's not in my nature. And now I haven't stopped since the wedding. I just needed to catch my breath. That was all. That's why I went outside. And then Alex was there and the world faded to black."

Max stared down at her upturned face, sensing something deeper in her words. "Why were you crying at the wedding?"

Violet hesitated, the silence so unlike her that he

thought she might not have heard him. He almost repeated his question when she pressed on. "Have you ever felt like that? Like you wanted to bind your life to someone forever?"

"I believe I asked you that question at the wedding."

"I know. And I was an ass to jump at you."

"You weren't an ass."

"I was—"

He cut her off, punctuating the intrusion with a soft stroke of fingers against her cheek. "You weren't."

"I've avoided it so far."

"Me, too."

"That's because you're Mad Max."

"I'm what?"

A small smile lined her lips—the first since he'd found her—and the sign that she might ultimately be all right shot straight to his heart.

"That's one of my nicknames for you. In my head."

"There are others?"

The smile grew wider. "A few. It depends on if you're being stubborn Max or grumpy Max or angry Max. You seem to trade off between the three."

"I'm not—" Well, hell. Yeah, he was. He'd always been short-tempered, and his time in the military hadn't morphed his personality toward bubble gum and flowers. Heck, his major job description had been blowing things up for a living for most of his adult life.

He simply did not have a hearts-and-unicorns personality. *Thank God.*

"So I'm not altar-bound because I'm a grumpy bastard."

Violet's smile fell and with it, the light teasing they'd drifted into. "I'm sorry. That's not what I meant."

"Doesn't change the fact you're still not that far off

the truth. And for the record, I'm not against marriage. I just figure you need to marry the right person."

"You've never found the right one?"

"Not by a long shot. Add on family members who made poor life decisions in that territory and I'll proudly own gun-shy with cold feet as a personality descriptor."

The words tripped off his tongue, as simple as breathing, but Max knew the ability to speak them so casually was hard-won. His parents had been screw-ups in every sense of the word, far more worried about the latest big-ticket item they could charge on their credit cards than the kid they'd brought into the world.

His grandfather had stepped in, well aware of the poor choices of his son and daughter-in-law, and tried to add balance and a sense of responsibility. The man's efforts had worked for the most part, but Max knew there were still holes.

And one that sat clear in the middle was the recognition that his grandfather had spent Max's childhood attempting to make up for his own poor parenting.

"Where'd you just go?"

Although he'd adjusted to the relative darkness of the loft, the shifting moonlight through the barn's upper windows kept changing the light as clouds moved in and out of position. Moonlight painted her face and in the soft light her eyes seemed to glow. In their depths, Max saw the clear interest and intelligence no amount of fear or uncertainty could erase.

"A memory."

"The one who got away?"

"Nah. Not unless you count Bellamy Moore in the first grade. But since she dumped me for a second grader, I suspect she doesn't truly count."

"Then what?"

Whether it was the moonlight or the adrenaline of the simple desire to help her forget the pain of her bruises, Max wasn't sure, but he found himself giving up information he normally wouldn't. "There was always my grandfather. He took me in when things at home got bad. First just overnight or the weekend. As I got older, more permanently."

"Were things bad often?"

"Nothing in the physical sense. But a kid who's ignored can get into a heap of trouble if no one's watching."

"And Max Senior stepped in?"

"He did."

The smile returned and with it a small sigh. "I do have a soft spot for him. Does he know you're here?"

"We thought it best not to call them until it's over. He's still in hiding with your landlady and Reed's mother. Reed's been managing the communication there so he can make sure his mother doesn't attempt to come back to Dallas."

"They've stayed put?"

"Mrs. Beauregard's still recovering from her run-in with Lange a few weeks ago. And if Reed's mother needed any further convincing, the fact her husband went after her son pretty much has her staying put while we deal with this."

"It must be driving your grandfather mad."

"He's staying busy with his charges."

"And a side of romance?"

Max shook his head. "For someone who doesn't feel romance is your thing, you certainly are quick to identify it in others."

"Because then it's fun."

"You do realize others think the same thing for you."

"Cassidy and Lilah know I'm not marriage material. I never have been."

The absolute certainty in her voice struck him with a swift slap, and for the briefest moment, he wanted to reach out and pick up exactly where they'd left off. Sex might not be love and marriage, but her response had been something more than a casual mating of lips, a careless connection of bodies.

Violet felt something. Something for *him*, to be more precise. And he knew damn well he'd had something brewing for her for some time now.

How odd, then, that she'd bring up her friends as a reason for the fact she wasn't going to marry. He'd have bet the next year's profits from his business that Cassidy and Lilah were more than convinced Violet Richardson would make excellent relationship material.

Since they'd seemed to shatter some invisible wall between them, he pressed on, curious about what new information he might learn. "It's your turn."

"For what?"

"For confessing. I told you my life story, including the pain of my broken first-grade heart. Your turn." He pressed a soft kiss to her forehead, the motion natural and unplanned. He almost cursed himself for it but stilled when the arms around his waist held on a bit tighter.

"No first-grade skeletons in my closet, but I did cause the breakup of the year in third grade. I had a crush on Simon Asher, who had been the boyfriend of Mallory Coltraine."

"Vixen."

"You're not kidding. I whispered in his ear at recess, and word got back to Mallory that Simon wanted to change his loyalties."

"And did you and Simon become the main squeeze of the third grade?"

"Oh, no. I dropped him like a hot potato when I found out he hurt my friend."

Max shook his head, fascinated that the challenges of dating and relationships didn't necessarily change with age. They got more complicated, but they didn't truly change.

Boy meets girl. Boy makes bad decisions over girl. Boy loses girl.

"Which takes me right back to where we started," Violet said. "I'm simply not wired that way. Something's clearly missing, because I've never had the urge to bind my life to someone."

Max noticed the small tinge of sadness belying the casual air. "There's nothing missing."

"I manage weddings for a living. You'd think something would rub off."

"No, I'm quite sure I'm right. Not because I'm always right, but because I'm right about this."

He smiled at the light smack to his arm, the exact reaction he was looking for.

"You're bright and vibrant. You're a catch, Miss Richardson. Don't forget it." It might have been the oddest conversation he'd ever had, but Max pressed on. "Someone's going to be lucky to have you."

If only it could be me.

The thought slammed into him so hard Max wondered how he didn't see stars.

Chapter 7

Violet shrank in fear as Alex seemed to grow larger before her eyes. Violence coated his skin in a grayish tinge, and she tasted blood on her tongue even though he hadn't touched her yet. Madness roiled behind his dark eyes, and for a moment, she found herself caught up in it.

How did one get to that place? Where the blackness of the soul literally poured out like lava?

She could see it on him.

The darkness of his eyes. The pallor of his skin. And the great, growing mass of muscle that levered up to its full height in front of her.

I'm going to play with you for a good long while.

"Violet!"

She screamed at the large hands that held her shoulders and then struggled even more when one hand covered her mouth.

"Violet. Shhh."

She struggled against the shackles, her only thought

the raw fear and panic that once again she couldn't move. Couldn't use her limbs. Couldn't run.

Something warm and strong penetrated the haze of fear, and she blinked her eyes open, only to look up into Max's gentle blue gaze.

"I'm sorry, but you screamed, and we can't have the horses agitated." He lifted his hand from her mouth. "Are you okay?"

"Fine." Her voice croaked out and with it, the last tendrils of the dream dropped their hold. "What time is it?"

"About six. The house hasn't stirred yet, but they're bound to get here shortly to feed and exercise the horses."

"Then we need to get out of here."

"I need to get out of here. You're going to stay put while I scout out the car and the damages. If you stay quiet, no one will even know you're up here."

Whether it was the lingering images of the dream or the return of her personal equilibrium, Violet sat up, the argument already spilling from her lips. "We're in this together."

"You don't even have any shoes."

"I've got the gloves, which worked just fine last night. And you mentioned there are clothes for me in the car."

"If there's still a car to retrieve them from."

"Then let's walk into town and call the guys. They'll be here in no time, and we can go home."

"You think Lange hasn't shored up his investment down here? He's bound to have tabs on his neighbors and the farm. And possibly even more people in his pocket."

"He's also bound to have an eye on the car, if the car's even there. It could be a burned-out pit by now. We need to head out on our own."

As arguments went, it wasn't the most cheerful, but Violet was damned if she was going to stay behind while he got himself into who knew what. There might be danger out in the world, but there was plenty of danger by herself.

She'd take her chances with Max.

At the realization that she trusted him with her life, images of the night before washed over her, filling her thoughts in a rush.

How patiently he'd held her, keeping her close as she shed the adrenaline and terror of her kidnapping. The feel of his hard body, wrapped around hers in a physical display of strength that went a long way toward calming her mind. The quiet conversation that had given her a chance to express the jumble of emotion that had kept her company far longer than she'd realized.

But it was the memory of their kiss that lingered in vivid Technicolor. The bold red of desire, woven with the vivid blue of want and the golden sheen of tenderness. For a man as large as Max, he was infinitely gentle, touching her as if she were precious. Treasured.

Revered.

She'd never given much thought to the flowery words her brides had used over the years, so many of them flustered with the scale and scope of details that went into planning a wedding, but there were a few conversations that had stuck with her. She still recalled the way one bride spoke of her fiancé and how he smelled like strength, vulnerability and the outdoors. Another had spoken of how her love listened to her as if she was the only woman in the world. And a third had practically glowed when she talked about the warmth and safety she felt in her new husband's discarded shirt from the day.

Touching flashes, shared in moments rife with happiness and hope.

She'd never put much stock in the fanciful words,

but she had to admit every one of those conversations had smacked of someone who knew—and observed—a person she cared deeply for. With that in mind, Violet admitted to herself it was more than a little strange to acknowledge just how much she noticed about Max Baldwin.

Max's disgruntled march around the small loft brought her back from the deep end of her memories, and she couldn't quite hide the smile. The two of them might not use flowery words with each other, but they had come to a funny sort of communication. Whether they'd become resigned to each other out of necessity or sheer, stubborn strength of will, she didn't know.

But as she slipped her feet into the funny little gloves, Violet had to admit that she and Max had cleared some hurdle the night before.

Was it the kiss? The conversation that came after the kiss? Or the almost *something* that came before the kiss? Although the pain had put a quick end to their exploration of each other, she still didn't think that was quite the root of their standoff.

No, it was their conversation that had been the revelation.

She knew he was close to his grandfather but had no idea their relationship had grown from the pain of his parental abandonment. And while she'd teased him about his grumpy disposition, she now suspected his lack of finesse was more about barreling his way through life on his own steam than any real intention to hurt someone.

Sort of like you.

The thought had her hands going still, the small stalks of straw she'd picked from the gloves dropping to the floor.

She'd seen a lot of brides come through the doors of

Elegance and Lace. And inevitably, the ones who always struck her as having the strongest shot at a happy marriage were the ones who were compatible with their spouses.

She wanted Max and had admitted as much to herself already. If she hadn't been hurt the night before, would they have gone further?

A quick glance down at her soiled clothing had her sighing. She wanted to think the lack of a shower and some lingering bruises had been the reason for interrupting their sexy moments, but maybe it was something more.

The lack of a shower was a convenient excuse, but that's all it was. An excuse.

Perhaps the real problem was that having sex with Max would have consequences. Such as acknowledging the feelings she had for him ran far deeper than she ever wanted to admit.

Alex stroked the gun in his lap, the barrel still warm from his early morning run-in with the property owner. His leg throbbed, and his makeshift stitches, while neat and even, were his own handiwork. Baldwin's intent had clearly been his knee, but the bullet had missed bone, instead nicking a sizeable ball of flesh out of his calf. It might have left him with greater mobility, but the damn wound burned like the fires of hell.

With a practicality born of years of self-control, Alex shrugged it off, well aware he'd soon have his revenge. The wound would heal. And he'd make Baldwin regret the fact he wasn't a better freaking shot.

A mistake Alex hadn't made with the farmer.

Alex had convinced Lange they needed to do a sweep of the area, but he'd almost overlooked the Rolling Acres farm. At the last minute he'd remembered from their initial tour of the region that there was a property about two miles away from the compound. The farm was modest, with limited production, and he'd have forgotten it if not for Lange's pronouncement that he'd lost Baldwin and Violet heading west. A quick review of the area online and he'd remembered the property.

He'd also done some additional digging on Baldwin. While he believed in living and dying by the sword, he believed even more strongly in the benefits of knowledge. And his homework on Baldwin had been extensive. Their opponent was ex-military, Army Corps of Engineers, before opening his architectural firm a few years prior. While his ostensible skills were around architectural and structural stability, the man had spent time on active duty. Which meant he had enough survival training to know how to handle himself when things got rough.

Baldwin he'd expected, but Violet Richardson was a surprise.

She was a hellcat. He'd give her that. Those dark green eyes and lithe body were sexy as hell, and he'd looked forward to spending time with her. There was nothing he enjoyed more than a worthy opponent, and the defiance in her gaze had given him all the clues he needed that she would be a rather enjoyable sparring partner.

Where he was more concerned, Alex admitted to himself, was the Duke's increasing instability. The man had proven himself an admirable leader, which made the past few days that much more concerning. Lange was devastated over his wife. His desire for the Renaissance Stones hadn't diminished, but his acquisition of the first on the same day his stepson spirited his wife away to safety had set off a strange sort of distraction that, at times, seemed to border slightly on madness.

Was it possible Diana Graystone had crept in and demolished the man's defenses?

Alex had emigrated from Germany in the last decade, and his father's old friend was already married when he arrived. He'd never believed Tripp Lange put anything above his goals and ambitions—a perspective Alex respected beyond measure—yet the last days had suggested otherwise.

He knew it wasn't his place to act without authority, but he'd not dealt with this version of Lange before. The man had been inconsolable last night, stumbling into the house with his eyes streaming tears, his ranting troubled and disjointed.

Diana. The rubies. Violet Richardson. He'd muttered about all three in an endless litany of frustration and deep-seated ire.

For the first time, Alex had to admit, Lange's fear had been evident, oozing from the man like a poison. It had pained him see his mentor and leader in that state, but those moments of madness had given him all he needed.

From here on out, he'd act on his own.

It was the only way.

And once he'd proven himself—and once his leader was more stable—they'd renegotiate his terms of service.

Max searched the barn before slipping out the back door. He'd had the last-minute hope he might have overlooked an old cell phone or ancient landline the night before, but a quick look through of the small structure had confirmed otherwise.

What he had managed to acquire, though, was baggage.

Despite his best efforts and most reasonable voice—one that lacked any grumpy notes—he'd acquired a stubborn woman who refused to listen to reason.

Hell, she was still battered and bruised, and she wanted to walk miles to get to help.

At the mental image of the large, mottled bruise on her stomach, he ground his heel into the dirt. The thud of the barn door slamming from his hand echoed in the morning air, and he quickly checked himself. They'd made it this far. He'd be damned if he alerted anyone now.

"Max!" Protesting the noise, Violet's quiet hiss resounded through the early morning air.

"I know." He slung his pack up and reached for her, forcing the image to the back of his mind. "Your feet will be okay in those gloves again?"

"They're fine. Let's go."

Just as with Lange's property, they had to cross a large field before they could find the additional shelter of trees and the dry creek bed. He and Violet had lingered a bit too long, and it was a wonder the house hadn't risen yet to check on the horses.

The thought stuck with him as they crossed the length of the property, jangling in his mind like a siren.

"What is it?"

"The farmhouse. There's something—" He broke off, acknowledging the concern was silly. They'd avoided detection, and besides, it was still early. They needed to keep moving.

"What?"

"Nothing."

"No, not nothing. What's bothering you?"

Max glanced back toward the farmhouse that stood proudly in the distance. "It's after six. The sun's up. Where's the farmer?"

"Sleeping in."

"Yeah, right. On a summer morning?"

"Well." Violet hesitated. "Should we go check on him?"

"I'll go—"

She held up a hand before he could say anything else, so it was a surprise when her gentle tone matched the soft glow of her green gaze. "What if something really is wrong? I'd rather be with you than waiting out here alone."

"Let's go check."

They crossed back the way they'd come, and Max couldn't quite shake the growing sense of dread. He trusted that feeling and knew it had served him well in his years on active duty. Farmers woke early, and the fact their farmer hadn't risen while they were hiding on his property was a problem.

Max slipped his gun from the holster. "Front or back door?"

"Let's take our chances at the back." Even with her gloved feet, Violet kept pace right beside him. They started with the back door but quickly moved on when the door wouldn't budge and they saw no sign of life through the windows.

Stepping off the back deck, they edged the house, peeking into each window they passed before rounding to the front of the house and the longer porch that ran the width of the home.

The subtle tingles that suggested something was wrong had turned into a full-on conflagration, and Max forced even, steady breaths through his nose as they continued their methodical search. He kept Violet between his body and the road as they climbed the stairs, then remained behind her as she checked each window.

Where was the farmer? And if something had happened to him, how had he and Violet escaped detection in the barn loft?

Violet saw the body a split second before he did. She

muffled her quick scream almost immediately, the hard slap of her hand to her mouth echoing like a gunshot.

"There. He's in there."

Max held his position behind her but leaned forward, pressing against her back so he could get a better view. Sun dappled the window, and it was only when he shifted against the glare that he saw the evidence he'd feared on their walk back to the house.

A large body lay sprawled beside an old living room couch, one bullet hole piercing the man's forehead.

On a hard whimper, Violet turned into his arms and pressed her face into his chest. "Max. Oh, no. No."

He held her, giving her a moment to adjust as he gently walked them several feet down the porch and away from the window. "Shhh. Shhh now."

Violet pressed her hands to his chest but didn't fully step out of his arms. "What is this?"

"Sadly, a gut instinct proven correct."

"It's madness. Wherever Lange goes, he creates destruction and death." Violet shook her head before tentatively turning back toward the house. "That man did nothing, absolutely nothing, and look how he's paid. If we'd only picked somewhere else."

Max shut down that line of thinking as fast as it began. "You can feel compassion and anger and sadness, but not guilt. We didn't do this."

His words had been harsher than he'd intended, but he was pleased to see them hit their mark.

She slipped from his arms, standing taller. "We are going to stop this. All that's come before is nothing. Charlie and Robert and Lilah's ex, Steven. They knew what they were getting into. They chose to live by greed and their own inner evil. But this man was an innocent."

Several thoughts had brewed as they searched the

house, but one began to clang louder now that they'd discovered the body.

How had he and Violet escaped detection? If Lange knew enough to find the farmer, he'd have known enough to come looking for them, yet they'd been unharmed, seemingly undetected while hidden up in the loft.

A hard frisson of awareness skated down his spine, curling at the base in a tight knot. "We need to go. Now."

"Where?"

"Right back the way we came."

"What? Why—"

Max grabbed her arm and pushed her toward the porch steps. The unease that had kept him company throughout their walk to the farmhouse morphed into something stronger, coalescing like concrete in his stomach.

Something was very, very wrong.

Max pressed Violet down the stairs, then reached for her hand as they were back on the front lawn. "Move!"

A light ping registered a second before the house exploded at their backs.

Chapter 8

Heat seared Violet's back, simultaneously burning even as it blew her several feet from the house. Violet belatedly heard Max's screams, but they were muted in the roar of the fire. She stumbled, the ground practically quaking beneath her, before a firm hand grabbed her upper arm, steadying her.

"Are you okay?"

The sweep of the fire consumed the air around them, but she was still able to read lips and quickly answered yes, punctuating her point with a nod.

And then they ran.

The wall of fire grew hotter, and again, Violet could only wonder at how loud it all was.

Or was that her heartbeat throbbing in her ears?

Their legs ate up the ground, and she and Max pushed as much distance between themselves and the burning farmhouse as they could. The hot Texas air that was normally so stifling in August was practically breezy compared with the conflagration behind them.

Soot and ash clogged her nose, a filthy counterpoint to the rampaging wall of heat.

And still they ran.

The same woods that had hidden them the previous night beckoned, and Max pulled her forward, over the broad expanse of the farmer's fields. Violet abstractly registered the dry soil as it flew up under their feet but kept on moving, desperately drawing air around the thick, lingering mess that clogged her throat and eyes.

So much dust and soot.

Her lungs squeezed and a hard cough gripped her, enough that she stumbled to a stop, tugging on Max's hand to slow him down.

"We have to keep moving."

"Can't breathe." She bent at the waist, struggling to gather breath.

"Violet. I'm sorry, but we have to keep on." Max dragged at the heavy backpack he wore, dropping it to the ground before he fisted his T-shirt, pulling it off over his head. "Wrap this around your mouth and nose. It's not ideal, but it'll do until we get some more distance."

Violet took the shirt, still warm from his body, and nearly had it up to her face when she caught sight of a car in the distance. The fire still raged from the rapidly disintegrating house, but it was the black sedan bumping sharply over the ground that caught her attention.

"He's—" She broke off as Max grabbed her hand before bending down for his pack.

"It won't be much farther. He can't follow us easily into the woods."

She lifted his shirt to her nose, covering her breaths from the worst of the fire, and began moving once more.

Although she wasn't fond of her daily trips to the gym, she offered up a small prayer of thanks for the conditioning and followed behind Max.

They zigzagged through increasing brush, the ground growing rockier as the landscape altered. The trees were still some distance away, but the change beneath her feet offered some solace they might have a shot at disappearing.

She risked a glance at Max, his hard form pumping beside her. Sweat glistened off his skin, and the hard curve of his shoulder moved in time with the motion of his body. A hard shot of awareness pooled in her stomach when her gaze drifted over the tribal tattoo that painted his biceps, and she cursed herself for the moment of awareness.

So not *the right time or place to notice, girlfriend.*

The distinctive echo of a gunshot only reinforced the thought, the bullet whizzing mere inches from their position, and Violet refocused on her feet. One foot in front of the other. Step by step.

A hard lance of pain lit up her chest, the exertion and lack of clean oxygen coalescing in her lungs like a hard knot. She stumbled and tugged hard on Max's hand, dragging them both into her staggering fall. As she tumbled forward, trying to catch her footing, another gunshot flew past them, embedding itself in the hard ground with an explosion of dust and clods of hard-packed earth.

Max's arms came around her waist and pulled her close. They fell into a roll to the ground. She hung on to him, the press of his body catching nearly all the force of the unforgiving ground. The moment they came to a stop, he moved on, rolling to his feet with his gun in hand.

"Wait for my mark!" Max hollered the words as he lined up his shot.

The car was still about twenty yards away from them, stopped in the middle of the field, with Alex visible in the open driver's window. Max wasted no time and fired off three rounds.

The shots lit up the morning air, and Violet watched as each pierced various points of the car.

Windshield.

Driver's window.

Gas tank.

Alex had ducked along with the bullet that struck the windshield, but it was the hit to the back of his car that had the man scrambling from the vehicle.

"Now! Keep moving."

Violet followed Max's lead, back on her feet and racing beside him when a thick horn lit up the early morning air.

Max never slowed, but he shifted direction, moving them in the path of the oncoming sound. "The train. That's our ticket out of here."

Her lungs burned in pain, every breath a painful wheeze, but Violet kept pace. She would not burden him any further, and she refused to relent.

They'd come too far.

The heavy clack of the train grew louder as it trundled down the tracks, several cargo cars evident in the early morning sunlight. Max tugged on her hand, running them parallel to the tracks as he searched for the proper train car.

When each one that passed was closed up tight as a drum, the adrenaline that had carried her through the last several minutes began to wane.

They'd come so far. *Too* far to end up empty-handed.

Max uttered a string of hard curses when another gunshot flew their way, again going wide. He dragged her farther, their run now a combination of outpacing Alex and searching for a miracle.

The hard-packed dirt of the field gave way to a scattered patch of rocks where the land morphed from private property to professionally maintained train tracks, and it was only when another shot rang out that their miracle appeared.

The back of the train cleared a small curve, and as it righted itself, Violet saw the open cargo door.

"Max! There!"

The renewed burst of energy gripped her, and she forced herself forward. Salvation was in sight, and they needed to time it just right. This would be their only chance.

"You know how to do this?" Max shouted over the roar of the train as he tossed his pack up through the open train car door.

"Not really."

"Stick with me, Richardson." The grim determination that had filled his features made way for a wide smile. "And don't be mad when I squeeze your ass."

Without waiting for her reply, he bent and juggled her into his arms, one palm flat on her rear while the other covered her thigh. That promised squeeze was more of a firm push, and then she was flying up and over the bed of the open boxcar. Her feet hit the metal floor, and she staggered forward several steps before righting herself.

And turned to nothing but empty air.

Another gunshot rang out, and Max toyed with stopping and simply ending Alex there, but he couldn't leave Violet. So he kept his attention on the train car, running alongside until he caught the small ladder that hung from the side of the vehicle. With a hard push off his feet, he swung up to grab the ladder, his fingers fumbling against the slippery metal.

He hung like that for a moment, one hand firmly wrapped around the bars of the ladder while the rest of him dangled against the moving train.

"Max!" Violet screamed his name, her body hanging half out of the train car.

He swung himself up, his other hand snagging the ladder. "Get inside before you fall off."

The muttered curse that greeted his ears had him smiling in spite of himself and his precarious position before she added the obvious. "You're stuck there."

"Get inside, Violet! I know what I'm doing."

"But you're stuck!"

He ignored the exasperation, only slightly convinced falling out of the train would make the damn woman believe that she was in danger, and climbed the ladder to the top of the car. Once he got to the top, the trap door he hoped for greeted him, and he jimmied it open, then slid through into the car.

The face that greeted him was as welcome as it was irate.

"How'd you know how to do that?"

He shrugged. "I played a hunch."

"What if you'd been stuck there?"

"I wasn't."

"But what if—"

Max dragged her forward, crushing his mouth to hers. He spread his legs against the swaying of the train and pulled her even closer, flush against his body.

It wasn't the time or the situation for romance, but he'd be damned if he let another moment go without touching her. Over and over, images of her, pale and wheezing as they dodged bullets, flew through his mind. He couldn't imagine what he'd have done if she'd been hurt.

Decimate Alex, his mind whispered, the dark vengeance at odds with the soft yearning the woman in his arms stirred inside him. With aching desperation, he plundered her mouth, greedy with the need to drink her in.

No, his mind corrected him. To inhale her.

Violet Richardson was a drug, and she'd intoxicated him from the first moment they met. Those long legs, the witchy green eyes and that agile mind that would keep a man on his toes for a lifetime.

He had the abstract satisfaction that she was as into the moment as he was, her hands at his nape, pulling him close. His fingers drifted lazily over her spine, and while he wanted her with an increasing sort of madness, for the moment he was content to hold her and connect in the most basic of ways.

A kiss.

As old as time, yet shockingly original and fresh with the right person.

Everything was original with Violet.

Her hands played over his skin, the heat of her touch branding him. From collarbone to shoulder to chest, paths of liquid fire lit under his skin, far hotter than the blaze they'd just escaped.

The memory of their near miss had him reluctantly lifting his head. "Are you all right?"

"Hmm?" Her eyes had a dreamy, unfocused quality, and Max stopped to enjoy it because he knew it would vanish momentarily.

"The fire and explosion. Did they hurt you at all?"

"No." She shook her head, awareness returning. "The smoke bothered me the most. Trying to breathe through it."

He risked another few moments of her goodwill and checked her over. The outfit she'd worn at Saturday night's wedding had clearly seen better days, but other than the bruising he already knew about, she looked amazing.

"I'm surprised they left this door open."

Max shifted his gaze to their train car. "So am I. The notion of the homeless riding the rails isn't nearly as plausible in today's world of cameras, security checks and vehicular management. This car's open for a reason."

"You think Tripp has influence over this? The train does run behind his property."

Violet was right. The man might have significant influence, but even he wasn't omniscient. "Fair point. He can't possibly be into everything. But I wouldn't underestimate his and Alex's knowledge of the local schedules."

"So we'll take the open train door as a spot of good luck—our first in several days. And stay on our guard."

She kept her legs wide as she moved in a small circle around the moving train car, inspecting the narrow space. "Do we know much more about Lange?"

"Reed's uncovered far more than he expected the past few days, but I still think there's a ton he doesn't know."

Violet settled herself on a small bench built into the train car wall. "His mother, too. She had no idea she was married to a monster."

Reed's mother, Diana, was currently holed up with Max's grandfather and Violet's landlady on a small property that Max had purchased while still in the military. He'd originally thought to send them to the ranch house that had been in the Baldwin family for decades, but he knew the risk of Tripp discovering the location was far too great.

His survival place was small and remote, and Max had paid cash. It would take Tripp Lange a bit longer to manage digging through the records to find it, especially since Max wasn't Tripp's primary target. That hadn't stopped Max from arming his grandfather with an arsenal as well as asking the town sheriff—ex-military, too—to keep an eye out.

But Max had confidence they were in a safe place until the danger blew over. "From everything Reed's said, Diana's a strong woman. She'll manage."

"Maybe."

Max sensed something beneath that single word but couldn't quite place it. "She has no choice."

Violet nodded, and Max was even more curious when she didn't offer up anything else.

"You hungry?" He took a seat on the bench next to her and reached for the pack he'd tossed into the train. "I've still got some granola bars and a few waters from the barn."

She took what he offered and remained silent throughout eating. It was only after she'd finished the water and stowed the empty plastic back in his backpack that he gave his curiosity free rein.

"You don't seem all that convinced Reed's mother will be okay."

"She might survive, but she'll never be okay."

The certainty in her voice piqued his curiosity, and while Max knew the answers weren't simple, he wasn't sure he totally agreed with Violet's assessment. "Tripp hasn't harmed her."

"But he has annihilated her trust. The bedrock of her life has been shattered. People don't recover from that. They can never go back."

"That's not always a bad thing."

"Having someone ruin your life is a good thing?"

Max finished off his own water, stowing the empty

plastic behind Violet's. "It is if it takes you to a better place. The woman's married to a monster. She's better off without him."

"That's callous."

"How is it callous?"

"She's suffering!" Violet stood on the last word, her pacing admirably steady despite the soft swaying of the train. "Her entire life has been ruined, and you think she's better off?"

"I'd rather know the truth and live without a monster than live in the dark with one."

Max knew Violet's arguments had an indelible stamp of female concern and compassion in them—and he agreed with her. Diana Graystone Lange had married a man and shared her life with him, and the whole time he'd hidden a side of himself that wasn't only secretive but downright evil.

But Max also knew how strong and competent women were.

Diana had raised Reed as a single mother, only meeting Tripp after Reed was nearing high school. She knew how to survive, and if the son she'd raised was any indication, the woman not only survived but also thrived.

She was better off without the bastard criminal she'd married.

Violet stopped her pacing and stood in front of him. "She's paying a horrible price. Her trust has been shattered."

"Yes, but Diana didn't do anything. Tripp's duped the entire business community of Dallas."

"So that makes it okay he lied to his wife?"

"Nothing about this is okay." Max ran a hand through the short military cut that made a cap over his head, rubbing on the ends that were too short to tug. "He played a part and lied to her. She did nothing wrong."

"But she's a victim."

While he hated the word—hated every single thing it implied—Max had to agree with Violet's statement. "Yes, she is."

"Which goes back to my bigger point. You simply can't account for it."

"Account for what?"

"Human nature. The things that lurk within. Secrets." Violet laid a hand over his shoulder, the gentle movement a discordant counterpoint to her words. "How is a person supposed to recover from that?"

Violet stood over Max, her legs bearing her weight as the train hummed over the wide Texas prairie, and wondered how she'd gotten here.

The immediate here was obvious. She'd fallen into the hands of a bad man and, through the help of a professional operative, had escaped.

But the bigger here—standing in the middle of a train car arguing with Max Baldwin—was something else entirely.

"Define 'secrets,' Violet. Because the last time I checked, most people weren't walking around with a secret empire, killing off minions they felt were no longer effective allies. Lange's far from the norm."

Lange wasn't the norm, and she knew it. Yet even with that knowledge, Violet was surprised by how much she wanted to spar with Max on this subject. Cassidy and Lilah were her best friends and they knew quite a bit about her, but even they didn't know everything.

Nor were they fully aware of her skewed view of the

world. People lied. They destroyed each other. And they left. It was simply the way things worked.

So why was she nearly bursting to spill all her anger and frustration and bleak worldview on a man who was practically a stranger?

Even if you don't think of him as a stranger. The thought stole in on sly feet, sidling up close and whispering in her ear.

"While I agree most aren't like Lange, people keep secrets."

"Which is their right," Max answered, his hand closing over hers in a warm squeeze. "Just because some people choose not to be open books, spewing forth every thought in their heads, doesn't mean they're hiding criminal tendencies."

"But they do hide disappointment. Unhappiness. Disillusionment." And sometimes a deep, desperate desire to start their lives over.

"None of which is criminal. Or even a bad thing."

"It's not love!" The words ripped from her throat with a force that surprised even her as she snatched her hand back from the comforting cradle of his.

She wasn't a yeller. Heck, she hated even raising her voice. She was responsible to a fault and had been since about birth, and raising one's voice was undignified and childish. So why now?

Why had the shadows of pain and loneliness reached up and grabbed her around the throat in a tight grip?

"What's this really about?"

"Making you see reason."

"Nope." Max shook his head. "Not buying it. If you were simply trying to give me the ol' Violet Richardson drubbing, you'd be having a lot more fun with it."

His hand reached out, folding over hers as he tugged her forward to stand between his knees. "What is it?"

"People do horrible things to each other. They live double lives. They hide their true selves. They change their minds."

It was that last one—that inevitable march toward change—that Violet struggled with. She loved what she did and was good at it, but way down deep inside, in that small niche she kept buried from everyone, she struggled with the fact that it was all for show.

Weddings. Ceremonies. Forever.

No one really got forever. They just got a series of promises that someone could choose to break at any time.

The strong, thick fingers wrapped around hers squeezed her back into the present. "People do change their minds. For reasons that make no sense, they wake up some days determined to be different from who they were the day before. People discard each other. They get hurt or selfish or just tired and bored and suddenly decide commitment's not worth it."

"Yet, we push for it. Seek it with a determination that borders on madness."

"Because it's out there. And because we spend our lives seeking out who we are and trying to build our lives with others who seek the same things."

"So how do you explain Reed's mother?"

Max cocked his head, his blue eyes the color of a stormy sea in the muted light of the train car. "Why does this matter to you so much?"

"Why do you want to dismiss it?"

"I asked you first."

Violet waited, the clacking of the train car lending an almost hypnotic rhythm to their exchange, before she exhaled a breath she hadn't even realized she'd been holding. "It's Reed's mother. And the couple who got married on Saturday." *And my parents.*

"What about that couple?"

"It's all a jumbled mess in my mind. I know they're distinct situations. Honest, I do. But I can't seem to separate the bigger idea that not everyone gets forever."

"Do you think the couple who got married on Saturday won't last?"

"I have no idea. They don't, either. But they took a leap of faith that they would." An image of Kim as she smiled up at Jordan while taking vows filled Violet's mind. "They believe they can make it."

"I don't think it's about belief."

"You don't?" She stared down at him, surprised to realize she'd placed a hand on his shoulder to steady herself. The firm roundness of his shoulder was as reassuring as it was tempting. She snatched her hand back and focused on Max's words.

And if a small smile filled his lips, she'd pretend not to notice.

"I think commitment has a heck of a lot more going for it than belief."

"But you need to believe in what you're doing."

"Of course. But you need commitment to stick around when it's not fun any longer. When there's no wedding dress and no party and no fancy tunes that get you on your feet dancing."

"Commitment for the bad times."

"And for the boring times. Life's not a party every day. It's routine and a daily grind."

"Cheerful."

He shook his head, the smile fading. "I don't mean it that way. But I've seen a lot of people wake up a few years married, well into their routine, who suddenly decide this wasn't what they signed up for. They don't appreciate the fact that having someone sit there every morning and share a cup of coffee is worth far more than exotic trips to Europe or an endless series of parties."

"You want to share coffee with someone?"

"Hell, yeah. If I settle down, I want it to be with someone I want to share my life with and all that goes with it. And I can tell you—" He leaned forward, his gaze full of the same intensity that had sighted Alex down the length of his pistol. "You spend more days of your life doing the routine than doing the spectacular. I expect someone who wants in for the long haul. And a hell of a lot of coffee."

The power and the sheer passion in that gaze sent something shooting through her system, more intoxicating than any champagne. And for the first time in her life, Violet realized there was no breezy response or lighthearted quip to push it away.

It still didn't mean she wouldn't try.

"You failed to mention the item at the top of most men's lists."

"Everyone wants sex." He winked before that cocky smile she couldn't quite resist returned. "That's the prize for putting up with all the routine."

While they'd sparred many times over the past year, Violet had to admit to herself that she saw Max through a new lens.

Sharing a cup of coffee.

Days spent together.

Commitment.

The man had depths she hadn't given him credit for. Worse, she acknowledged to herself, she hadn't even tried.

"You've missed your calling."

"Oh?"

"I should hire you to give marriage counseling to some of my clients. You've managed to make practicality sound sexy and fun."

"I hope I made it sound worth it."

Chapter 9

Reed paced the small office Lilah maintained off her kitchen at Elegance and Lace before returning to the desk and the large highway map he'd dug up from the back of his car. He had traced the route Ryan had outlined for them the day before, then analyzed the various points that spread off the homestead they'd earmarked as his stepfather's.

"He's got this, Reed."

Tucker Buchanan stood at the door, two mugs in his hand. He offered one with a smile. "Full of cream and sugar, courtesy of Lilah."

Reed relaxed in spite of himself, the mention of his fiancée doing something funny to his heart. He'd never felt anything like it before, but since meeting Lilah, his heart had garnered the oddest ability to flip over at the mere mention of her.

"We have no idea how the property's outfitted. They could both be kidnapped by now."

"We both spoke to Max on the drive. He's prepared. And he knows what he's doing."

"So, apparently, does my stepfather."

Reed dropped into the swivel chair Lilah used so infrequently it had a stack of three chef's coats layered over the back. The warm scent of vanilla suggested they were earmarked for the cleaners.

"I should have known."

"Last time I checked, clairvoyance isn't in the job description."

"It's beyond the job. He's family. He's my mother's husband."

"And for almost two decades, he's been a role model, too. I get it." Tucker's dry, sober tone didn't go a long way toward assuaging the anger that still roiled inside, but even Reed had to acknowledge the man understood.

"Damn it!" Reed slammed the mug down, the milky coffee sloshing over the rim. "What if something happened to them? What if he didn't get to her in time?"

"I trust Max Baldwin with my life. He's one of the best damn men I've ever met, and he knows how to take care of himself. He hasn't called for a reason. When he can, he will."

"Don't underestimate my stepfather."

Tucker's retort was whip quick, tossing Reed's words straight back at him. "Don't underestimate Max."

On a nod, tension Reed hadn't even realized he held slipped from his shoulders. "I won't."

Tucker sighed. "But you should probably prepare yourself for a drive. If he hasn't called, it's likely because his plan went off the rails in some way. At some point, he's going to need a ride."

"Why don't we head that way now? He's only an hour south of town. He can't have gotten too far from my stepfather's house, and then we'll be near when he calls." The sense of taking ownership of the problem went a long way toward altering his mood.

"I'll go get Cassidy and Lilah."

Reed stilled. "They can't come."

Tucker shot him a dark look over the rim of his coffee mug. "You don't actually think either of them will stay here."

"I—" Reed shook his head. "I guess we'll take Lilah's delivery truck. There's plenty of room in there."

Violet knew they hadn't been on the train long, but the steady clacking that had initially meant safety was quickly becoming a monotonous bore.

She didn't even have a seminaked man to ogle, she thought morosely. Max had dug a fresh T-shirt out of his bag a short while earlier and slipped it over his impressive physique.

Even as images of that broad chest still lingered, a fresh question surfaced in her mind. "Why didn't you carry your phone when you came to get me?"

"I didn't want to give Lange any possible access to my grandfather or Lilah or Cassidy. I did a pretty solid wipe on it before I left the car, but still—" His lip curled. "Clearly that plan worked out."

"It's—" She swallowed hard at the implications of his forethought. "You put yourself in an awful lot of danger, being without it. What if you needed backup?"

"I didn't."

"Yes, but what if you did?"

Max glanced up from rummaging in his backpack. "But I didn't. Besides, it's just a phone. It can't shoot bad guys, and taking it along was more of a liability. Of course, now that the car's a pancake on the side of the road, Lange's got access to it anyway."

"Only if it's not crushed or if he thinks to look for it."

"Even if he doesn't think to, Alex will."

The mention of Lange's sidekick sent a wave of loathing over her skin, followed by very real, sharp pinpricks of fear.

"He depends on Alex."

"Probably more than he would ever admit."

"When we get home, we should have Reed do a deeper check on the man. He seems to be content to play in the background—" A hard shudder hit her when she thought of how he stepped forward from behind Lange, his expression nearly gleeful, before he beat her.

"We'll let Reed know all we know."

"What if they get away?" The question snaked out before she even fully realized it had lingered in her mind like a poison. Slow-acting yet terribly deadly.

Max wrapped an arm around her shoulders. "They won't."

"That's not an answer."

"Of course it is." He shifted beside her so they were looking at each other. "Tripp Lange, his man Alex and whomever else he's still got in his employ will pay."

"You're not a cop. And Reed's proven pretty conclusively that there's a bunch of dirty brass at the heart of this. How can you know we'll be successful?"

"There are also a lot of good men. Men like Reed. Men like his colleague, Ryan Masterson, who helped us find you. Don't let a small cancer of corrupt individuals convince you everyone on the force is bad."

Violet wasn't sure how, especially with the thick, ambient noise from the empty train car, but somewhere underneath Max's words she heard it. That lingering voice of experience that suggested he knew what he was talking about.

"You seem pretty sure."

"If you paint everyone with the same brush, you're going to get the same results. That's why corruption works. People think they don't have a voice and remaining silent is a better alternative. They believe if they open their mouths, it won't matter because they can't effect change or positive results."

"When did you speak up?"

His arm tightened briefly before he dropped it from her shoulders. "I didn't."

"But—"

"I didn't, Violet. Drop it."

Silence descended between them, about as comfortable as a wool blanket in August. Violet knew she should choose to stay quiet and leave him to his thoughts, but something inside her welled up in a hard rush of curiosity.

Why hadn't he spoken up?

And what did he even have to speak up about?

And where did he think he got off dispensing wisdom like some all-seeing guru?

"You're awfully quick to pass out advice."

As potshots went, it was fairly lame, but she knew Max was as tense as she was. And the fiery retort she was secretly hoping for didn't take long to come.

"What part of *drop it* didn't you understand?"

"Oh, I understand plenty. You march around, all stoic and wise, and expect the rest of us to fall in line."

"I don—"

"You spout pithy remarks about not judging the entire Dallas PD through the eyes of a few, yet refuse to even acknowledge your own experiences."

"It was a long time ago, Violet. Leave it alone. It had nothing to do with the Dallas PD."

"Then what did it have to do with, Max? Because whatever it is, it rides around on your back like a silent partner, dragging you down."

That stoic demeanor she accused him of took over, and as he stood before her, silent and frustrated and mad at the world, she recognized him.

Knew him.

And knew—with bone-deep certainty—what lived and breathed beneath his skin in a roiling sort of anger that couldn't be assuaged.

Violet's dark green eyes had flashed from bright and curious to stormy and irritated without even a blink. How had they gotten here?

He didn't discuss his past. With anyone. Of course, now he had a she-cat on his hands and nowhere to run.

So it was a good thing he wasn't a man who ran easily.

"You sure don't like it when you're not in the know."

"I—" She stopped, closed her mouth, then seemed to think better of it. "Information is my business. And understanding what makes people tick is also part of my business."

"I'm not in your business."

She gave a light snort before staring him down. "All evidence to the contrary."

"I might be *up* in your business but I'm not *in* your business." He pressed his luck and leaned a bit closer, just to that delicious spot where her cheek angled into her ear. "Don't tell me you don't know the difference."

Although the light inside the train was dim, he didn't miss the flutter of pulse at her throat or the steady heat that rose off her body beside him. Need and frustration filled the small space between them, lapping up that heat and pushing it back on both of them tenfold in their close quarters.

Violet didn't move, but he could sense the thick beat of her pulse because of their proximity. "Why'd you come for me?"

She'd asked the same question before and he'd managed to deflect it, but in that moment, he sensed how important it was to her. Lifting his head, he stared down at her, the air fraught with everything neither of them had said for the past year. "Why are you so surprised I came for you?"

While she'd doggedly pursued her line of questions, he was fascinated to watch her close down at his. Utterly and completely. "Why, Violet?"

Her green gaze that flashed from battle to desire and right back again revealed something he'd never seen before.

Pain.

"People don't come after strangers to rescue them."

"You're not a stranger."

"I might as well be. You barely know me. Two weeks ago we were basically just acquaintances who saw each other every month at the local Design District business meetings."

"And two weeks later we do know each other."

The urge to touch her—to punctuate his point—was a fierce need inside him, but he held back. Stilled, really, afraid she'd fly away if he made the slightest move toward physical intimacy.

"We're strangers to each other."

"Whatever you may be to me, you're no stranger, Violet."

"We barely know each other."

"You keep saying that."

"But we don't."

While he would never admit to firing with a full set of brain cells so close to a beautiful woman, Max knew there were far too many things left unsaid between them. His own urge to know her and what drove her nearly had him pressing her for more information, but even he wasn't that big of a hypocrite. He had his own secrets and was still reeling from the sheer relief of keeping them to himself.

So he went with instinct.

And the one thing neither of them could run from.

He leaned forward then, pressing his lips over her soft flesh. Her pulse thrummed beneath his lips, and he took a moment to press his tongue to that sensitive spot, gratified when the tempo sped even faster in response.

"Don't confuse time together with knowing." He flicked his tongue once more against that sensitive spot.

"Max." His name drifted past his ear on a lazy sigh, in distinct counterpoint to the hard clench of her fingers on his shoulders.

"You know me, Violet."

"Yes." Once more, her breath fanned out in another featherlight sigh. "Yes."

Violet's pulse notched up on a hard kick as Max's lips pressed to hers. She was still frustrated he'd avoided her attempts to understand what drove him, but she couldn't argue with how he wanted to pass the time.

And to think she'd considered herself bored.

The wonder of that thought faded at the gentle pressure against her mouth. The tip of his tongue probed the seam of her lips, the gesture sweet and at odds with the power that stretched his body into tight planes of muscle, bone and sinew.

Here was a man in his prime. His body was the result of years of hard work and effort—work he still maintained even after leaving active duty—yet his movements were tender. Soft. And deeply respectful.

The hands he'd settled at her waist grew restless as the kiss heated. Her nerve endings lit up as his fingers found the folds of her blouse, then drifted beneath the material to rub the soft skin of her stomach.

Had she ever felt anything like this before? Or wanted anyone more?

Attraction that she'd diligently attempted to avoid wouldn't be sated as each moment with Max grew more and more precious.

More *necessary*.

The hard peal of the train horn interrupted the quiet moment that cocooned them, and Max lifted his head.

"What is it?"

"That might be our stop." Max crossed to the heavy sliding door, his grip firm on the handholds before he shifted it open. Even though he had his T-shirt on, Violet couldn't miss the play of muscles across his back as he moved the heavy door.

And in that moment, she wondered why she'd spent so many months resisting him.

Even before the break-in and the gems and the threat that was Tripp Lange, she'd been attracted to Max Baldwin. From their monthly Design District business meetings to the occasional run-in around town, she'd been interested.

More than interested, truthfully.

It wasn't just his strength, though she could admit with honesty that she liked his body. Liked the way he looked. But more, she liked how that strength translated to his business and his work ethic. Dallas was a big market, and the city's large architectural firms had a lock on most major projects.

Yet Max and Tucker had managed to carve out a strong niche for themselves, and in a rather short time as well. Max Baldwin showed, day in and day out, he was a man who believed in the value of hard work.

And that appealed.

"How much do you like dirt?"

Violet pulled herself from her musings, Max's vivid blue gaze direct on hers. "What do you think?"

"I think we probably need to avoid the upcoming station stop and get off a bit early."

"You want to jump off?" When he only nodded, she added, "This train?"

"We jumped on."

"We had handholds. And you gave me a boost."

A quick grin flashed at that statement. "And more's the pity I won't get another shot at that spectacular ass. But—" He broke off, his gaze serious. "We can't risk the stop if Lange has mobilized somewhere along the line."

"How fast are we moving?"

"We're not going to jump at this speed."

"And we're not jumping while it's still, so give me some idea of what to expect here."

If their moments wrapped up in each other had been full of a delicious sort of madness, Violet had to admit the admiration stamped in his gaze offered a different sort of heady excitement.

He respected her. And he believed in her. Both were as powerful as his kiss and, if she were honest, far more potent threats to her heart.

"From what I can see, the train has to make a broad curve about a half mile from here. The conductor will have to slow for that curve, and that's likely our best shot."

"You can see that?"

"Gotta love Texas and its wide-open spaces."

Violet snuck up behind him, secretly thrilled when he wrapped a solid arm around her waist, holding her firmly to him against the heavy bumping of the train. She ignored the sudden trip of her pulse and bent to stare out the open train door.

Max's assessment had been spot-on. What he'd failed to mention was the banked drop-off between the tracks and the flatter ground traveled over. "That's a steep drop to the actual ground."

"It's probably about ten feet. We're going to throw everything else out and dangle over the edge before we push off. That should reduce the impact to about eight feet."

"And you think we can do this?"

"Yes."

On a hard nod, Violet stared down at the ground speeding past beneath them. They could do this. They had to.

Because if Tripp Lange and his henchman were at the stop ahead of them, they were never going to make it back to Dallas.

Max watched the play of emotions across Violet's face. He didn't want to press her, but they were losing time to make a decision, the upcoming curve of track closing in on them. "What do you say?"

"I'm in."

He pressed off the door, and retrieved his pack from beneath the hard bench seat. Her long, lithe form silhouetted in the light of the open train door and he offered up a quick prayer he wasn't making a disastrous decision. He'd jumped from higher, but he'd also had training. And he had nearly a hundred pounds on her to help pad his fall.

Max was careful to keep a tight hold on her so she didn't fall out instead of waiting for the proper moment to jump, his other hand tight on the handhelds that framed the door. "Get down on your butt and scoot toward the edge."

She nodded, her eyes wide as she dropped to the hard metal floor. The gloves still covered her feet, an incongruous counterpoint to the pencil skirt and untucked blouse.

Damn, but she'd been through so much.

The anger he thought he had in check rose up to choke him, a tight fist around the heart and throat that cut off the air.

She *had* been through so much, yet she had gamely followed wherever he took them. The inherent trust in the gesture only tightened that fist harder, squeezing his throat into a solid knot.

He couldn't fail her.

He cared for her—knew there was a steady, simmering attraction between them—but even he hadn't been prepared for the wave of protectiveness that filled him when he was with her. Despite the fear, it was the streak that pressed him on. He'd calculated all the angles and estimated their best chances for escape.

It was time to take the shot.

With quick moves, he sat next to her, keeping close so he could maintain a hold on her against the hard air rushing past the train. They had to time this perfectly, and they weren't far from the curve.

"You see that?" He pointed toward a stretch about two

hundred yards away. "That's our best bet. The falloff between the track and the ground is the least of any point.

"Scoot to the very edge of the floor and then push off as much as you can with your arms. Try to bend your knees when you land, and don't be afraid to roll to help the impact."

"Got it." She nodded hard, her gaze never leaving the upcoming curve in the tracks. "Bend. Roll."

The curve beckoned, but Max couldn't help himself. He dragged her close and slammed his mouth to hers. He knew he had little to offer, but he had this. A solid promise to protect her.

With one last hard press of his lips, he lifted his head. "Ready?"

"Ready."

"Go!"

She stared at the ground, then pushed off and in mere seconds was flying through the air.

Max wanted to wait—wanted to see how she landed—but knew the kiss had taken precious seconds they didn't have. On a hard push, he went flying behind her.

Chapter 10

Violet landed with a heavy thud, already stumbling forward from the force of her fall. She tucked her shoulder as Max instructed, the ground rising fast against her body. Soft grass surrounded her along with a cloud of dirt from the hard-packed, summer-dried earth as she tumbled. The impact thudded through her shoulders and on down to her rib cage.

With one last, graceless thump, she came to a halt, her back flat on the ground. Dust rose up around her face, and she coughed against the offending particles.

Well. That was fun.

Violet struggled to a sitting position, brushing at the dirt on her skirt until she was forced to acknowledge it was a useless effort. She shifted focus and took quick stock of her body, inordinately pleased to discover nothing worse than a few bumps.

"Violet!" Max was already up and headed her way, his strides long and sure as he crossed the wide expanse of field between them. Violet had a brief vision—inspired by far too many romantic movies—of her conquering hero, striding across the moors.

A dusty Texas field was a far cry from the Scottish Highlands, but the image stuck all the same.

He'd come for her.

Watched out for her.

Even rescued her from the violence and pain Lange and his henchman were sure to mete out.

He closed in on her, his hands at her waist. His head was already bent, his hands roaming down over her hips, then thighs, then knees. "Are you hurt? Any injuries?"

The clinical nature of his perusal was at direct odds with the heat that flamed everywhere he touched. Violet held still, willingly submitting to his perusal.

"I'm fine. Fine."

When he finally lifted his head, he pointed into the distance behind her. "Let's get the pack and go find a phone. It's time we got you home."

Violet followed him, pleased the aches that had seemed minimal on first standing were just that. She'd end up with a few bruises but could congratulate herself on a drop well done.

She was okay and they'd be fine. The worst was over.

What she couldn't quite figure out was why the thought of returning to Dallas actually filled her with a small pang of sadness.

Max had the pack in hand, his focus once again on her. She saw the concern stamped across his features, even with the layer of dust that covered his cheeks from their jump. "Are you sure you're okay? That was a pretty hard fall."

Violet ignored the urge to either scream or cry—really, what was *wrong* with her?—and stiffened her shoulders. "I'm fine. And I can withstand a few bruises."

"You just looked—"

"Tired?" That insult had been a favorite of her father's to her mother, so it was a surprise when Max's words suggested something different.

"No, sad. Just very, very sad."

The comment derailed her internal negativity, and she reached up to brush the dust from his cheeks, surprised when his palm came up to cover her hand.

Violet stilled for a moment, the feel of his hand a singular support in a world that seemed to have gone off its hinges.

Maybe it was time to get back to Dallas. Back to their lives and back to finding a solution to the mess they were in. And maybe it would be just a tad bit easier, knowing she had the support not only of her friends but also of Max.

"Come on. Let's go find a phone."

The train horn echoed in the distance, yet near enough that she knew some sort of town center was close by. They walked in silence beside the tracks. Violet toyed briefly with a list of subjects that might irritate him but quickly discarded each and every one. She hadn't quite gotten over his unwillingness to share on the train and simply didn't have the energy to dive into another prickly conversation.

With a side glance at Max, she opted for something safe, yet intriguing enough to assuage some lingering curiosity. "How have you adjusted to civilian life?"

A wry grin filled his features, and Violet couldn't quite deny the hard catch of breath in her throat. "You mean prior to getting involved with my crazy neighbors and going on a chase halfway across Texas to find one of them?"

"Yes."

"Good days and bad days. I'm happy to have my own business, but I do miss active duty from time to time."

"Was it hard?"

"Some days. It was also full of a shit-ton of monotonous, boring hours with nothing to do but wait. I can't say I'm sorry to have given that up."

"You've got quite a reputation for your ability to blow things up." Violet hesitated, the reality of the past few weeks coming back in a wash of memories. Max had rescued her from Lange's home using explosives, and then they'd blown up Lange's office back in Dallas while attempting to capture him the first time around. "I never expected to see the skill firsthand, and now you've used it twice."

"Definitely one of the job's high points."

"How'd you end up in the Army Corps of Engineers?"

That grin was back, along with a knowing sheen in those blue eyes that matched the Texas sky above them. "Checking up on me, Richardson?"

"No, I'm not checking up on you." *Much.*

In fact, finding out about people was her business. She used the tools at her disposal—social media, friendly gossip and even the not-so-friendly—to do her job. So it was only natural that she'd know about Max. Her best friend was marrying *his* best friend, for heaven's sake.

And if she'd filed away details, meticulously hoarding any and all information about Max Baldwin, well, no one needed to know.

Seeming to recognize she wasn't going to elaborate on her *no*, he pressed on. "The corps was a natural fit. I've always had an aptitude for blowing things up."

"Men and their love of fire and things that go boom."

"Pretty much, and mine started earlier than most. I'd gotten into a few spots of trouble until my grandfather had the brilliant idea to channel my focus. He had an old buddy he grew up with who had been part of the corps. Old Al took me under his wing. Explained how you needed to understand structures and supports to know where to make an explosion really work. Turns out the structures and supports were even more fascinating than the things that go boom."

"So why leave? Certainly more of your brethren work in civilian jobs for the corps instead of on active duty."

One lone eyebrow shot up. "You've done your homework. So, you have been checking up on me."

"No." On a hard breath, she gave in. "Okay. Fine. I have asked a few questions. It's only natural since your best friend's marrying my best friend that I'd like to know your and Tucker's backgrounds."

"Uh-huh."

She gave him a light punch. "Leave a woman to her illusions."

That small shot of honesty seemed to do the trick, and he nodded, then continued. "I was offered several civilian jobs and almost took a few that interested me. But in the end, I decided to come back to Dallas. Back to Pops."

"He's happy you're here. His pride practically beams off of him in waves."

"He'd be happier if I got him out of lockup and let him come back home."

"Soon."

The joviality that had momentarily filled his features faded as reality descended once more. "Not soon enough for him."

"Who knows? Maybe the forced proximity will give him and Mrs. Beauregard a chance to mend some fences. They're not technically locked up, but you've given them something to focus on by taking care of Reed's mother."

"You're on that kick, too?"

"What kick?"

"Cassidy's been all over Tucker to find out if my grand-father is back to getting it on with your landlady."

"I hardly think octogenarians 'get it on.'" Violet sniffed. "I was merely suggesting they could rekindle an old flame."

"And get it on."

"Max!"

"Don't pretend to be shocked."

"In this case I don't think—"

He leaned into her, halting their movements, the force of that gaze causing the words to dry up in her throat. "You can stand there all wide-eyed and innocent, but I have no doubt you've got urges beneath that prim exterior, Miss Richardson." He traced the line of her jaw, the wide pad of his forefinger settling into the small dent at the base of her chin before he lifted a thumb to trace her lower lip. "I don't plan on saying goodbye to that part of my life just because I've got a few more candles on my cake, and I think you'd be silly to do the same. Why should we expect anyone else to?"

"I—" She swallowed hard. Max's thumb never left the edge of her lips.

For the briefest moment, images of them growing old together, snuggled tightly together under an old quilt, rose up in her mind's eye. She wanted him now, and she couldn't imagine fifty years would change the need all that much.

Hell, she hoped it wouldn't.

But she needed to get control of this situation and quickly. Tilting her head, she cut the direct connection of their bodies and began walking again, focused on her point. "Mrs. B. is still recovering from a heart attack. I'd hardly think your grandfather would take advantage of her in a weakened state."

"She's expected to make a full recovery."

"Fine. Then when she's recovered, they can decide what they would like to do. About. *That*."

"That's a sweet blush, Richardson. But I bet I can make an even prettier one."

When she only shot him a dark look and kept marching through the dusty field, he leaned toward her and whispered, "Come closer and I'll show you."

"You're awfully sure of yourself."

"You're the one who's been researching my background."

Whether it was the sheer overwhelming drama of the past few weeks or the simple acknowledgment that running from Max was getting her nowhere, Violet didn't know. But she stopped once more and turned to face him.

She could *do* this. Could share how she felt. No hiding behind a well-placed sneer or staring down her nose to humble her opponent. She had given him everything she could throw his way, save one thing: honesty.

"What if we take that leap and end up causing a mess?"

The cocky smile and teasing words vanished, his features going as slack as if she'd hit him with a blunt hammer. "You want this, too?"

"I don't not want it."

Storms lit up the blue of his eyes as the corners narrowed. "Yes or no, Violet."

"It's not that simple and you know it."

They'd danced around each other for a year, but their time in proximity had only exacerbated the sparks that were already there. Violet knew damn well, despite his pushing and pressing, that Max would have left her alone had she truly given him the brush-off.

But she hadn't brushed him off. At all.

"The biggest decisions actually are the simple ones. Besides—" He pressed closer, the heat of his body a solid match for the Texas summer that wrapped around them both. "Last time I checked, making a mess is part of the fun. People who look the same as when they started sure as hell aren't doing it right."

"Why do we keep circling around to sex? First your grandfather and Mrs. B. Now you and me."

"Because it's out there, circling us."

"And you think we can't resist it?"

"I think we have been resisting it and the attraction won't be put off."

All thoughts of resistance fled as shots lit up the air. Max had her in his arms and was diving for the ground before she could even register the abrupt change.

"Damn it!" Another explosion of expletives met her ears as Max shielded her with his body before he shifted off her.

"There!" He pointed toward a long row of buildings about seventy-five yards in the distance. "He's over there."

Before Violet could say anything, Max was off the ground and running straight into danger.

Recriminations raced through his mind as Max hot-footed it over the expanse of dry, cracked ground. He was a damn distracted fool. He'd counted off what he felt was a fair distance on the train, but of course it wouldn't have been that hard for Alex to follow their path in a car. And since he'd been near Lange's property, he'd gone back to retrieve a new one.

Damn it, but how had he missed the possible threat?

Max could ask himself the question all day, but he knew exactly why he'd missed the threat.

Violet.

The woman had filled his head so there wasn't room for anything else.

It was his job to keep her safe. And a madman on their heels—one who obviously wouldn't be deterred—wasn't making that possible.

Brushing off the litany of failures—there'd be time to count them later—he kept Alex in his sights, unwilling to let the man circle back around to grab Violet.

Although he didn't want to lose Alex, the distance worked to Max's advantage. He'd already dragged his gun from his ankle holster and immediately went on the offensive, firing shots while running toward his opponent. The forward momentum put Alex in the position of dodging bullets or running.

Curiously enough, the man ran.

Which meant he had no backup.

The thought struck swift and hard, and again, Max cursed himself for the slow realization. Lange might be a sometime partner, but Alex had no one else matching his agility and age.

He was pursuing them alone.

Alex slipped around the edge of one of the buildings, and Max used the temporary reprieve to look backward. Violet was visible, her movements swift as she crossed the expanse of field at his back.

The urge to follow Alex was strong.

But the urge to protect was stronger.

With his gaze still on the line of buildings, he walked backward until they met. "You okay?"

"In one piece for the moment."

"And you're going to stay that way." He dug into the pack, his hand closing on extra firepower in the form of a semi-automatic pistol. He handed it over, his gaze lingering on hers briefly before shifting to keep an eye on the row of buildings. "You know how to use this?"

"Yes."

"You okay with using this?"

"If you'd asked me three weeks ago, I'd have said no."

Max returned his gaze to hers, surprised at the admission. "You don't like guns."

"Hell, no. That's why I took the shooting class."

Max grinned in spite of himself. "You're quite a woman. Fearless as all get-out."

"I'm not fearless. I just refuse to be dominated by my fears."

He dragged her beneath his arm, almost sorry to mar her with the day's grime until he really looked at both of them. "We need to go after him."

"What if he has the town in his pocket?"

"We have to try." He pressed a quick kiss to her forehead.

"Shoot-out at the O.K. Corral?"

"I sure as hell hope not."

Violet kept her arm steady, the gun at her side. She hadn't been lying to Max—she hated guns and all they stood for—but she'd be damned if she wasn't going to use one to keep both of them safe.

They cleared the remaining distance across the field, the wall of buildings that made up what had to be the town's main thoroughfare greeting them with their backs.

Max gave her hand a quick squeeze. "Alex swung off about three buildings down. Which means he's either headed out of town or is waiting on the other side. You ready?"

"Yep."

Max took a small alley between three-story buildings. His hand was at her side, and he gently pressed her against the bricks. "Keep your back covered."

She nodded her confirmation and used the wall as her guide as they both slid down the alley. It was only when they came to the edge that Max stilled her once more, the sound of voices drifting toward them in the heat.

"Officer Davis. It's good to see you."

"Mr. Ebner. I wasn't aware you were visiting. Welcome back."

"It's a quick visit. I never get to stay as long in these parts as I'd like."

Violet wanted to roll her eyes at the forced congeniality but held still, unwilling to make any extraneous moves for fear of being overheard.

"Officer. I was hoping I might get your help with something. Mr. Lange has had some interlopers on his property." A light *tsk*ing sound wavered on the breeze. "Thieves, really. A man and a woman. Heavily armed."

"I haven't received any alerts. Why haven't you called it in?"

"Mr. Lange. He's—" Alex broke off. "He's admittedly concerned about broadcasting some of his more valuable assets."

"I see."

"I am a licensed security professional. I work inside the law, and am hoping to handle this matter myself. But support is always welcome. Mr. Lange and I have the highest opinion of local law enforcement in these parts."

Whatever foreign tongue Alex had grown up speaking had vanished in the "aw shucks" demeanor. Violet wanted—with a desperation that bordered on madness— to run forward and call the man out.

And then gripped the gun even harder and knew that wasn't a possibility.

Max shifted a hand to her waist, pushing lightly to get her moving backward. She took the unspoken cue and sidled back the way they'd come, Alex's final words ringing in her ears.

"I'll just keep looking around a bit if you don't mind."

"Let me help you. We can start—"

The rest of the officer's words were inaudible because of their physical distance and the slamming of her heart. Violet kept a steady pace, not even aware she was holding her breath until she and Max cleared the end of the building.

Backs pressed to the wall, he turned to face her. The sharp relief of his cheekbones framed the dull reality in his gaze.

"Lange's got the damn town in his pocket."

Max had never fancied himself a thief, but his time in the corps had taught him that there were times a man had to take what was needed to fulfill an op. Although he didn't like it, he managed his guilt with an oversize scoreboard in his head and hoped he could even out those moments of necessity with contributions to several local charities as well as a ton of pro bono work with his business.

It wasn't much, but his heart was in the right place.

Or so he consoled himself as he lifted a cell phone off a harried mother juggling two toddlers at the entrance to the Main Street pharmacy.

He'd even held the door for her.

He moved off quickly to the small service station they'd discovered at the far end of town, just where Main Street branched off into a small two-lane road that crisscrossed this part of the state.

Violet had batted her eyes at a bored teenager manning the register and secured the key to the women's room. The two of them were holed up in there, the door locked at their backs. The lock had barely flipped when Violet rounded on him. "Where'd you get that?"

"Somewhere."

Not one for an easy dismissal, Violet pressed her point. "Come on. You disappear for fifteen minutes and come back with a cell phone? Where'd you get it?"

"I relieved a young woman of it. I'll see that we find a way to get it back to her after we finish using it."

Violet stared at him for several long moments before giving him a hard nod. "Fair enough."

In moments, Tucker's voice was booming out of the receiver. "Where the hell are you, man?"

"A women's bathroom."

"Why am I not surprised?"

Although Tucker would normally have given him quite a bit more ribbing, he punched their location into GPS and promised Max they weren't far away.

They? "Seriously, Buchanan? Who's with you?"

"All of us. We're in Lilah's van."

"Because that's not all freaking kinds of conspicuous."

"It's what we've got. We'll see you in twenty."

Tucker cut the connection, and Max dropped the phone in his pocket.

"I would have liked to talk to my friends."

"You'll see them soon."

The tentative truce they'd settled into earlier vanished. "I wasn't going to keep them on for an hour. But it would be nice to hear their voices."

"Come on, Violet. I get it. And on a really high level, I understand why you and Cassidy and Lilah want to be involved. But we don't know who's outside or who that kid might tip off. And making a ton of noise calming your friends down over the phone wasn't a good idea."

"I wasn't going to yell and scream."

"And I need you to give me an ounce of credit that I know what the hell I'm doing." The thought spit out with such force that he wasn't surprised when she moved a few steps away from him. "Doing everything in a pack isn't safe. I don't know why the hell Cassidy and Lilah are even with them."

"Because staying home alone like sitting ducks is a good idea?"

Max nodded, the truth of her words slicing deep, knocking the wind from his sails. "No. No, it's not."

The single light over the bathroom sink cast a florescent pallor over the small space, reinforcing the danger they were both in. He'd initially been tempted to leave her there and go after Alex himself, but he had no idea how many other cops Alex's new friend on Main Street had mobilized.

"Why'd you come for me?" Violet's voice was quiet and bereft of any sass, totally at odds with her normal approach.

"Because you needed me."

"But why not the police? Or why not bring Reed and Tucker with you?"

She'd asked the same question before, and he'd managed to deflect it. "Why do you keep pressing this?"

"Why do you keep giving me the runaround?"

"Why are you so surprised I came for you?"

Although neither of them was quite willing to sit on the floor of the bathroom, Violet had settled herself against the wall, the grimy tiles supporting her weight. At his question, he saw her change, her long, lithe frame seeming to shrink as she closed down. While she still stood against the wall, the structure appeared to be the only thing holding her up.

The only source of strength left available to her.

"Why, Violet?"

Her green gaze that flashed so easily from battle to desire and right back again revealed something he'd never seen before. Pain.

"I told you before. People don't come after strangers to rescue them."

"And I told you before, you're not a stranger. It's like a lifeline you're clinging to, and it's no longer true."

He deliberately tossed her words right back at her, scrabbling at anything handy to make his point.

"Don't you see? It is a lifeline. And I'm scared to death to let go."

Fists he hadn't even realized he'd made relaxed as he reached for her. Max placed his hands on each of her shoulders, pulling her toward him, one of his thumbs playing over the hollow of her throat. "Let go, Violet. I'll catch you."

He leaned forward then, pressing his lips where his thumb had just played over her soft flesh. Her pulse thrummed beneath his lips, and he took a moment to press his tongue to that sensitive spot, gratified when the tempo sped even faster in response.

"Max." His name drifted past his ear on a lazy sigh, in distinct counterpoint to the hard clench of her fingers on his shoulders.

"Let go."

"Yes." Once more, her breath fanned out in another featherlight sigh. "Yes."

Chapter 11

Violet felt the press of Max's body, thick with muscle, and could do nothing but hang on. Oh, how she wanted him. The knowledge drove her—made her reckless—and even knowing that, she couldn't find the will to stop.

Why do we keep circling around to sex?

Their conversation earlier provided an odd backdrop to her thoughts as her body took whatever comfort and solace it could. His tongue slipped inside her mouth as firm hands gripped her hips, pulling her determinedly toward him. She reveled in the moment—in the man—as her last threads of self-control snapped.

And you think we can't resist it?

Resist? Why would she want to resist? Why would she want to walk away from something that felt so good? So life-affirming.

She ran her hands over his shoulders, the flex and bunch of muscles an enticing dance beneath her fingertips. Continuing her exploration, she ran her hands over his chest, then on down to the ridge of muscle over his stomach.

He was perfect. An absolutely perfect specimen of male strength and perfection.

I think we have been resisting it and the attraction won't be put off.

Why resist?

Why…why…wh—

Violet broke off the kiss, the reality of exactly why she needed to resist rising up to swamp her. She gulped for air as if drowning, the long, endless years of her childhood digging for purchase against the haze of sexual attraction.

Of sexual *madness*.

Because that's all it was. Hormones and loneliness and the lingering adrenaline caused by several days' worth of fear.

Nothing more.

It couldn't be something more.

"Violet?"

She shook her head, slipping from his arms to move across the small space. She caught sight of her appearance as she passed the scratched and silvered mirror, barely recognizing the woman who stared back.

She'd been through a war. Physically and emotionally.

And no matter how tough he looked, there was no way she was dragging Max Baldwin into her hell.

Cassidy, Lilah, Tucker and Reed filled Lilah's delivery truck with steady chatter. Violet couldn't deny her relief at their arrival a half hour before, but she'd found her energy quickly waning in the face of an endless stream of questions.

Reed drove the pink monstrosity that signified to anyone who saw it that its owner was a purveyor of cakes, pastries and sweets, and Violet vacillated between horror at how noticeable they were and delight that news of the van would no doubt reach Tripp and Alex.

She suspected the arsenal packed in the back had also gone a long way toward calming her fears.

"Since when do we carry guns with our cakes?" Violet pointed toward a row of weapons strapped securely to the floor of the van.

"You can save your smart-ass snark for someone else." Lilah pulled her close on the bench seat that lined the back half of the van. "I'm so glad you're safe and with us again."

"I am, too."

"Do you want to talk about it?" Cassidy patted Violet's knee, a lingering gesture she continued to make off and on, as if she were convinced Violet would suddenly disappear.

Violet laid a hand over Cassidy's. "Would you be upset if I said not right now?"

Her friend's blue eyes grew serious. "Of course not."

"No one stopped you in town?" Max had already asked the question several times, but their friends remained patient, and Violet was grateful. Although she wasn't crazy about kid-glove treatment as a general rule, she couldn't deny how good it felt to see them again.

"No, no one. Although we did get several stares as we drove down Main Street toward the service station." Lilah smiled. "No one can miss the pink."

"No, they can't." Violet nodded, unable to resist the small smile at one of Lilah's favorite sayings.

Fortunately, she and Max hadn't had to wait long. Tucker's assessment they were about twenty minutes away had been a good one, and she and Max had had to sit in silence for what amounted to no more than ten minutes.

Even if it had felt like ten hours.

A dull flush still washed over her neck and chest every time Violet thought about her make-out session with Max in the bathroom. Heights of ecstasy counterbalanced with the thick weight of memory and hurt and anger that never seemed too far from the surface.

So why had she given in to the memories instead of the man? One was a phantom and the other was real. Flesh and blood.

"Why not take a different car? We'd have all fit in Tucker's SUV."

"We wanted to be noticeable." Reed tossed back the comment from the driver's seat.

"But why? Max and I were hiding in a bathroom so we *wouldn't* be noticeable."

"We need my stepfather back here. In Dallas. And what's more of an enticement than a large pink van driving smack through a town he thinks he owns?"

"And you think he knows?" Violet was torn between the sheer simplicity of their idea and the fact that they were setting a trap. A bright, shiny pink trap.

"Of course he knows." Max was solemn when he spoke, but his tone held absolute certainty. "It's only a matter of time before he and Alex head straight back to Dallas."

Gabriella puttered around the cavernous kitchen at Elegance and Lace and waited for her friends to return. She knew she should probably avoid being inside the shop alone, but she'd locked all the doors and had given her brother, Ricardo, a heads-up she was there and waiting for her friends. He'd already driven by several times on his patrol, shooting her texts to confirm there was nothing out of the ordinary.

She'd kept the news of the jewels from her broader family—her mother would lapse into full-on insanity if she knew what Gabby's friends were currently dealing with—but Ricardo was a member of the Dallas PD. He'd already heard through the grapevine about what was going on and the suspicion that had fallen on several high-ranking officials since Tripp Lange was let out of county lockup.

No, Gabby mused. It was better that she kept this to herself. Violet, Cassidy and Lilah would get through this. And once they did, with the situation wrapped up in a bow, *then* Gabby would tell her mother.

In the meantime, she'd cook.

Cassidy had called her shortly after they got a call from Max, providing their location and the confirmation he and Violet were safe. She had wanted to go along on the pickup but knew she could offer something even better. Warmth and a sense of haven when they arrived back home.

As she'd mixed up her grandmother's chicken enchiladas—the very best recipe to be found in the entire city—Gabby had taken the time to reflect on all that had happened.

Her friend was safe, and for that she gave thanks.

But it was the road Violet still had to walk that gave Gabby the bigger concern.

The violence that had hovered over them all since the break-in and subsequent discovery of the rubies would haunt the women of Elegance and Lace for a long time to come. But an actual kidnapping had taken the situation to a whole other level. Gabby hadn't gotten much from Cassidy's call beyond the clear confirmation that Violet wasn't hurt, but she suspected more would come out over the next few days.

With swift movements born of years in the kitchen, she wrapped each enchilada, gently nestling each filled tortilla side by side in the glass pans she'd dug up in Lilah's kitchen. The woman might bake for a living, but she had all the necessary tools of an industrial kitchen, and Gabby had made good use of them.

She'd also made extra since Max, Tucker and Reed could eat a bull under the table. And, of course, she'd promised her brother a plate after he ended his shift. And since every good meal needed a good plate of leftovers, she'd send everyone home with another dinner's worth.

The Sanchez family knew the old adage that food was love, and she was determined to let everyone know exactly how she felt.

With cheese now covering the rows of tortilla-wrapped chicken, Gabby settled the pans in the oven. But it was the hard knock at the back door that had her slamming the oven door harder than she intended.

Damn, but she was jumpy.

She shot a glance at her phone, but there were no waiting texts from Ricardo, and Lilah had already confirmed she didn't have any deliveries scheduled. So who was it?

The knock came again, and Gabby moved to the small, high window in the back of the kitchen. She couldn't see whoever stood at the door, but she did see a white sedan parked where Lilah's delivery van typically sat. When the knock came once more, she moved toward the door. "I'm sorry. We're closed."

"I need to speak with the owners." The voice was muffled, but she caught the distinct notes of Britain through the thick panel of wood.

"They're not here."

"So who are you?"

The retort was fast and smooth, and Gabby wasn't sure why the quick comeback had her on edge.

"I'm sorry, but I need you to come back another time. I can give you the number, and you can call for an appointment."

"I need to speak with them now. Today."

"That will be difficult since they're not here."

The thin mail slot fluttered in the vicinity of her knees, and she jumped back, surprised to see a compact billfold fall next to her left foot. The disembodied voice filtered back through the door. "Take a look at my credentials and then let me in. Or flag down the police car I've seen troll through here twice already and ask them to come join us."

Gabby picked up the small fold of leather, flipping it open to some rather official-looking credentials.

MI5?

Gabby turned the black billfold over, her fingers tracing the well-worn leather that had smoothed with obvious use. While she'd admit to having no knowledge of official British documentation, the credentials appeared real.

And something about the worn leather struck her as legit.

With the sure knowledge her brother would be back for another round relatively soon—and curiosity riding high on her shoulder—she opened the door. And nearly stumbled backward at the vision who stood on the other side.

He was tall, because he had several inches on her five-seven plus four more from her heels. His hair was a thick, burnished gold, the sort that would age with him instead of fading out. But it was his eyes that drew her in.

Ice-blue and shockingly vivid, even behind a pair of wire-framed glasses.

Oh, the glasses.

Gabby felt a quiver in her knees and took a step back for balance. "Who are you?"

"Didn't you read the badge?" The voice she'd pegged as British slid over her with all the finesse of warm honey, and she forced herself to stand in place.

"I read it."

"So can I come in?"

He extended his hand for his identification, but Gabby moved the billfold just out of reach. "Who *are* you?"

"Knox St. Germain."

"No way."

As responses went, Gabby knew it was crass in the extreme, but who the hell was this guy? And who walked around with a name like Knox St. Germain? He sounded like a cross between a boxer and a liqueur.

Oddly enough, the boxer reference fit. As did his dark black suit jacket, over what appeared to be a rather fit frame.

"Excuse me?"

She flipped open the leather billfold once more, her gaze focusing on the larger type that bore his name. *Knox St. Germain.*

Was this guy for real?

"That's an awfully serious name."

"I do an awfully serious job." His face remained set in stoic, craggy lines, but she didn't miss the cheek in his voice. A life spent with five brothers and an endless pack of cousins had her well versed in male amusement.

His was simply veiled behind a rather delectable accent.

"Would you care to tell me why you're here?"

"Do you work for this establishment?"

"No."

"Then I can't tell you."

"Yet you were adamant about getting in."

"It's essential I speak with the owners."

"They're not here." Gabby handed him the billfold. "So I'm afraid you're out of luck."

"When do you expect them back?"

He stepped through the door, despite the lack of invitation, but stopped just past the entrance. His gaze roamed over the mess she still hadn't cleaned up on the counter. "You appear to be cooking."

"It is a kitchen."

"Does this mean you're cooking for one or more of the individuals who owns this establishment?"

"I'm—" She broke off before changing tacks. "You're nosy."

"Also part of the job description."

"They should be here in about an hour. Why don't you come back then?"

Knox St. Germain moved past her and settled himself on a large stool at the kitchen counter. "Why don't I just wait?"

Max had to give Reed credit—the man maneuvered a large pink van with all the panache and style of a small roadster. He'd also made what should have been about a two-hour trip back to Dallas in just over ninety minutes.

What he couldn't get his mind wrapped around were the shadows that lurked beneath Violet's gaze.

A bone-deep weariness seemed to settle over her like a blanket, and for the first time he sensed her ordeal was finally drawing a physical response.

She smiled at Lilah's sweet jokes and patted Cassidy's hand at the woman's many small touches, but the threads beneath her composure were frayed to the point of snapping.

Reed pulled up to the delivery entrance at Elegance

and Lace just as the late summer sun began its descent toward the horizon. The evening hues of gold and red reflected off the back door of the business as well as a strange white sedan.

"Whose car?" Tucker asked.

Reed shook his head, leaning forward over the dash as he pulled behind the sedan, effectively boxing it in. "No idea."

"Is someone here?"

"Gabby's waiting for us. Said she wanted to cook dinner." Lilah craned her neck to look out the passenger window. "That's not her car, though."

Tension immediately filled up the air like a thick mist and Max already had his hand on the door. "Let's go see who it is."

Reed left the van running, gesturing for Lilah to take the wheel once he got out of the driver's seat. His voice was low but firm when he instructed her to leave at any sign of trouble. Max eyed the guns in the back of the van and at a nod from Reed was nearly out of his seat to snag protection when the back door of the business opened, Gabby framed inside.

"You're here!"

She raced down the back steps on heels that resembled ice picks and rushed to the van. She had the back door open and Violet in a tight embrace, tears flowing freely as they hugged. "You're home, *chica*. You're home."

The urge to grab a side piece faded, but Max was itchy to move the reunion inside. "Gab. Whose car is that?"

Gabby kept Violet in her arms but laid off the tight hug. "MI5 has decided to pay you all a visit."

Alex poked through the rubble of the battered sedan, careful in his search. He'd already towed the vehicle from the back of The Duke's property and was even now sifting through what was in easy reach in the full privacy of the compound's eight-car garage. The events of the day rumbled through his mind, culminating in the vision of that idiotic pink truck barreling down Main Street.

He'd almost acted—had nearly given into the thought of firing round after round of bullets into the gas tank and watching it burn—but had held back. Hasty actions never produced good results.

Never.

Take his current problem. A sedan nearly crushed beyond salvage. He'd pull out a blowtorch later and cut away what blocked the interior, confirming he hadn't missed anything. In the meantime, he was going on a quick fishing expedition so he wouldn't need to go into the house—and run into Lange—empty-handed.

Because that was what he was.

Damn empty-handed, with his quarry rapidly departing back to Dallas.

While he knew he'd find them again, the fact that Violet had gotten away with her protector was a slam to his pride. He'd admit that to no one else, but he could to himself.

He didn't fail.

Ever.

Yet he'd stumbled several times over the past few weeks.

What should have been a simple job had proven to be otherwise. Far from simple, in fact.

His former associate, Trey, had lost his life in their last scuffle with Lange's son, Reed. They'd still not been able to secure more than one of the three rubies. And he and Lange had ended up in jail.

Although the stay had been brief, any time spent in lockup was loathsome.

But the loss of Trey was the worst.

Alex had thought his partner nearly invincible. And while he knew even the best soldiers fell to an ambush, the man's loss was keenly felt. Although dim and relatively unable to think for himself, Trey had provided considerable brute strength to their operation. He'd also followed orders to a *T*, more than willing to do what needed to be done. No job was too large or small; Trey would see it through.

Oh yes, did he miss the ever stoic and stalwart Trey.

The Duke had spent far too many years in the rarified air of order-giving to be all that useful at even the basics.

Alex kicked at the car, disgusted when his efforts failed to dislodge the back panel over the wheel.

This damn car was a perfect example.

Lange hadn't simply made it impossible to drive. He'd pushed it beyond its limits so Alex could barely open the freaking doors to the secrets housed within.

Impulse. The Duke acted on impulse, and it'd only gotten worse of late. He wanted to be loyal—believed himself so—but the increasing lack of focus was…disillusioning.

Perhaps one day soon he'd be free of it.

Shrugging off the disloyal thoughts for fear they'd somehow show on his face, Alex refocused on his task. Unlike his boss, his temper didn't run to the juvenile and impulsive, and that control had served him well. He'd think his way through their current problem and find a way to get back on track.

Images of the small bridal boutique on Dragon Street filled his mind's eye as he methodically worked over the sedan. Where had he gone wrong?

What hadn't he planned for?

Three women who owned a bridal shop. They should never have posed a threat. To him and his partner. To the Duke. Or to their overarching mission.

Yet they'd managed to thwart every planned effort at every single turn.

How?

Even as he asked himself the question, Alex knew the answer. The women had help. Help in the form of Lange's surprisingly well-trained stepson of a cop and the two ex-soldiers who worked down the lane.

What he hadn't accounted for was something intangible that hovered just out of reach. Although Alex had no time for the purported curse that lay over the Renaissance Stones, he couldn't deny they'd seen precious few dividends from all their methodical planning to ultimately possess the stones.

Curses were for fools, and only the weak-minded put any stock in them. No, Alex marveled to himself, the stones' real power was in their many, many facets. The rubies were worth unimaginable sums.

And, therefore, people did—and would do—unimaginable things for them.

Curses meant nothing. It was action that moved the world forward. Yet none of it explained the nearly impossible run of luck that had favored the women. Although Tucker Buchanan's discovery of Cassidy Tate the morning after her shop was broken into was simply bad luck and timing, what had ensued was so much more.

How could he have known the ex-soldiers who now owned an architectural firm would get their rocks off playing hero?

Alex kicked at the back panel of the sedan once more, irritation simmering beneath his blood like a witch's brew. The whole damn op had been fraught with issues from the start. With another swift kick—this one for the loss of Trey—he let the zing of bone connecting with metal echo through his nerve endings.

And then again. And again.

Orders. Responsibilities. Strategies.

He'd fulfilled them all, and it had gotten him nowhere. He believed in the old ways. Believed in following his leader.

Yet here he was, unable even to dislodge a damn car part because his *leader* had acted like a child.

With one final kick, the hard crunch of metal gave way, the back door of the car tilting on its hinge. Alex stepped forward, working the metal frantically as he sought whatever might have been left behind in the car.

The hard screech of metal on metal echoed off the cavernous garage, but he ignored it, now manic to find whatever lay inside. As the door finally came off with a hard wrench, Alex threw the metal aside and leaned forward. The front passenger seat was nearly flush with the back bench, but after a quick search, he saw the dark army-green material covering the floor of the backseat.

Dragging the thick duffle free of its mooring between the now-ruined seats, Alex stumbled momentarily before righting himself.

Dropping to the garage floor, he dug through the layers of female clothing, bottles of water and energy bars before his hand closed over something small.

Perhaps their luck had finally taken a turn.

He threw the bag aside, several silky items floating to the floor along with the hard thud of several water bottles. Alex ignored it all and instead watched as a bright light flooded the face of a sleek black cell phone.

Chapter 12

What the hell sort of name was Knox St. Germain?

The thought had stuck in Max's craw since inspecting the Brit's credentials, and he still hadn't managed to come up with a satisfactory answer. Reed's affirmation that the badge looked legit had helped, but it was St. Germain's production of a card that gave a business address of Thames House, London, and the number for his supervisor that had sealed the deal.

None of it changed the fact that Max would have preferred to bundle Violet up in the back of the van and whisk her home instead of dealing with an interrogation. Sadly, the choice wasn't his to make.

Violet had slipped into her office after arriving and had changed into a new outfit. He suspected burning wasn't good enough for the clothing she'd been wearing, but the bonfire would have to wait. Instead, her smile was firmly in place when she returned to the broad seat-ing area of Elegance and Lace, clad in slacks and a fresh blouse, her hair twisted up in a clip.

Worn.

The thought struck as Violet settled into the large, oversize couch in the main sitting area. The woman appeared worn to the bone. Their adventure had taken its toll. Worse, the shadows he'd noticed in the van had only become more pronounced, especially with her hair upswept, displaying the fragile bones of her face.

Tired or not, Violet moved on the offensive the moment she took her seat. "I can't imagine your arrival is coincidence, Officer St. Germain."

"No, it's not."

Max wanted to dislike the man on sight, but the officer had proven himself above reproach. He'd also turned down Gabby's enchiladas, which had earned Max a perverse satisfaction as the stoic officer had to watch the rest of them dig into the steaming meal.

The enchiladas had proven themselves as perfect as all of Gabby's food, and he'd barely restrained himself from a third helping. Only the knowledge she'd made extra and was sending them home with leftovers had stilled his hand.

Violet's plate, however, lay untouched on the coffee table where Gabby had set it earlier.

"Why don't you tell us, then, why you're here?"

The officer eyed everyone assembled around the room. "I'd prefer to speak to Miss Tate, Miss Castle and you, Miss Richardson, alone."

Tucker and Reed both braced as if to argue, but Violet proved herself more than in control of the conversation. "Everyone sitting here is well aware of what's going on. We speak together or you'll need to take more official action to speak to us."

"I can do that if I must."

Violet shrugged. "I spent the last forty-eight hours under the control of or running from some rather unsavory individuals. If you think you can scare me with empty threats, you've picked the wrong girl."

St. Germain nodded before settling back in his seat. Max's overall impression was of a man who didn't acquiesce easily, so the quick capitulation must mean he needed answers. Fast.

That focus on expedience had alarm bells clamoring in Max's mind, lifting the hair on his nape. His days of service came back in a rush, his own experiences still shockingly fresh.

He *knew* the root cause of that focus.

Hell, he'd lived it himself.

Someone well above St. Germain was pulling strings and wanted answers. And as a good officer, their new friend, Knox, was expected to get them. His response only confirmed Max's suspicions.

"Fair enough, Miss Richardson. As you might imagine, the Renaissance Stones are of considerable interest to the British government."

"That's a change of heart." Max took the first jab. "Especially since the very reason the stones are on US soil is that the British monarchy couldn't have cared less about them."

"I wouldn't say that is fully accurate. The Queen Mum had…concerns about the gems. When she found a way to remove them from Britain during wartime, she took the opportunity."

St. Germain's diplomacy earned a sizable snort from Cassidy. "If by *remove* you mean smuggle them out of the country with our landlady's family, then we're in agreement."

"Removal of the gems was a sanctioned event, Miss Tate. I'd hardly use the term *smuggle*."

"I would." Cassidy refused to back down. "I'd also add that our landlady is so upset about this that she had a heart attack and subsequently had to go into hiding."

The delicacy that had imbued the officer's actions up until that point faded in the face of Cassidy's comments. "We're aware of the removal of the stones but not the illness. Where is the landlady now?"

"She's safe." Max interjected once more, the comment as much a response as a warning to his assembled friends. He might give St. Germain the leeway to ask questions, but he'd be damned if any of them were giving up the location of their loved ones.

Reed's subtle nod of agreement only added reinforcement to the approach.

Max Senior and Mrs. B. might want out of their confinement on the ranch, but Reed's mother's life depended on the secrecy. She hated going into hiding as much as Max's grandfather, but Reed had worked hard to convince Diana she needed to stay put until they had her husband back behind bars. They'd all be damned before some nosy officer put her at risk now that she'd agreed.

MI5's focus was three priceless rubies, and Max had no interest in his grandfather, Reed's mother or Mrs. Beauregard becoming collateral damage as the British government worked toward their own ends.

At this point, Max trusted very few to keep the secret of where they had his grandfather in hiding. A badge and a formal British accent weren't going to change that.

Max's gaze drifted over Violet once more. She'd more than held her own—on their trek to safety and now with the officer. The delicate skin around her eyes was dark with exhaustion, but her deep, honeyed voice was as firm as steel when she spoke next. "Officer St. Germain. We can bat this one around or we can get to the issue at hand. Why don't you tell us the real reason you're here?"

Violet took Knox St. Germain's measure, curious to see how he'd respond. She hadn't been kidding earlier—she was tired, and she was beyond being cowed by a government operative who knew he didn't have the upper hand.

What she hadn't quite figured out was why the man was dancing around the matter as if he held live snakes.

Of course the British wanted the rubies back. The individuals originally involved with the gems had wanted them off British soil, but they were all long gone, along with the threat of war. A new generation—one who valued what had been so easily brushed aside—would want the stones returned to England.

Things that were considered priceless had a way of raising interest, no matter the time or place.

What Violet couldn't quite shake was the sense that St. Germain was here for a more urgent reason.

At the heart of the matter, she, Lilah and Cassidy had no claim to the rubies. Beyond watching them for Mrs. Beauregard and ensuring they remained in safekeeping—Lilah's missing stone the current exception—they had no claims. MI5 had to know that.

So what was the man's end game?

"I'm here to see this matter handled. If word of the stones' disappearance got out, it could be a considerable embarrassment for the British monarchy."

"Embarrassment?" It was Gabby who spoke up, and Violet didn't miss the anger that flashed in her friend's dark brown gaze. "My friends have all been put in life-threatening danger because of these jewels, and you're worried about a little PR dustup?"

If St. Germain was surprised by their friend's ready defense, he gave little overt indication. But Violet didn't miss the appreciative gaze—albeit a quick one—that traveled down Gabby's long, curvy form. "I'm not dismissing what has happened, Miss Sanchez. I'm simply explaining why it's essential we get this matter under control."

Gabby snorted. "By thinking you can order home something that was already given away."

"This matter needs to be dealt with. It's why I'm here and why I'm asking you all to reconsider your position on this." Knox pulled a few more cards from his suit jacket pocket and settled them on the table. "I've already given Detective Graystone my supervisor's information. I suggest you call him and confirm that what I'm sharing with you is legitimate, backed by an even more legitimate set of orders. We need to get these stones out of your possession and off US soil. It's for your protection."

"And your reputation." Lilah smiled sweetly, her comment, Violet thought, surprisingly restrained for Lilah.

"I think Miss Richardson's recent scare reinforces my point." When the officer's words landed with a heavy thud, he stood. "I'll leave you now."

Tucker saw St. Germain to the door, and they all waited in unspoken agreement until the door was firmly closed and locked behind the officer.

"Son of a bitch," Max muttered under his breath before he stood to pace the sitting area. The various dressmaker's forms, clad in some of Cassidy's more elaborate creations, made a strange backdrop to his large frame and murderous gaze. "Damn Brits want to just swoop in and take the gems."

"You think they've kept tabs on them this whole

time?" Tucker's gaze was sharp as he took a seat next to Cassidy, her hand quickly vanishing beneath his.

"I think it's safe to say the secrecy Mrs. Beauregard and Max's grandfather were insistent on these past decades was misplaced." Violet glanced down at her own hands, abstractly focused on the chipped polish on her left ring finger.

And the fact that her hands lay in her lap instead of wrapped in Max's.

"How so, Vi?" Gabby spoke first. Although she'd remained quiet throughout most of the officer's questions, Violet hadn't missed her friend's interest or hard scrutiny of Knox St. Germain.

To be fair to Gabby, Violet knew the officer was the exact sort of man who'd have caught her interest as well. The clipped British tones that twisted up a woman's insides. The cool gaze behind a sexy pair of wire-rims. Even the fine cut of his dark suit gave an aura of power and authority that was appealing.

Unbidden, her gaze drifted to Max.

So why couldn't she see past a pair of shoulders that were thick and rounded, a surly personality and a stubborn will that bulldozed through life at warp speed?

At the expectant silence from her friends, Violet brushed off the curious comparison. And the very tangible realization that Max Baldwin had no comparison.

Or equal.

She added a small yawn behind her hand for effect as she remarshaled her thoughts. "From the start, Mrs. Beauregard was insistent she had to keep this big secret. That her father's role as jeweler to the Royal Family and creator of the fake Crown Jewels during World War II was meant to stay quiet, never to be spoken of. She even went so far as to bury everything here in the floor."

"My grandfather only reinforced the secrecy component. He took helping her seriously," Max added before snatching a handful of tortilla chips Gabby had placed on the coffee table next to the platter of enchiladas.

Violet pressed on. "So they kept the secret, but they wouldn't have been the only ones to know. The Royal Family knew."

"But they have no reason to tell anyone," Reed pointed out. "The removal of the stones was their idea. It would be in their best interest, in fact, to say nothing. Especially since the jewels were a gift, given on a diplomatic visit."

"Which means even more people know."

"I'm not following," Reed said.

Violet had made it her life to read people, and she knew one thing with certainty. People talked.

It had been the truth of her life—first as a child of parents who flagrantly socialized around town and now in her daily interaction with any number of individuals. People were unable to keep the exciting or the salacious or the secret to themselves.

Violet caught Max's gaze, that same sense of approval she'd gotten while on the train shining once more from his eyes. He got it.

And he gets me.

The layers of exhaustion that had kept her company since they drove back to Dallas faded slightly in the excitement of finally getting down to the heart of the matter. She'd initially resented Officer St. Germain's arrival but had to acknowledge he might be exactly what they'd waited for.

Someone who truly had the power to end this whole mess and let them get back to their lives.

"You're on to something." Max snagged another handful of chips. "Follow it through."

"We've been operating under the assumption Mrs. Beauregard and Max's grandfather were the only ones who held the secret of the gems. But we've completely discounted everyone else on the other side of the pond who knew about them, too."

She fired the spark and watched as it rapidly lit up the room.

"Do you think the Royal Family has been tracking the gems all this time?" Cassidy nodded, her eyes widening. "Keeping tabs, as it were?"

"The Royal Family. MI5. A team of royal advisors." Violet ticked them off on her fingers. "It could be some or all. But people in a position to know are well aware of those stones."

"Then they're not going to take lightly the fact that I gave mine away." Lilah's voice was a whisper as loud as a gunshot in the cavernous room.

"You didn't give it away." Reed pulled her close. "You had no choice."

"I didn't have to carry it around, persisting in the ridiculous idea it was safer with me." Lilah paused. "Or that I was somehow safer with it as a bargaining chip."

Max spoke first. "Coulda, woulda, shoulda, Lilah. If you want to point fingers, then I shouldn't have taken them off the top of the cache after we unearthed it from the floor. Or we shouldn't have dug them up in the first place. What's done is done, and now we're focused on the cleanup."

All the air vanished from her lungs as Max spoke, warmth and compassion layered through his words. With a brief "Excuse me," Violet stood and headed for the kitchen.

"Vi?" Cassidy's voice echoed behind her. "You okay?"

"Yep!" She kept her tone friendly. "I just need a quick minute."

She didn't stop, just kept a steady walk toward the back of their business to her office—her sanctuary.

Max saw the change and the concern that filled the faces of Violet's friends. Cassidy was nearly out of her chair when Max stood. "I'll be right back."

"Max—" Lilah was already on her feet, but he stopped her, laying a gentle hand on her small, delicate shoulder. He didn't miss the stiffness or the subtle quiver of concern that matched her voice.

"It's okay. She's got a lot on her mind. Why don't you let me talk to her?"

He knew Lilah struggled—and knew there was still a strong layer of guilt over the loss of one of the rubies—but she finally nodded. "All right."

"I know I've got the girlfriend cavalry right here. I won't hesitate to call for backup."

"She's our girl, Max." Lilah pulled him close for a tight hug, her small body far stronger than he'd have expected. "And she's a lot softer inside than she lets on."

"I know that, too."

Lilah released her hold, the concern that had clouded her eyes fading to something that looked a lot like acceptance. "Go."

Although he hated being on display—and had always hated it—somehow the gazes that bore into his back as he left the room filled Max with an odd sort of comfort. Quite unexpectedly, he and Tucker had stumbled into something special. Extraordinary circumstances, but special all the same.

It would be easy to chalk up the experience as unique

because of the jewels that had been discovered, but Max knew it was something more.

The women who owned Elegance and Lace had the exceptional about them. Their ironclad friendship. The business they'd built from scratch. Even their role in the community was special. Despite all those things, Max knew it was something more.

Violet, Lilah and Cassidy had a core of unfailing loyalty that meant they would do the things that were hard. They had uncovered their landlady's lifelong secret, and rather than dumping it back on her, they'd stood for her.

And they continued to fight an exterior threat who wanted nothing more than to end them in a blaze of greed and madness.

Max had fought beside men he'd trust to the gates of hell and back, with Tucker Buchanan sitting at the top of that list, but he'd never seen such an unflinching dedication to responsibility. And it humbled him.

He knocked on Violet's door, then pushed on through.

"I—" She sat huddled at her desk, a wad of tissues in her hand and a delicate layer of red rimming her eyes and nose. "I didn't say you could come in."

"That's why I didn't wait for an invitation."

She kept a small love seat in the corner of the room, and he took it instead of one of the chairs opposite her desk.

"I just need a few minutes."

"So take them." He lifted a thick book of fabric swatches and tossed them to the floor.

"Those are silk."

Max glanced at the pile of fabric that now lay next to the couch. "Okay."

"They don't belong on the floor."

Since vacuum lines were still evident in the carpet, he

failed to see the problem. "You could eat off the floor. They'll be fine."

"Why do you do that?"

"Do what?"

"Just…" She stood, her gaze roaming wildly around the room, never really landing anywhere. Oddly, he noted, those warm green eyes kept skipping right over him. "You just infiltrate!"

"I'll grant you that. I'm a persistent man."

"Stubborn as a bull crossed with an elephant."

"Why, Miss Richardson. That might be the sweetest thing you've ever said to me."

Her gaze swung straight back to his, her shoulders stiffening at his words. "Don't mock me."

"I meant it."

"It wasn't sweet."

"No, but it was honest. And I'll take honesty over useless words, flattering or otherwise, any day of the week." Max leaned forward, his elbows on his knees. "I think you feel the same."

The stiff posture and irate visage seemed to deflate before his eyes. "People don't like the truth."

"No, they don't."

"They like comfortable platitudes that tell them everything is going to be okay."

"Yep."

"So why are you here?"

Max stayed where he was, even though all he wanted to do was cross to her and wrap her up in his arms. "I thought you needed a bit of honesty. And someone to take it out on."

"And why would you think that?"

"Because something changed out there." He hitched a

thumb toward the outer area of the store. "I saw it in your face before you leaped up and disappeared."

"I didn't disappear." She hesitated before adding, "It was something you said. To Lilah."

He wasn't sure what he could possibly have said but saw she'd been affected. "I didn't mean to be insensitive."

"No. You weren't." Violet let out a hard breath before coming around the desk. "You were the opposite of insensitive. You reassured her when she got upset about giving up her ruby to her jackass ex. And. Well. I just thought it was awfully sweet, and it made me realize how hasty I've been."

"Hasty?"

"About you."

"Hasty how?" Max barely dared to breathe, the moment powerful. Shockingly so.

"I want to think of you as some big clod, grumping your way through life."

Although he did prefer honesty, he couldn't deny her words were harsher than he'd have expected. "Oh?"

"And you're not. You're big and brave, and you care. Even if you don't want anyone to know it, you care. You've protected your grandfather and Mrs. Beauregard. You've protected us at considerable expense to yourself." She stilled, those exotic green eyes so wide they nearly engulfed her face. The long sweep of dark eyelashes only accentuated the color, making that shock of green even more vivid. "And me. You've protected me. Rescued me. You saved me, Max."

Whatever hurt might have come at the word *clod* vanished at *big and brave*, and he was honest enough with himself to admit the flattery was effective.

Highly so.

"Come here."

She hovered by the edge of the desk, indecision warring with exhaustion to the point he thought the slender figure might just topple over. The urge to go to her was strong, but he sensed it was important she come to him.

For her *and* for him.

"Come on." He shifted over on the couch, creating a small space for her next to him.

That same indecision hovered there a moment longer before something snapped. She slipped out of the heels she'd insisted on wearing for the meeting with St. Germain and sat next to him on the couch. Without waiting for permission, he pulled her beneath his arm, tucking her head into his shoulder. He pressed his lips to her hair, breathing in the soft scent of her. "That's better."

"I smell." Her tone still bore the same petulant traces she seemed to love tormenting him with, but buried in the notes was something else.

Vulnerability.

"You smell wonderful."

"I smell like a train."

He pressed another kiss to the crown of her head. "Maybe I like train."

She snuggled deeper, leaning into him and wrapping her arms around his waist. "Then you have no taste."

"We'll go with that if you want."

He had extremely good taste, and the proof of it was currently snuggled in his arms. The tension that set her shoulders in hard lines slowly faded beneath his palm, and rather than talk to her, he simply let the moments pass. There'd be plenty of time for talking later.

Now she needed comfort. And some blessed relief from the monsters that lurked in the shadows.

Chapter 13

Knox St. Germain sat down at his government-issued laptop and considered the email he needed to send. A double cross was a delicate matter, after all.

In the end, he kept it short and simple.

MADE CONTACT WITH THE WEDDING BOUTIQUE. ALL PROCEEDING ACCORDING TO PLAN.

He hit Send, then sat back and considered the bourbon he'd poured earlier. While his mates would hardly consider his choice a proper English drink, preferring pints at the pub or an increasing favorite, vodka, he'd gotten a taste for bourbon after an assignment in the States a few years back. He sipped about half the contents before the customary ping winged its way back to him.

KEEP ON THE TARGETS. REPORT TOMORROW.

Equally short. Equally simple.

Keep on the targets.

He took another sip of the bourbon, intent on marshaling his thoughts from his earlier meeting, cataloging all he'd learned so he could identify what he'd share and what he'd alter.

And was surprised when, instead of a mental review of his conversation with Violet Richardson, Cassidy Tate and Lilah Castle, his thoughts drifted straight to Gabriella Sanchez.

Although not technically one of his targets, she was an interesting one. A spitfire, he'd give her that. She was also a fascinating contradiction. The long hair and the equally long legs, smooth as silk on five-inch icepicks suggested a woman with more body than brains, yet she'd gone toe-to-toe with him.

And she'd been fast about it, too. Sharp. And most definitely nobody's fool.

All evidence that suggested there was a sizable brain beneath that gorgeous swath of dark brown hair that spilled down her back in lush waves.

Knox shifted, a slight twitch at the base of his spine as he considered the interesting puzzle that was the lovely Miss Sanchez. Well, he assumed the *miss* part.

She wore no rings at all, despite large earrings, a prominent necklace that sat on an equally prominent— and impressive—chest and several bracelets that jingled when she'd set down what looked like an incredible tray of enchiladas.

But no rings.

Curious.

He drained the rest of his bourbon and opened up a quick search. No use sitting there wondering when the information was his for the taking.

Knox tapped into the agency's database, running a query on one Gabriella Sanchez of Dallas, Texas. Several women came up, and he scrolled through the results until he clicked on *caterer*. She'd never shared her job description, but the enchiladas were a pretty large clue, and he cursed himself once more for passing on a plate.

Knox rubbed at his stomach, the answering growl a further reminder of what he'd missed out on. He navigated a few more clicks into the data, pleased when a few newspaper articles led him straight to a website.

He scanned the home page, then her bio, taking in the references to heritage, home cooking and the fact that she came from a large family.

And still no mention of a husband or children.

He scanned to a photo page and saw some of her accomplishments. She looked as if she'd won every cooking competition in Dallas and the surrounding areas, her smile broad and welcoming in every shot. Each photo also showcased a large cadre of family surrounding her, a proud set of parents flanking her in every situation.

Interesting.

Knox flipped back to the database details, noting her age was thirty-two. Three years younger than him. They were even born in the same month.

He knew it was patently unfair to question why she wasn't married yet—he'd roundly avoided that noose since his first sexual escapade—but it still left a curious open spot in his mind.

Especially when you factored in how she looked. The woman must have any number of men beating down her door.

You could learn a lot from observation, Knox mused, and he toggled back once more to the photos. People who were obviously family members surrounded her in the various images on screen, many showcasing couples with small children. And the woman beside her was clearly her mother.

The mother wore a warm smile in every shot, but there was something implacable beneath the glowing facade. And in a flash of insight, he suspected the delectable Gabriella Sanchez just might be fighting an uphill battle to live her life.

Parents who were proud of her accomplishments but who questioned her method for getting there.

Recognizing the observation hit a bit too close to home, Knox snapped the laptop closed and crossed his hotel room to retrieve a bottle of water. He'd hit the gym and forget about Miss Sanchez.

And instead, he'd figure out how he was going to get in, get out and get what he came to Texas for.

Violet woke on a start, a slight crick in her neck dragging her fully awake. She wasn't sure how it had happened, but she was half-curled into Max with the rest of her body squinched oddly between his large frame and the end of her office love seat.

How did they...

The question faded as she slowly came back to herself.

He'd followed her into her office after she'd gone on all squinty and sad. Which meant everyone else was still outside her office.

Max's even breathing suggested he was asleep, but she didn't dare turn her head for fear of waking him with the movement so near his face. Instead, she moved inch by inch, sliding from his arms. She nearly fell onto the floor of her office but caught herself in time and rebalanced to a standing position.

Thank goodness for squats three times a week.

Her door was closed, so she turned the knob with careful movements.

"They've all gone home."

She slammed a hand on the door frame, nearly screaming at the surprise of Max's words in the quiet room. Summoning up some sense of calm, she turned in the direction of that dark, sexy voice. "How long have we been in here?"

"A few hours. I don't know. Two or three, maybe."

"I thought you were asleep."

"Light sleeper."

She tugged on the hem of her blouse. "Why didn't you wake me? I could have gone home with everyone else."

"You were asleep. It's as easy for me to take you home now as it was three hours ago."

Home.

The thought struck her so hard she felt her knees buckle. Her own bed. The comfort of her things around her. "Let me just get a spare set of keys."

"Lilah brought your purse back from the wedding." Max gestured toward the desk. "I think she stowed it in your bottom drawer."

Violet retrieved her purse, oddly touched to see her belongings. "She thought about it."

"Your friends don't miss much. Lilah did a sweep for your things while Cassidy closed out the event."

The wedding.

She'd initially worried about Kimberly and Jordan when she first awoke in Lange's house but had forgotten them in the ensuing hours. Had it really been only two days since the wedding?

Max laid his hand over hers. "You okay?"

The thick strap of her purse hung from the tips of her

fingers like an anchor, steadied by his firm grip. "I can't get my bearings."

"You've been through a lot."

"I know." And she did know. No matter how strong she believed herself to be, nothing changed the fact that two days ago she was drugged, kidnapped and attacked. She'd survive—she was counting on that—but it would be nice to feel like herself again. "You certainly seem bright-eyed and bushy-tailed."

"Like a bunny."

The image did the trick, and she laughed in spite of herself. "Sure you are."

"Well, you know, the big and brave ones who sort of clod around."

Her words—albeit mixed up—came back to haunt her, and she touched his shoulder. "I'm sorry. That was insensitive of me."

"I liked it. Not the clod part, but I can do big and brave."

Before she could reply or make up for her remark, he had her back against the door, his hands on either side of her face.

His lips drifted down to her ear. "I can definitely do big and brave."

The comment was so like Max, and Violet toyed with being obstinate just because, but the large warm male body currently boxing her in quickly pushed her thoughts in another direction.

"Oh, yeah?"

"Absolutely."

And then there were no words—stubborn or otherwise—as his lips came over hers, enveloping the sigh that drifted up her throat.

Nothing was rational with Max. But everything was just right. The upheaval in her life might still be fresh in her mind, but she also knew the moment for what it was. Desire, yes. Need, yes. But there was something even more potent that beat underneath.

Life.

He made her feel alive, and that was something to hang on to.

Although his hands never moved from either side of her head, she used his arms-up position to run her palms over his chest, then down the sides of his body without restriction. Firm muscle bunched and tensed beneath her fingers as she traced the thick line of muscle over his ribs before narrowing on his stomach. The hard ridges she'd already seen firsthand on the train rippled beneath her hands as she touched his stomach, the tactile exploration an erotic counterpoint to the play of lips and teeth and tongues as he deepened the kiss.

"What do you do to me?" He exhaled the words on a hard groan before tracing another line of kisses over her jaw and on down to her throat.

What did they do to each other?

She wanted him. She'd known that for days—months, really—but in that moment, Violet was forced to admit the truth. She wanted him with a fierce need that refused to be sated. "I want you, Max." She kissed his chin. "I want to be with you."

"I thought you didn't like me."

"I thought *you* didn't like *me*."

"I hate to disappoint you, sweetheart, but I'm a man. That part's usually immaterial."

She wanted to be shocked—knew she should be—but again, the honesty was refreshing. And the exact opposite of her lifetime of experiences.

"Of course," he drawled, his words as smooth as the

hand that had drifted down to trace a line across her stomach, "I do like you. A lot. And I have from the start."

Violet could only stare up at him, her mouth gaping like a fish. "But you don't like me."

"Of course I do. You're smart and talented. You don't take crap from anyone. And you're sexy as hell. What's not to like?"

"But we argue. And snap at each other."

Max shrugged, those large shoulders lifting and dropping with enticing movement that seemed to beg her to just hang on. "It's foreplay."

And there it was. Raw truth, plain and simple.

A conversation she'd had briefly at a party the previous spring came back to her at Max's words. She'd struck up a conversation with a woman on the elevator ride from the lobby to the host's condo. Marina, as she remembered. The two of them had quickly fallen into conversation, discussing those light and airy odds and ends that filled party conversation.

It was only when the woman had remarked about her lack of a date that Violet had thought of Max. Unbidden, an image of him filled her thoughts, and she'd made a few comments about how stubborn he was and how ill-suited they were.

Marina had lit up at the discussion, and Violet could still remember the woman's gentle tease as she probed for details about Max. Even more curious, Marina had ended up using the same descriptor, despite Violet's protests that Max wasn't at all suited to her.

Foreplay.

Was this what they'd been working up to? All the long months of sniping and lingering glances had brought them here.

Unwilling to analyze it any further, she smiled for the

sheer joy of it and wrapped her arms around his neck. "I like the way you think, Baldwin. But first, I need a shower."

With aching slowness, he traced the line of her cheek, over her jaw, before following her neck to the hollow of her throat. Violet gave herself up to his touch, the delicious counterpoint of such a large, capable man so gentle and delicate in his movements. It was only when he hesitated, his fingers stilling, that she questioned him. "What is it?"

"You're—" A light flush colored his cheeks. "It's just that you're so soft."

"I'm filthy."

"Doesn't make you any less soft."

"And as we confirmed earlier, I smell like train."

He traced the line of her cheek once more. "No need to go fishing for compliments. I already told you I like that smell."

Now it was her going still, the gravitas of the moment striking somewhere deep inside. She didn't fluster easily, so it was more than a little shocking to realize the effect of his words.

Soft.

He thought she was soft. It wasn't a term she typically associated with herself, nor was it an image she tried to cultivate. Yet she felt the compliment all the same.

Half amused, half annoyed with herself for analyzing the moment, Violet felt her brain cells vanish as he took her mouth once more, his tongue playing over hers and coaxing forth a need she'd never experienced. Shockwaves pulsed through her body, tightening her skin with delicious sensitivity. Her fingers flexed at his waist as she pulled him closer, anxious for the contact of Max's large body flush against hers. But it was the hard length of him, more than evident in the press of their bodies, that sent an answering need rocketing through her core.

Oh, how she wanted him.

His fingers drifted over her skirt, moving to the front and flicking open the lone button at her waist.

An image of closing that button two days before had her hands covering his, stilling his movements. "I don't want to ruin the moment." She whispered the words against his lips.

"Then don't." Clearly intent on ignoring her, he covered her mouth again. Violet felt herself going under before finally pulling away.

"I mean it. I can't think when you do that."

"Good." He nipped her lips. "Thinking's overrated."

"Yes, but clean isn't."

Recognizing he wasn't going to make things easy on her—and knowing full well a few more minutes in his arms and she likely wouldn't care—Violet slipped away, putting a few feet between them.

"We probably should head home. I definitely need a shower."

"You're a determined woman, Richardson."

"It's only right. We're—" She stopped and acknowledged it was way more than just a few layers of dirt that needed to be washed off.

Before she could say anything, his quiet sigh punctuated the moment. "We need to wash off what the last few days meant. Let's get out of here and do just that."

He understood. Way down deep, Max understood.

And with that understanding came a wave of roiling confusion that nearly cut her off at the knees. They didn't know each other. Not all the way down deep where it mattered. Men could be nice—could be considerate or thoughtful or empathetic in a moment—but they always defaulted to their own selfish needs once they got what they wanted.

Right now, Max wanted sex. If he had to delay it for an hour to appease her, he would. She'd do well not to confuse acquiescence with anything more meaningful.

Alarm bells jangled in the back of her mind, and she tried to ignore them—did her level best to do so—but the distant memory of voices rose up to swamp her.

"You have to look so freaking perfect all the time. A damn illusion for Dallas's finest."

"You expect your wife to play a part. Your beautiful doll, projecting the image of a perfect family. It's your damn illusion and I'm just playing my part."

"An act. It's all an act. For our family. Our friends. Even in front of our child."

"Don't get sentimental on me now. You're the one who's created the act. The illusion for others that we're happy. That we matter to each other. Hell, that we even give a damn about each other."

"You're awfully accommodating." Violet mentally winced as the accusation slithered out.

The warm blue of his eyes, hazed over with the heat of passion, cooled off a few degrees. "What?"

"You say you want me, then are fine with a big interruption to drive home."

"I do want you. And I thought I was showing you basic consideration and understanding."

"Consideration? Or a play to get what you want? Me, in bed."

Max moved up into her space, passion morphing quickly into ire. "What part of the past half hour haven't you understood? Hell, what part of the past year haven't you understood? I want you. It's humbling to realize just how damn much I want you. But I'm not a freaking manipulator, Violet. I don't operate that way, and I sure as hell wouldn't insult you by behaving that way."

Misery squeezed her in a vise. "It'll fade. We'll screw around a bit and then this will all fade. The adrenaline rush will be gone, and we'll go back to being two people who bicker and argue and drive each other nuts." Where were these words coming from? And why wouldn't they stop?

"What?" Max backed away at that, and she saw the very result she was aiming for.

Pain. Hurt. Confusion.

"What's the matter with you?"

"Just coming back to my senses. You are quite skilled at scrambling a woman's brains."

Max moved forward once more, retracing his steps back to her. She nearly gave it up right there, because the confusion mapping his face in craggy lines gave way to a small bead of hope that lit up his eyes. "Talk to me, Violet. What's this about?"

Holding the ravages of her parents' failure in an emotional fist, she now took the steps away from him. "Let's just say I'm coming up from the adrenaline haze I've been in since Saturday night."

"Whatever's going on here has nothing to do with Lange. And it sure as hell has nothing to do with being kidnapped."

Without giving her a moment to respond, he ground out, "Get your things. I'll drive you home."

He was out the door of her office before she could say another word.

Alex turned the cell phone over in his hands, the tinkering he'd done with the piece paying him sweet dividends. Although somewhat damaged, he'd managed to retrieve the SIM card and had worked his way through the data. Baldwin was good, Alex had to give the man credit. The ex-soldier had done a pretty solid surface wipe of the data.

But Alex was better.

He dug beneath the data and bit by bit parsed out the information he was looking for.

And was now sitting on a fifty-acre property in the Hill Country that belonged to one Maxwell Paul Baldwin. The land was purchased about a decade ago, but it was only recently built upon, based on some county permit records he'd also managed to unearth.

Armed with the information, he made his way to Lange. The man had locked himself in his study, his anger over Violet Richardson's escape and the lingering frustration over the loss of his wife putting him into a state.

Alex had always believed his boss above reproach, but the past week had given him increasing doubts. Where he'd believed Lange strong and crafty, powerful and wise, he'd begun to see the cracks. The man's dependence on his wife—and distraction at her disappearance—was downright shocking.

Alex had come to America seeking a leader. How disappointing to see the veneer of strength he'd always admired crack and crumble, fading away to dust at a few small setbacks.

That's all they were. Setbacks.

Alex believed to his very marrow that they had prepared better. Planned more effectively. And had the sheer drive necessary to reach their ends. They simply had to keep pressing forward.

Otherwise, what had all the time and effort—years' worth—been for?

Tripp Lange had operated in the shadows, hiding his less savory choices behind a public face of charm, hard work and cutthroat business acumen. Even his wife had been unaware of her beloved husband's shadowy maneuverings. It had been masterful.

And now it was just weak.

To allow it to fall to pieces was simply unacceptable.

Relaxing his face, he set his features in calm lines and knocked on Lange's door. A muffled "Come in" greeted him, and Alex entered the office.

And was speared clean through with the evidence of his misplaced trust and loyalty.

A dim light reflected from the desk, highlighting Lange's features. He hadn't shaved in two days, gray stubble painting his cheeks like those of a haggard old man. His hair, normally pulled back from his forehead in an elegant sweep, was disheveled and greasy. But it was his eyes that aged him.

Lange's most powerful feature had always been his eyes. A pale, nearly reptilian green, their ability to stare down an opponent with all the calm and predatory grace of a snake had given the man an unwitting edge.

Now they were dull. Lifeless. And fixed, almost unseeing, on the lone ruby at the center of his desk.

Alex had believed the promise in those eyes. He'd devoted his life to the belief that Tripp Lange was well able to seek restitution for the ravages faced by their homeland during the war. Even more, he'd committed himself fully to Lange's service, knowing his vow to his dying father would be realized by his alignment with Lange.

He'd failed.

Once more, Alex held back disgust as he looked at the man he'd allied himself with. His pulse beat a hard thud in his chest, but he maintained the calm outward demeanor. It would do no good to tip his boss off to his disillusionment.

Retribution would be swift, and it was no use to give up that edge.

"I have some news."

Lange's gaze remained fixed on the ruby. "Yes?"

"I've worked out our next move."

"Dallas. Tomorrow. We already discussed it."

"I believe I have something better."

That pale gaze remained dull, but Lange did lift his eyes from the ruby. "We already discussed attacking the women in their place of work."

"Let's hit them with something harder."

Chapter 14

Max prowled around the kitchen looking for something to eat along with the beer he'd already popped. He was still full from Gabby's enchiladas but eyed the package of leftovers she'd made him. At least it was something to do.

Which was ridiculous.

He shouldn't even be here right now. He should be wrapped around Violet Richardson, delightfully wet from the mutual shower they'd have already completed. Or were still in progress of completing. Instead, he was standing in his damn kitchen, staring at an open refrigerator and attempting to cool the fire in his blood. Hell, he'd taken the edge off in the shower and it still hadn't done much to drive away the gnawing desire that clawed at his gut with razor-sharp nails.

So here he was, with nothing but his damn thoughts to keep him company.

What had he done? Had he pushed her?

He saw the No Trespassing sign. It came on fast, like a hairpin curve out of the blue, but it was as clear as the drop off a sheer cliff.

What had happened to her?

He'd suspected it, even if he couldn't quite identify what he sensed underneath her often prickly shell. Had another man hurt her? A former relationship?

Ignoring the enchiladas, he drained the rest of his beer in the cool air of the open fridge, then reached for another. He wasn't interested in getting drunk, but a few more beers might help take that edge the rest of the way off.

The knock on his door interrupted his thoughts, and he was about to ignore it when he heard his name.

"Max. Open up. It's me."

He moved through the small living room, suddenly grateful he'd remembered to vacuum Saturday morning, and opened the door to Violet standing on the other side. Her hair was still wet, she wore no makeup and he knew, without question, he'd never seen anyone more beautiful.

So why the *hell* was he thinking about his vacuum? "What are you doing out of your place? With all that's going on, I figured you were smart enough to stay put."

"I had my old phone with me and had 911 programmed and ready to go if I needed it."

He pulled her inside, slamming the door behind her. "Stupid risks. Why the hell—"

Violet never let him finish. She slipped into his arms, her body flush against him as she pressed her mouth to his. The past hour vanished as if it had never happened and he pulled her close, barely holding back the growl that centered in the back of his throat.

She was *here*.

Max buried his hands in her still-wet hair, desperately pleased she'd come to him even as the ravages of their conversation still lingered. They needed to talk. Needed to come to some sort of understanding.

But right now, all he wanted to do was kiss her and sink into the one thing between the two of them that did work.

"Max." She squeezed his shoulders. "We need to talk."

The rational part of him knew she was right—having her back in his arms didn't negate any of the reasons he'd dropped her off at her apartment alone—but the irrational part just wanted to hang on and never let her go.

"That's what got me in trouble earlier."

"Not true." She squeezed his shoulders once more before putting some distance between them. "Give me a chance to explain. Please. You deserve it."

Violet shook her head. "No, that's not quite true. *We* deserve it."

Max led her to the couch and took the seat beside her. "Do you want anything?"

"No, I'm good." A small, tremulous smile tilted her lips up. "And I've finally taken a shower and cleaned off two days of grime, so I've already got a clearer head."

He brushed at several strands of hair that had already dried and tucked them behind her ear. "So I see."

"You do." She gripped his hands in hers, and he reveled in the feel of her slender fingers holding him tight. "You see a lot. And it's bothered me. More than I've understood or been able to explain to myself."

"Violet—"

"Please. Let me finish."

Max nodded even as his own words caught in his chest. He wanted to tell her she was beautiful. That he wanted her in a way he'd never wanted another woman. That it wasn't just sex, even though he wanted her body with a desperation that bordered on madness.

But more, he wanted *her*.

In his bed. In his arms. In his life.

"I'm not comfortable letting other people in. I find emotional intimacy intrusive."

"This from a woman who helps people create one of the happiest days of their lives."

"The great contradiction of my life." She squeezed his hands once more before continuing. "But it's easy to create that for someone else when you know it's just a fantasy. Every wedding I help put on is just someone else's play."

"And you don't believe the people you're helping are in love?"

"It's none of my business if they are or aren't. It's only my business what they tell me and what they ask me to help them create."

It was on the tip of his tongue to poke a few holes in her approach when Max considered his own work. Yes, as an architect he created, but more, he was responsible for helping someone's vision come to life.

They knew what they wanted. It was his role to create it in the physical. It never mattered if he liked Spanish tile or French Colonial or cathedral ceilings. It was his job to create to his clients' demands.

"Do you hope the couples you help are in love?"

"Of course." She did smile at that. "I'm cynical, not mean. And if it makes you feel any better, Cassidy and Lilah both think I just need to find the right man and I can shake off this funk."

"It's not a funk if you feel it deep inside."

The smile faded. "No, it's not. Especially since the roots are deeply seeded in my personality."

"What did they do? Your parents?"

The reference to roots moved her reticence out of the

realm of an old love or a relationship gone bad. But it was in her quiet pause that Max knew he'd guessed right.

"They never loved each other. And they put me in the middle as they figured out how to strike back and forth."

"How long did that go on?"

"It still goes on from time to time, but lucky for me they've both gone on to second and third spouses and have spread the striking out across more people."

Max knew about those moments. When you wanted to hide from the very people who should create a warm, safe haven. When their inability to live with each other— hell, even to function with each other—took away any sense of comfort or safety or roots. He'd spent his childhood that way, and if it hadn't been for Pops, he didn't know where he'd have ended up.

Or who he'd have ended up being.

"Sounds like a miserable way to live."

"I think so." She glanced down at their joined hands, and Max had the fleeting thought that she was surprised to find herself hanging on so tight. "But it's the norm, don't you think?"

Was it the norm?

Had she asked him even a few months ago, he'd have likely said yes. He'd spent his adult life with a rather cynical view on love and reveled in the role, always re-assuring himself that his view was based on reality. On seeing things as they actually were.

But in the past month, he'd begun to think differently. He'd had an attraction to Violet, but since becoming involved with her and her friends, his view of the world had started to shift. He saw how happy Tucker was with Cassidy and saw the same with Reed and Lilah. He didn't know Graystone all that well, but the man had proven himself well suited to their somewhat motley group. He'd also proven himself more than devoted to his new fiancée.

While Max had no crystal ball, his gut told him those three couples had what it took to see a relationship through all its ups and downs.

So maybe it *was* possible.

More than possible, he thought, as he took in the woman sitting opposite him on the couch.

He wanted to experience all those ups and downs with her.

Her normal battle armor was nowhere in evidence. Instead, the woman who could corral a hotel staff of a hundred or plan a wedding for four times that had faded, replaced with someone who had dropped her guard.

For him.

Since she still waited for his answer, Max thought about what he wanted to say. He didn't want to brush off her question—and the cynic in him hadn't fully vanished—but he couldn't deny his perspective had changed. Evolved, really.

"For some, breaking up or fighting or general apathy is the norm. For others, their experience is the exact opposite. Look at our friends."

"What if they're just lucky? What if that's not meant for everyone?"

"You think what Cassidy and Lilah found is just sheer dumb luck?"

"I—" She swallowed hard, her gaze narrowing. "They've both worked hard to give themselves to their relationships. To be true partners to Tucker and Reed."

"So it's not just luck."

"Why are you twisting up what I'm trying to say?"

"Because it's not as simple or easy to dissect as you'd

like to make it. Maybe none of this is about being lucky at all. You make your own luck, after all."

"You don't choose who you fall in love with."

"No?" Max had always believed that to be true, but increasingly he wasn't so sure. The idea of cosmic forces acting upon him when he had no say in the outcome—and no ability to recognize genuine feelings for another—struck him as patently misguided.

"Of course not. Lightning strikes and sometimes it's a good thing, and other times—" She faltered, and Max knew the depth of her pain wouldn't be solved by a few philosophical questions. "Other times it doesn't work out."

"There are no guarantees. But I believe we control how we treat others and how we temper our expectations. You're not like your parents, Violet. You are capable of love. I see it every time you're with your friends."

"That's different."

"Why?"

Where he expected challenge, he saw only more confusion in the determined set of her jaw. "Because they're my friends. You and I are different. We're talking about sex, and sex changes things."

"I sure as hell hope so."

"Then you admit it is different."

Max squeezed her hands and tamped down on the grumbled retort that threatened. She'd been hurt before, and brushing off her concerns was tantamount to brushing off her. "Sex may add spice, but I'm talking about the core emotion of love. You're capable of that. More than capable if what I've observed is true."

"But we're not in love."

Weren't they?

The thought hit with such a swift punch Max wondered that he didn't see stars.

But of course they weren't in love. He'd be a fool to get caught up in that notion, and he wasn't a fool.

A besotted one, at that.

No, Violet was right. And if the acknowledgment of that simple fact left him with a raw-boned cold way down deep inside, well. He'd live with it.

Of course they weren't in love.

"Max?"

"Hmm?"

"You seemed—" She hesitated, then shook her head. "We're talking too much."

Her comment gave him the opening he needed, and he latched on to it like a lifeline, dragging on a lightness he didn't feel. "Seems to be a mutual problem."

"What are we going to do about it?"

"Maybe we shut up and just be friends who have really great sex."

The warm smile that greeted him went a long way toward thawing that deep freeze. And when she moved into his arms, Max took what she offered willingly.

Violet wanted to believe him. Wanted to reach out and take what Max offered with effortless simplicity.

She wanted that more than anything. But years with her parents and their endless acts against each other, with her locked in the middle, had taken a toll. She loved them still, in spite of the endless drama, but she couldn't deny they disappointed her over and over.

But the idea that she and Max were leaping into just sex?

That went down harder than she expected.

What were you expecting? Promises of everlasting devotion?

Violet knew she was overthinking things. Heck, she'd begun overthinking when it came to Max Baldwin the day the man walked into one of the local Design District meetings and stood up to introduce himself. Even then, she'd been intrigued.

And attracted.

Which only added to her internal debate. Physical intimacy between them, while a big step, was also easy. It was a moment in time. A physical need fulfilled.

But the possibility of something more?

She wanted a relationship. And when she looked at Max, she could even see herself in one. But the lingering ghosts of her parents' messy relationship hovered in cold silence beside that image. A reminder that no matter how well-intentioned at the start, things ended. People moved on. And love died.

What if you're different? A quiet voice she barely dared to believe whispered through her mind.

And more importantly, what if he makes you different?

He made her feel alive. Wonderfully, magically alive.

But was she committed to seeing this through? It was a gamble, and Violet wasn't sure she had what it took to make the proper wager.

But she did have it in her to take tonight.

To keep all the shadows at bay—the ones she couldn't quite escape and the others that still lurked outside, waiting to attack. "I want you. More than I've ever wanted anyone, I want you. But I can't promise you anything. I don't know where this is going to go."

"I don't know, either."

Violet cocked her head. "You're awfully reasonable. Is it the promise of sex talking?"

"If it helps, I can promise you I've heard every word."

She did laugh at that, the fear of what still lingered in the shadows fading at the raw hunger that filled his sky-blue gaze. "There you go with that honesty thing again."

"I can't be anything else, Violet. I hope you understand that." He shifted closer and pressed his lips to her ear. "And I do want you. But it hasn't completely shut off my brain or stopped me from hearing you."

She settled her hands on either side of his face. "I do love a man who can multitask."

"Did I also mention I was skilled with my hands?"

The tension that had set her shoulders in hard lines on the short drive to Max's apartment began to fade in the simple joy of being with him.

He made her happy.

Somewhere deep inside the denials and the questions and all the rational reasons why she should walk away, Violet had begun to think about all the reasons she should stay.

"Those are awfully promising words, Mr. Baldwin."

"I've got the skills to back up the promise."

"Why don't you prove it?"

Max's apartment was small and spare, but the walk from the living room to the bedroom seemed endless. Now that she'd made her decision, the desire to be with him overtook everything else. The need to join with him—to welcome him inside her—became as steady and as necessary as her heartbeat.

Max never broke contact as they kissed and touched their way to the bedroom. The clever man even managed to remove the thin summer tank top she'd paired with shorts, the silky peach material floating behind them in their wake.

She should have felt briefly self-conscious to stand before him in her bra, but instead she was empowered. Emboldened by the way he made her feel and the sensual power that beat beneath her flushed skin.

So it was with no small measure of embarrassment that she nearly retrieved the tank top at the dark look that filled his eyes as his gaze roamed over her bra-clad form.

"What's—" The question died on her lips as she realized what he was staring at. Several round bruises that had turned a mottled yellow and green stood out on her pale skin, just beneath the line of her bra.

"I should have killed him." The words were spoken so softly Violet barely heard them, yet their lethal edges were unmistakable.

"Max. I'm fine. It's fine."

Her protests seemed to have no effect as he knelt before her, his hands roaming over her stomach in gentle, probing motions. "Does this hurt?"

She settled her hands on his shoulders for lack of any other place to put them, intent on using the position to pull him back up to standing. To return them to the lighthearted teasing and sexual promise that awaited them at the end of their walk to the bedroom.

Instead, her position only telegraphed her pain when he indented her flesh with the tender press of his fingers. She fought a wince but couldn't stop the instinctive reflex of her fingers against his shoulders. "It's fine."

He only shot her a dark look as he continued his inspection, moving his hands to the other, more prominent bruise, low on her right rib cage. The ache still lingered, but something else rushed in to take its place at the supreme gentleness of his touch.

She'd have thought the marring of her body and the remembered violence would intrude on their moments together. Instead, sharing it with Max helped to put it in its proper place.

"I really am fine." She ran her fingers through the military-short cut of his hair, the strands soft against her skin. He read the implicit request in her motions and lifted his head once more, his attention fully focused on her. "And I'd like you to stand up."

His blue eyes darkened like a winter's day before the snow came—a brilliant shade shot through with the impending storm. "I can't get past it. You have to understand what it does to me to see these marks on you."

She thought she'd understood, but now, faced with his smoldering anger, she realized just how far she'd underestimated his emotion.

"You rescued me, Max. You stopped them and made sure they couldn't do anything else to me. We need to focus on that." She bent her head, pressing a kiss to the soft swirl of hair at the crown of his head. "We need to celebrate that."

He finally stood but left his hands on her waist. "Maybe we shouldn't do this. I don't want to hurt you."

"You're not going to hurt me."

"There are marks on you, Violet. You can't tell me they don't hurt."

"Until you decided to focus on them, I hadn't given them much thought."

"Stubborn woman."

The petulance in his tone matched hers, and she couldn't help but smile at the pair they made. "I'm tougher than I look. And I'll be really pissed if Lange manages to ruin this, too."

Indecision wrapped around those storm clouds in his eyes as the gentleman he was did battle with the sexual desire that had haunted them both for nearly a year.

Determined to force the innate gentleman to take a

backseat, she lifted up on tiptoes and pressed her lips to his ear. "Please."

She nearly had him, the widening of his pupils a dead giveaway to the needs of his body. Since his T-shirt had vanished along the journey from living room to bedroom, Violet used every tool in her arsenal to gain victory.

She ran her hands over the broad expanse of his chest before working her way toward the button of his jeans. Heat radiated off his stomach muscles, and she traced the thin line of hair that slid beneath the waist of his briefs before taking him fully in her palm.

The hard breath that whooshed past her ears had Violet smiling, and she couldn't resist massaging the hard line of his erection, anxious to draw the same response again.

He cupped her face in his hands, the liquid blue of his eyes lit with a fierce passion. "What do you do to me?"

She'd meant to keep things light—she'd had every intention of breezing through sex with Max—but the repetition of the same question he'd asked earlier stopped her.

Was it the raw honesty she saw reflected in his gaze? Or the gentleness of his touch, even as his muscles practically quivered with need?

Or the realization that he had her as deeply in his thrall as she seemed to hold him.

What do you do to me, Max Baldwin?

A pithy retort sprang to her lips, but she held it back. Somehow saying anything during such a momentous moment seemed wrong.

He grazed his thumb over her cheekbone before speaking once more, his voice husky. "What have you done to me?"

The only answer lay in the needs of her body. That culmination of the sensual dance their souls had understood long before either of their minds had processed the inevitable.

So without thinking of what she didn't have to offer Max, Violet focused on what she did have.

Herself.

With the long months of endless aching finally at an end, she continued her ministrations, the solid length of him still cupped in her palm. He gritted his teeth and covered her hand with his, halting her motions. "I think we're both wearing too much."

"You're sure this isn't some plot to put you in the driver's seat?" With aching slowness, she stroked the length of his erection. She was rewarded with the dropping of his eyelids and the hard clench of his throat as he fought for control. When he finally spoke his voice was hoarse, strained to the breaking point. "I'm a very good driver."

Before she took another breath, Max had her in his arms, his movements sure as he strode to the bed. She wanted to argue—was she actually being carried to bed?—but the sensation was so sweet and sexy she didn't have the heart to say anything that might ruin the moment.

Max laid her down, then followed with his body. He created a cage with his arms as he settled his hips between her thighs. The same erection she'd so recently cradled in her hands pressed against the apex of her thighs, and Violet saw stars as she adjusted to his weight.

"Happy to see me, Mr. Baldwin?"

His wolfish grin was his only answer before he bent his head and began to nibble his way down her body. Her bra went first, sacrificed to his clever fingers, followed quickly by her shorts. When his hand slipped beneath the silky material of her panties, Violet nearly came off the bed.

"Max!"

He maintained his silence, his only acknowledgment he even heard her the increased pressure from his fingers and the slide of silk down her legs, which he managed with his free hand. On a hard moan, Violet gave up any attempt to speak. Instead, she closed her eyes and let the long drafts of pleasure wash over her.

The fear of the past few days faded, along with the loneliness she'd increasingly accepted as a part of her life. She gave herself up to the moment. To the need and the fire and Max.

Sweet, wonderful, surly, amazing Max.

And then there were no adjectives—no thoughts at all—except for the raw pleasure that suffused her body in bright, warm waves. Violet took the moment, clutching Max's shoulders tightly even as she allowed her body to go hurtling through the heavens.

But it was only on her descent back to earth that she registered the soft words, crooned in her ear over and over.

How magnificent she was.

And how beautiful.

And amazing.

Tender words that praised and adored in equal measure.

Abstractly, she realized that she hadn't stopped touching him, her hands roaming a steady arc over his shoulders, down his chest, around to his back. There was power here, Violet thought. Raw power, barely leashed.

Max lifted up onto his forearms again. "Are you okay?"

She nodded, still shimmering with the aftershocks of her orgasm, her hands splayed across his thick muscles.

"Good. I'm good." And then, before she could stop herself, she blurted out, "You're so big."

His eyebrows rose for the briefest moment before her words registered more fully, and he moved off her. "I'm sorry. I'm crushing you."

"No." She was quick to pull at his shoulders to hold him still, but he'd already moved to stretch out beside her.

Damn, why did she keep fumbling with him? The man had just given her the best orgasm of her life, and she'd managed to insult him before the afterglow had even left her body.

"You weren't crushing me. At all. I just can't get over how big you are. I mean, I know you're a solid man, but you're like a rock."

"I'm not lean and graceful like Buchanan. Never have been, even as a kid." He snaked out a hand, tracing a line from her collarbone down over her breast. Her already sensitized body stirred under the soft touch, her nipple growing even harder as the pad of his finger brushed over the tip before continuing to her rib cage. "Don't think he doesn't know it, too. The bastard beats me every time we go for a run."

"Is that why you make him run alone?"

"I make him run alone because he's fond of the crack of dawn. Staying home to avoid getting my ass kicked is just a side benefit. Of course, paybacks are hell if he bothers to come with me to the gym after work."

The gym wasn't a surprise in the least. While she knew he hadn't been on active duty in a few years, he maintained the solid physique of a man used to operating in his prime. His visits to job sites for their firm's architectural work also ensured he needed to remain nimble and strong.

"I like your body. You're big and broad and sort of raw-boned, like a prize fighter." Violet traced the line of his collarbone, then down his chest, mirroring the same path he'd traveled over her own body. "It's sexy." She pressed a kiss to his lips. "So sexy."

The ebb and flow of desire reached out and grabbed them both once more. Like a roller coaster beginning its ascent to the next thrill, their touches grew more urgent, their breathing more ragged.

Max removed his jeans and briefs and in moments had a foil packet out of the bedside drawer. She expected him to resettle himself over her body, but he again defied expectation. He pressed a line of kisses over the same trail his finger had traced previously, stopping to linger over her breast. The unfulfilled urgency that drove them both only added to the pleasure, his teeth and tongue drawing sensation after sensation as he lingered, tormenting her with his mouth.

Restless with need—with the completion that would come only from the joining of their bodies—she pulled him close, guiding him back to her in welcome. He hesitated for the briefest moment, his eyes once again upon her.

Neither of them said a word, but she heard his thoughts as clearly as if he'd spoken and knew her answer had to be as obvious.

We can't go back.

I don't want to go back.

And then there wasn't a choice. She gripped his hips, lifting to meet him as he thrust, taking her fully. A harsh moan of pleasure filled her throat and spilled over in a soft cry as he embedded himself once more, then again. She matched his movements, quickly slipping into an urgent, elemental rhythm that imprisoned them both.

Violet held on to that large body, reveling in the elemental—and the essential—as they made love. Rapturous pleasure filled her even as fulfillment hovered just out of reach, growing closer…closer…

And then she fell, her hands tight on the curve of his buttocks as she sought to fill herself with him.

With Max.

Rich moments of pleasure suffused her limbs, a delicious elixir poured from the simple act of giving and sharing pleasure.

As her heart raced and her mind whirled in the simple joy of the moment, she knew she'd been given everything.

Max hovered in that delightful state between dreaming and waking, when he still had control of his thoughts but didn't much care where they went. He had Violet in his arms, her warm body and soft scent only adding to the contented drift.

"I've been thinking about Knox St. Germain."

Max's eyes popped open at her words. "What?"

"The MI5 agent. What do you think he wants?"

"We just did *that*—" he shifted up onto an elbow "—and you're thinking about another man?"

"I wasn't thinking about having sex with him."

"You just had sex with me. There should be a no-fly zone for at least an hour before another man can even enter your thoughts."

"If it weren't for St. Germain, I wouldn't have gone to my office in a huff. Which meant you wouldn't have followed me. Which means we wouldn't have ended up here. You should be thanking the man."

"We'd have ended up here sooner or later."

She tickled a hand over his ribs, her smile broad. "Yes, but you have to admit you liked ending up here sooner instead of later."

"No argument there."

She'd neatly boxed him in, with both words and gestures, but he wasn't quite content to let the subject go. "It's still a hit to a man's ego to share his bed with a beautiful woman and a ghost. A male ghost at that."

"So noted for next time. In the meantime, I am thinking about him, and I want your opinion."

Resigned to the fact that she wasn't going to let the matter drop—and pleased at the idea of a next time—Max bunched a pillow behind his back and leaned against the headboard, pulling her beneath his arm. "What about our British friend has captured your attention?"

"He got here awfully fast."

"So, there's this invention. It's called an airplane."

She swatted at his stomach, her giggle punctuating the moment. "I know that. But Reed just put in a call the other day to that friend of his at MI5. And we had a weekend in there slowing things down. Yet here comes a British officer, plain as day, all prepared to discuss the stones and their rightful return to the British government."

"You got that subtext, too?"

"Beneath the whole 'I want to help you get rid of the stones that can only cause you problems'?" She nodded. "Came through loud and clear that the real end game is returning the rubies to England."

"We can ask Mrs. B. again what her father's agreement was when he removed the rubies from British soil. He was a renowned enough jeweler to make pieces for the Royal Family. He had to have maintained the provenance on the gems. From her initial retelling to us, they belong to him, and by extension, to her, fair and square."

"Have you talked to your grandfather?"

"I've talked to him almost every day. I had Tucker contact him on Sunday while we were—" The comment faded, the memory of her extraction and their subsequent race across the Texas countryside still raw.

Whether it was insistence on making her point or a simple unwillingness to go back to the dark place that had nearly derailed their lovemaking, Violet gently shifted their conversation back to his grandfather. "So he's due for a call. We can check in on him and then ask Mrs. B. how her father ultimately handled the removal of the gems."

"It's been a long time. We may be asking an awful lot for her to remember."

"Maybe." She traced a repeating infinity loop over his stomach, fast causing him to lose his train of thought. "But none of it explains how St. Germain has gotten on this so quickly."

"I hate to work against your theories, Sherlock, but the government can mobilize awfully quickly when they want something. The normal laws of time, space and general slowness are irrelevant when you have a fleet of high-end planes at your disposal and an endless supply of money."

"But it still doesn't make sense why they'd mobilize at all. The rubies aren't theirs to want. They were given away to Mrs. Beauregard's father. Or whatever deal was struck that made the man more than willing to spirit priceless gems across the Atlantic."

"It's all moot, Violet. All someone needs to do is claim that the decision was made in the haze of wartime and, Bob's your uncle, the government gets involved."

"For future reference, British slang doesn't work all that well with a Texas twang."

He pressed a kiss to her head, smiling in spite of himself. "Just working on my Knox St. Germain impression."

Violet lifted her head from where it was pillowed

against his chest. "I don't recall him saying anything so silly and old-fashioned."

"He did in my head."

"Why?"

"Because if he sounds like an old man, I might be less inclined to beat him up."

"You know, you're sort of bloodthirsty." She shifted up to meet his gaze head-on, staring deep into his eyes. Max was tempted to shrink from the perusal, but he could only be who he was. "I like it."

He released a breath he hadn't even realized he'd been holding. "If it makes you feel better, we can consider it an occupational hazard."

"Why? It would be tantamount to hiding your light under a bushel basket."

"Geez, Violet. I don't go around drinking the blood of innocent virgins."

"I'm not suggesting you do. But you're a man who's comfortable with the power in his body and comfortable with unleashing that where necessary. Why are you getting so prickly?"

Did he dare tell her? Or did he leave the truth buried the way he always did? Hell, even Tucker didn't know the full story, and the idea he was even contemplating saying anything was an indication of just how far gone he was.

Sex with Violet was amazing, but he'd be damned if he was going to imagine it into something more.

Willing their conversation back onto more comfortable ground, he pushed more cheek into his voice. "I'm not getting prickly. But I do find it odd you seem so enamored with my ability to destroy things. For a woman accustomed to helping others build things, it's an odd juxtaposition."

"I'm a woman of many facets."

He ran a hand over her cheek, pleased to have avoided the blunt edge of her questions. "Each one more fascinating than the one before."

"You do realize this is the oddest postcoital conversation I've ever had."

"Coital?"

"You know what I mean."

"It's the clinical terminology that tripped me up." He pressed a quick kiss to her lips. "Yet another fascinating facet."

She shot him a dark look that promised future retribution, and Max marveled once more at how good he felt. He enjoyed being with her. It was just that simple.

From the silly to the stubborn and a million other stops along the way, she engaged him and refused to let go. Her mind. Her dry wit. Even her temper. They all combined to create a woman of passion and ambition and true beauty.

And if bitter memories lurked in the shadows, well... they could damn well stay there.

Violet Richardson was a bright, vivid light, and he'd be damned if he was going to do anything—confess anything—that would mar that warm glow.

Alex made the last turn onto the Baldwin property, the monotony of the old farm-to-market road they were on and the poorly marked turnoff causing a near miss. He swung the SUV hard right and followed the recently paved drive.

Yep. This had to be the place.

The information he'd secured had indicated Baldwin had finished the house after coming out of active duty, and the fresh paving of the driveway only reinforced they were in the right place. The drive had taken them a few hours from Lange's compound, and the sun was just coming up on the edge of the horizon.

"You're sure my wife's in there?"

"Yes, sir." Alex had provided the same answer, in a variety of ways, for the past two hours.

"And you know to retrieve her at all costs."

"Of course."

And so it had gone, over and over, the same conversation. Yes, he'd retrieve Mrs. Lange. Yes, he'd ensure her safety. Yes, he'd be gentle.

Alex relaxed his grip on the steering wheel, the drive and the ceaseless questions nearly at an end.

"We'll get inside and subdue the old man and the landlady. The plans I found for the house have two bedrooms on the east end and a third on the north side. We'll secure them, and then you can deal with Mrs. Lange."

"That's my wife, Alex. *Deal with* sounds like such a dirty term. Have more respect."

"Yes, sir."

Alex drove over the smooth path, the thin strip of sunlight on the horizon his sole focus.

Respect?

If Lange only knew how badly he'd damaged that and how tenuous his own position was, the man would be bargaining for his life.

But Alex remained silent and left Lange to his illusions. There was plenty of time to enact his plan. In the meantime, he needed to set each piece in motion.

The gleam of a police car stood sentinel, parked about ten yards from the house. Alex slowed the SUV and kept his hands visible on the wheel. He even added a small wave and smile as two cops stepped from the car.

He didn't miss their shift in stance, each quickly slipping guns from their holsters.

"Who the hell are they?" Lange's protest lit up the inside of the SUV.

"Imagined protection."

Alex waved once more and rolled down the window, extending an empty hand in friendship. "Good morning!"

One of the cops hollered for them to stop. His free hand went up while the other maintained a firm grip on his gun.

"Why are you listening to him?"

Alex barely glanced at Lange, just nodded and kept his smile firm. "Due time, sir. Due time. Follow his instructions for the moment."

Alex imagined the timing in his mind, mapping out the charade. He stopped the SUV and turned off the ignition, making a large show of placing his keys on the dashboard and then leaving his hands in plain view. With quiet instruction he whispered to Lange. "Step from the car, sir, with your hands up. And trust me on this."

A hard grunt was his only answer as Lange stepped from the car. Alex followed suit, his demeanor easygoing and friendly. Although the cops didn't lower their guns, their stances relaxed slightly at his acquiescence.

Just the signal he'd waited for.

"What are you doing here?"

"Visiting friends. Heard old Mr. Baldwin's been cooped up with nothing to do."

"And what would you know about it?" the second cop asked.

"Quite a bit, actually."

"Why's that?"

Alex didn't even take the time to answer. In a move he'd practiced over and over with his old partner, he charged low on the cop who was closest, gambling on surprise and fear to make any possible shot go wild. With his other hand, he had his side piece out of the back of his slacks and firing before the second cop had even reacted to his movement.

His first shot still echoing, he wasted no time in planting a bullet in the cop who'd given the order to get out of the car. Without slowing his movements, Alex pointed toward the front door, his orders as crisp and clear as a drill sergeant's. "Let's go get your wife."

He stepped over the second fallen cop, ignoring the wide-eyed gaze still locked on the brightening sky.

Chapter 15

Violet glanced at Max, his broad form stretched across the bed. She'd stood at the window for the past half hour, watching the barest glow of dawn work its way toward morning. A soft yellow now lit the room, lending a warm golden sheen at odds with the coldness that gripped her.

She'd originally figured it was just the blow of the air conditioning from the overhead vents, a necessity in Texas in August. But as her thoughts had twisted and turned, she knew it was something more.

Beneath the horror of the past few days—from the fear while in Lange's clutches to the race away from Alex to the new, more questionable threat posed by MI5—she'd hung on. She'd believed she could survive—could even get her life back—and ultimately move beyond the horrific circumstances that had descended into her life.

But now she knew there was something even more threatening—and a million times more hurtful—on the horizon.

Max held something back from her. Something big and terrible and life-changing.

She'd sensed it since their first meeting but had continued to ignore her instincts. His naturally gruff personality made it easier to chalk up his reticence or quiet to general surliness, so she'd left her impressions there and avoided probing any deeper. It was an effective cover, she knew now, and one that allowed her to place him neatly in a box, compartmentalized in her mind.

But there was no hiding from it now.

She loved him.

Heart-and-soul love. Deep and committed love. The have-coffee-together-every-morning love.

He'd painted the image in her mind as they'd ridden the train, and she'd been unable to shake it—or dismiss just how badly she wanted that reality. That daily commitment to another, through life's ups and downs, highs and lows. Always dependable.

Always *there*.

Accepting that sort of love in her life was a scary leap into the unknown, but more, it was acceptance that perhaps she'd been wrong all this time. That maybe there *were* people who wanted a relationship for all the right reasons. Not to have a partner as a showpiece or to advance their own social rank or to keep themselves company against the unbearable thought of loneliness.

Instead, there were people who believed in a relationship for the long haul.

Like Max.

So how daunting, then, that she'd finally opened herself up to the possibility, only to find a door slammed in her face.

Max did have something in his past. Something that haunted him in ways he likely didn't even realize.

She'd seen it on the train. How he'd shut down when she'd probed into his past. And earlier tonight, when they'd spoken of Knox St. Germain. Yes, Max had been a soldier. One who'd seen the horrors of battle and wartime. But the thought continued to press at her that there was something *more*.

Something else that haunted him.

"You're a man who's comfortable with the power in his body and comfortable with unleashing that where necessary. Why are you getting so prickly?"

"I'm not getting prickly. But I do find it odd you seem so enamored with my ability to destroy things. For a woman accustomed to helping others build things, it's an odd juxtaposition."

Even at that moment, lying in each other's arms, as she'd provided him an opening to share, he'd avoided it. Oh, he'd been deft about it. He'd lightly teased her but then turned the conversation firmly back toward her.

With an abstract rub at her shoulders, Violet turned back toward the window. How did she get herself into these things? She was smart. Secure in who she was. She didn't need a man to make her whole. And she damn sure wasn't ready to share all of herself with a man who gave her only a portion of himself in return.

Yet here she was, all the same.

In love. Wildly, fiercely, heart-breakingly in love.

The jingle of a landline echoed from down the hall, and Violet was almost happy for the interruption of her circuitous thoughts that took her everywhere and nowhere all at once.

Max's voice, thick with sleep and oblivious to her roiling emotions, followed her down the hall. "Tell Buck to leave us alone. Just because he gets up at the crack of dawn to go running doesn't mean anyone else cares."

The ringer pealed again, drawing her toward the spot where the cordless phone lay on a bar, dividing kitchen from living room. "Hello."

"I suspected it was only a matter of time until you'd screw Baldwin."

If Violet had believed herself cold earlier, she knew now that was only an illusion. Ice—bone-deep with edges like razors—ran down her spine. "What do you want?"

"What I've always wanted."

"They're not mine to give."

Lange's *tsk* echoed off her ear with the slippery finesse of a snake. "You persist in this notion that ownership matters to me, Miss Richardson."

"And you persist in this notion that I'm going to change my mind."

"It's hardly a notion."

The retort had nearly spilled from her lips when Violet heard the cry in the background. Soft and aged, the cry was distinctly feminine. And as Josephine Beauregard's voice traveled down the phone line, Violet knew Lange had gotten the upper hand.

"Violet! He's here. He's got us."

Violet stared down at the same cache of weapons she'd noted on their drive the previous day and had to admit, once again, that Max's skill and experience with violence was as foreign as it was reassuring. After Lange's call, they'd contacted their friends, and in less than an hour, they had all mobilized at Dragon Designs. The large, spare industrial space only added to the gravitas of the moment, and Violet found her gaze wandering, sizing up what Max and Tucker had built.

She'd been here before—several times—but the presence of enough firepower to take down a small city, all laid out on a large common table that dominated the center of the main design area, had her restless.

"What did Lange say again, Violet?" Reed asked.

She knew he was scared for his mother and trying to hide it behind action, but no matter how many times he asked, she had no other answer to give him besides the one she'd already shared.

Lange—and she assumed Alex in tow—had penetrated Max's ranch house. He had everyone under his control and expected her and Cassidy to arrive later that day with their rubies.

"And you couldn't hear anyone besides Mrs. B.?"

"No, not at all. And at the end, I tried to ask her about your mother and Max Senior, but Lange disconnected. We tried to dial the number back, but it came up unknown."

"It doesn't matter," Max ground out. "They're at the ranch and they want us there this afternoon."

"Yeah, but how'd they find it?" Tucker looked up from a laptop he'd settled on the corner of the table.

"How the hell does anyone find anything these days?" Max shot a dark look at Tucker and pointed at the laptop. "Information is everywhere. And Lange and his man Alex have proven themselves industrious. Clearly, thinking I was off their radar was the worst thing I could have done."

"Max—" Violet attempted to comfort him, shocked and more than a little hurt when he flung her hand off his arm.

"Damn fool I've been about this. Taking the damn jewels in the first place and now this. I'm responsible for them. I promised them they'd be safe." He stalked off before any of them could respond, closing himself in a small conference room in the back of the office.

Violet caught Cassidy's sympathetic gaze, but it was Lilah's harsher one that caught her unawares. "What?"

"Go to him."

"After he acted like a bastard?"

"*Especially* since he acted like a bastard."

If told at that very moment an alien had descended and taken over her best friend's body, Violet might have believed the description. "What is wrong with you? Cass I'd have expected it from, but not you. He's acting like a jerk."

"Well, I wouldn't have expected you to act like such a superior, cold-hearted bitch. You care for him and he's hurting. His grandfather is in danger. The least you could do is have some understanding."

"I do have—" Violet stopped, the truth more than evident. But it was only made harsher in the light of her best friend's dark glare. "I do have compassion. And I know he's hurting."

Lilah refused to budge, any and all of the usual traces of warmth in her gaze gone. "So why are you still standing here?"

Violet stalked off, following the same path as Max, her strides practically matched to his. Just because Lilah was correct didn't mean she had no right to be upset.

Max had shaken her *off*.

Who sat still and just accepted that?

She dragged on the door of the glass-walled office, diligently ignoring the pain that washed Max's face in a sick pallor. The urge to go to him suffocated every last ember of anger, but still she held back.

And waited to see how he'd react.

Comfort was one thing, but with sudden understanding, Violet knew if she gave in now, she wouldn't follow through. and she needed him to see reason. Needed him to understand he wasn't alone, nor was he solely responsible for all that had happened over the past few weeks.

So she'd use her lingering anger and hurt to make her point and hope like hell it was the right strategy.

"Go away, Violet. I just need a minute." He turned to stare at the whiteboard that filled one side of the walled-in space, his shoulders so stiff she wondered they didn't shatter.

"Nice attitude."

He whirled on her. "I want a minute. Is that so damn hard to understand?"

"And there's that old Max Baldwin double standard again."

"What the hell?"

"You hike off,.leaving everyone staring after you, and have the nerve to want to be left alone."

He stalked back and forth in front of the whiteboard, the movements so indicative of a caged lion that her thoughts came to a grinding halt.

All save one.

And as realization flooded over her so quickly she could barely catch her breath—Violet *knew*. She knew the secret he carried and protected as if his very life depended on it.

He was a predator.

And someone very important and high up had used that. They'd seen that quality, too, and had taken advantage of him.

Yes, he was upset right now. And fear for his grandfather and the others under his protection was a living, breathing fire burning in the belly of the beast.

But it wasn't the answer.

"What happened to you?"

"Three vulnerable people under my protection have

been kidnapped." He hesitated for a moment, then rubbed a hand over the back of his head as if trying to scrub out his frustration. "Three people who trust me and who I told would be safe."

"That's not what I meant."

Max stilled, the utter lack of movement only reinforcing her impression of a predator waiting to strike. Then Violet stilled, curious to see if he'd say anything and suddenly apprehensive that if he did speak, neither of them would ever be the same.

In that pause, Violet finally had to acknowledge the truth. Whether voiced or kept in the shadows, Max did hold something back from her. And until they brought it into the light, they had no hope for a future.

So when he remained silent, she asked once more.

"What happened to you?"

Blood thundered in his ears, obliterating everything around him with a steady roar. The urge to rabbit from that unceasing gaze consumed him, even as he remained rooted in place.

"Please don't make me ask again." Her voice was quiet, all the more powerful for that fact.

"How did you know?"

The light of battle faded from her eyes, but she remained still, standing firm across the narrow width of the conference room. "On some level, I think I've known for a long time. Your reticence about some things. The expectations you place on yourself. Even little things like how you size up a situation or watch a room. But just now, it all came together."

And there it was, Max thought ruefully. No matter how hard he tried to run and hide from his past, it was always there. Lurking. Waiting. Watching.

And always more than willing to stamp out any possibility for happiness.

With a soft sigh born of long years of acceptance, he pointed toward a conference room chair. "Have a seat."

"I'll stand, thanks."

"Tucker and I were Army Corps of Engineers. You know that."

When she only nodded, he pressed on. "We found success in the corps, both for our skills and our ability to blend into the team. We might have been the geeks who knew how to blow up bridges or divert water sources, but we were soldiers, too. Damn good ones."

"And someone saw that skill in you."

"In spades. I was put on a special mission. Covert ops to suss out and destroy a terrorist cell."

"Was Tucker on the mission, too?"

He shouldn't have been surprised how neatly she zeroed in on that fact, but he was. His own damn best friend didn't have a clue about the most important event of his life. "No. Buck doesn't know about it. We'd already been told we were splitting up for separate missions. Hell, I shouldn't even be telling you about it."

"I can handle it. And I can handle the secrecy of it."

He nodded, recognizing the truth of her words. She might be pushy and demanding and way too all-knowing, but Violet was a vault, and he didn't question her integrity.

"We had to ingratiate ourselves with the locals. Tell them we were going to find a way to help them get out from under the thumb of the local oppressors. They knew the terror cell was gaining strength, and several villagers had already been tortured for sport, so they were all too happy to listen to our guidance and advice."

"But?"

"We were really there to set a trap."

Images of those dark days filled his mind's eye. The plotting and planning, the damn *strategy* someone far above his pay grade decided upon. They'd use the poor villagers as bait and lure the terrorists into the camp.

And once all were assembled—including several high-ranking terrorists who led the cell—Max and his team perpetrated an ambush, followed by complete annihilation of the camp and all its inhabitants.

He walked Violet through it. Step by step, waiting as he uttered each and every word for her to turn from him in horror and disgust. Waiting as he told her the truth of what he'd done. That the trusting innocents who had put their faith in him and his fellow soldiers ultimately lost their lives along with forty-two of the most brutal terrorists on the planet.

"But you stopped more cruelty and violence than anyone could have possibly imagined. Those villagers were already being slaughtered, Max. You saved others from the same fate."

"By blowing them up? By playing God?" The words tore from his chest, finally free. The doubts and the self-loathing that had been his constant companions spilled forth. Like a genie released from a bottle, now that they were out he knew he'd never get them back inside.

"You did what you were ordered to do."

"That's no excuse."

"Isn't it?"

She moved toward him, narrowing the space between them, but he sidestepped her. He didn't deserve comfort or sympathy, and he damn well knew it.

"No. It's never an excuse. And it's why I got out as fast as I could. When I entered the corps, I understood my role and I did it willingly. But after that—" He broke off, tears clogging his throat.

"After that mission, I couldn't stay and keep any sense of myself."

Before he could move out of her reach, she touched him, her hands gripping his. That urge to flee grew even stronger, but Violet remained immovable.

And that was when Max knew the truth. His back was against the wall—literally and figuratively—and he had absolutely nowhere to go.

In supplication or acquiescence, he had no idea. But as he dropped to his knees and wrapped his arms around her waist, the firm beat of her heart beneath his ear, Max knew he'd finally found his home. He felt her soft hands, soothing as they roamed over his shoulders, before she stilled, clutching him tight. And he felt the warm press of her lips against his head, broken only by soft, soothing sounds of comfort.

It was only then, locked in her embrace, that Max finally let go, his silent, bitter tears falling to the floor.

Tripp Lange clutched at the ruby in his slacks pocket, the stone like a talisman as he faced his wife. She looked different. Cold. Immovable.

In only a few short days apart, she looked like a stranger. Or worse, like an enemy, prepared to do him harm.

He'd believed it impossible. On the drive with Alex to the property, he'd known in his soul that his wife would welcome him with open arms. Would see the error of her leaving and would come to him.

Yet now, as they stood across from each other, he wondered if his belief—his blind trust—had been the biggest mistake of all. Her son and his friends had brainwashed her.

And they'd turned her against him.

From the moment they arrived, she'd been cold and unwilling to even listen to him.

Alex's efficient dispatch of the local police, followed by his disarming of the old man and the landlady had been jarring for her, he'd admit. But Diana was his wife. And he damn well expected her loyalty.

Tripp had expected the old couple to end up like the police, but Alex seemed to believe there was a use for them. His man of business had carried them this far, so he opted to trust a bit longer.

They'd likely take care of them before they left anyway.

But his wife was another matter entirely.

Could she be persuaded?

A glance at her slender form had memories racing through his mind. They'd had so many good years, and she'd been the model partner. She understood the demands of his business. She kept a welcoming and beautiful home. And she took care of him.

Until her son brought it all crashing down.

Yes, he'd kept his less savory business dealings a secret. She didn't need to know how he provided for her, but simply that he did.

"How could you do it? All of it? How could you do that to us?" She stood with her back to a large window, the early morning Hill Country sun framing her like a halo. Yet even in the bright light, she kept her arms wrapped around herself as if to ward off a chill.

"I don't discuss my work."

"Answer me!"

Her outburst echoed through the room like a gunshot, and Tripp simply stopped and stared. What had happened to his wife? His partner?

He had always sensed the need to keep his less savory

business dealings private from Diana. He trusted that area of his life to a small circle of advisors, and meeting her hadn't changed his view on the need for secrecy.

But her fury was something else entirely.

"You can't be so juvenile as to think that your life was funded solely by the profits of my business."

"Yes, I did."

"Then you're beyond naive. I might not have shared the specifics of my business dealings, but I never took you for a woman who didn't understand the way of the world."

Fury painted her features at his words, an anger so raw she shook. "I trusted you."

Tripp paused, the ruby in his pocket like fire beneath his fingers. Were the gem and its siblings worth the loss of his wife? The discovery by his stepson? Even the need to lie low for a while once he had the rest of the Renaissance Stones?

Absolutely.

None of it changed the fact that she might be useful for a while longer. "Diana. You're being unreasonable."

"Unreasonable? You tried to kill our son!"

The change in subject—and the immediate jump to Reed—had him rapidly clicking through possible responses, discarding each and every one until he hit on the right approach. He did need her for a while longer, and if he could win her back to his side in the process, all the better.

"You can't honestly believe that."

"I believe my son. How you cut the brake lines in his car. Or had them cut—" she flung a hand out "—since I'm sure you refused to get your hands dirty doing the job yourself."

"He's got a dangerous job, Diana. He's a detective.

And he's into something risky and unsafe. It doesn't mean I'm at fault."

He saw it—that single moment when doubt crept in, replacing the anger—and he leaped. "I hate what's happened to Reed. And I've always hated the danger he's put himself into, even as I've supported his goals and dreams."

"You tried to kill Jessie. She's been coming to our home since she was a child, yet you tried to kill her."

Of course Reed had shared the information of their showdown the previous week with her. He and Alex had used Jessie, Reed's partner and one of his oldest friends, to pull his stepson out into the open.

The beginning of the end.

The thought stuck with swift force, large black dots swam before his vision. On a hard breath, Tripp focused on the stone in his pocket, its hard facets and heft slowly bringing him back into focus.

Back into control.

It wouldn't do to show any weakness to his wife. His love. And now his opponent and betrayer.

Although he'd hidden much of himself from her, she knew him. Almost two decades together had seen to that. Despite her naïveté about his business, she was a savvy woman, and she knew how to take care of herself.

And she'd always been better than most at figuring out his tells.

All he could do now was work the situation to his advantage.

"Diana—" He kept his voice calm even as his own anger threatened to seep through the cracks. How dared she stand there and accuse him? As if she understood the work he did that kept her in the home they shared. The clothing and the jewelry she wore. Her status around town.

"Stay away from me." As she shrank against the far wall of the room, that large window pressed against her back, Tripp finally accepted the truth. He'd believed he could change her feelings. Could build on nearly twenty years of marriage.

But he'd been a fool.

"How could you do this to us?" she cried.

"I've done nothing to us. What I've done is for us."

"Lying and scheming and stealing. And killing? That's for us?"

"You know nothing of my business or my choices. The sacrifices I've made to build a life for us."

"I know what I've been told." She flung out a hand, her movements large and sweeping. A strange awareness settled over him as he watched her as if from a distance. As if the woman before him was on a stage, murmuring words written for her by another.

She didn't understand. She didn't understand his world or his life or his choices.

"I trusted you. Believed in you and the marriage we built together. I'm your wife!"

"And as my wife, you should support me." Clutching the ruby, he hollered through the door. "Alex!"

Diana's eyes widened at his bellowing before darting toward the open door. He saw the calculation as clearly as if she'd broadcast it. "I had hoped to make this easier on you. Alex has tied up those old goats, but I thought I'd be able to have you join me as my full partner. I'm sorry I was wrong."

Alex slipped into the room, his large, ever-dependable form as quiet as a wraith. The man held a length of duct tape and stalked toward Diana.

"No. Tripp, no!"

Her protests swam in his mind like buzzing flies—

annoying and quite beneath him. That image of a stage
play again consumed Tripp as he watched Alex—his only
ally—immobilize his wife. The man's motions were swift
and efficient, economical even. And in a matter of moments, her hands and feet were bound, strapped to a desk
chair in the corner.

With one last glance at his wife, Tripp left the room,
his focus on preparing for the imminent arrival of his
enemies. He never broke his stride toward the front of
the house, even as he left his wife weeping in his wake.

Violet clung to Max, unsure of how much time had
passed. She knew she was playing with fire, pressing
him to share the demons that haunted him, but even she
hadn't been prepared for what he'd shared.

The horror. And the pain of living with those memories, locking them away day in and day out. It must have
been unbearable.

Yet despite it all, he'd worked so hard to build a new
life for himself. She knew he and Tucker had been instru-
mental in the construction of a local facility for veterans
that had recently opened its doors. And she'd also heard
through the local neighborhood gossip that he'd spear-
headed a fundraising committee for a wounded warrior
project.

He lived with his scars—and worked hard to create
something special for others—but that didn't make the
scars any less painful.

"I'm sorry." The words vibrated off her stomach,
where his lips pressed against her blouse.

"Why?"

He lifted his head, a light sheen of moisture still filling his eyes. "Because I just bawled all over you."

"You needed to get it out. Grief is a horrible burden,

and—" Before she could even finish her sentence, her words vanished in the speed of his movements. He was on his feet and had her in his arms, pulled tight against his body. The kiss was all-consuming and shockingly intimate, the emotions they'd just shared painting the press of his lips with something deeper and more meaningful than she could have ever imagined.

What has happened to me?

The thought dazed her, even as the heat between them had her rapidly losing the ability to think.

Caring. Intimacy. Devotion.

They shared something real and deep and life-affirming. And in a matter of hours, they were going to put it all at risk.

With that foremost in her thoughts, she gave herself up to the kiss, hot and carnal. Violet felt as if she'd been branded. His hands roamed over her body, seeming to touch everywhere at once, all while he maintained a steady pressure with his mouth.

She gave herself up to the power of what was between them, willing it to fill up all the dark spaces she'd kept locked up tight for so long. When they finally broke contact, she struggled to surface from the beauty and excitement of new love to what awaited them.

"You know Lange's setting a trap."

"We'd expect no less."

"Well, we can't go marching in there without knowing what we're up against."

Max pressed another quick kiss to her lips. "*We* aren't doing anything."

"You can't tell me we're honestly going to have this conversation."

"And you can't tell me you're surprised."

Violet shook her head, the reality of their impasse slamming into her as if she'd taken a header into a brick wall. "Lange's instructions were more than clear. He wants the rubies still sitting in safe-deposit boxes."

"Which you and Cassidy will retrieve this morning. Reed and I will make the delivery. Buck will stay behind and keep watch."

"I'm sure he's thrilled about that."

"Hardly." Max snorted. "But he recognizes the need for safety and knows there's no way Reed and I are staying back."

"It's not going to work. They've got all the power. You have to bring them here."

"There's no way they're going to buy that."

Violet hesitated, an idea taking shape she knew he wasn't going to be crazy about.

"I can see you thinking."

"You're not going to like it."

Max sighed and laced his fingers through hers. "Tell me anyway."

"We have a new friend at MI5. If he wants the rubies so badly, maybe it's time he put his fine British ass in the game and helped us."

Chapter 16

For as long as he could remember, Max had loved blowing things up and setting things on fire. He'd generally taken great joy in the process of destruction. He counted himself fortunate that he had an equal love of building in place of what was destroyed but—if pressed—he'd always acknowledge destruction offered up a hearty degree of fun.

He'd never have pegged Knox St. Germain as a kindred soul.

The man looked like he'd stepped off Savile Row in his dark charcoal suit and what Max assumed were Italian loafers. Yet even deep in the heat of battle planning, St. Germain's eyes glowed like a small boy's on Christmas morning as he stood over the large table in the center of Dragon Designs.

If the man had any issue with the level of available firepower occupying said table, he had refrained from commenting. He'd had no such concerns about attempting to shoot hole after hole in their approach. "And you really think you can lure him here?"

"We have what he wants." Reed tapped several photos of the rubies. "He's not in a position to bargain."

St. Germain didn't hesitate, just continued to push question after question. "No risk he'll take it wrong and eliminate one of the hostages?"

At the word *hostage*, Max felt a shot of something dark and evil line his stomach.

Hostage.

His grandfather was a hostage, all because of him. He'd believed he was keeping the old man safe. Instead, he'd left him out in the open like a sitting duck.

"He's coming home, Max. We're going to get him back." Violet had maintained a respectful distance, sizing St. Germain up from her perch across the room ever since the man arrived. At the decided shift in the conversation, she'd moved up to take Max's hand in hers.

"None of it changes the fact that I put him there. What a freaking miscalculation."

"Then it's one we all made." Reed tapped the photo of the Renaissance Stones once more. "And it's one we're going to solve. My stepfather has killed repeatedly for these stones. He's proven himself maniacally dedicated to possessing them. Berating ourselves for making decisions in good faith won't get us anywhere."

Max relaxed a fraction at Reed's earnest words. He knew the detective had a point—Lange's influence and reach were one thing, but his devotion to the stones had gone on for a long time. The man was finally close to his goal—especially as he already possessed one—and it was ridiculous to think he wouldn't move heaven and earth to see this game through.

"Baldwin will make contact." St. Germain pointed to a legal tablet he'd scribbled on. "Then we'll—"

Reed interrupted the officer. "I'll make contact. I know him, and I know what we're dealing with."

St. Germain shook his head, cutting Reed off in return. "That's the problem. It's too personal. Baldwin's got a heavy stake in his grandfather, but he's already put a chink in Lange's armor. He's the best choice for this. He can rile Lange up. Taunt him with how he swooped in and rescued Violet."

"Taunts won't keep my mother or Max Senior or Josephine Beauregard safe."

"You'd be surprised, mate."

Sensing an impending impasse, Max interrupted the two of them. "I'll make it more than clear to Lange that if anyone's harmed, we're not handing over the rubies. It's the one bargaining chip we have, but it's a powerful one."

When no one made any move to argue, Max palmed his phone. "I know what I need to do. Let's make the call and get this moving."

St. Germain slid the legal pad toward him, with several key pieces of information outlined. Time. A drop location. And the requirements to make a deal. Max scanned the same details he'd already committed to memory and reached for his phone.

Gabby had run out and secured replacements for him and Violet, dropping off their phones and another tray of food before she headed to her shop. The simple gesture of help and sustenance was as welcome as it was necessary, and they'd all tucked into a tray of lasagna like a pack of wolves.

Even the Brit had helped himself to the lasagna, his expression after the first bite suggesting he was still cursing himself for skipping the enchiladas the day before.

Max also hadn't missed how the man had sized up Gabby when she'd delivered the lasagna, but he kept his observation to himself.

And took the small satisfaction in the fact that the guy was actually human.

Setting aside his plate, Max dialed the number for his house. His sanctuary. A home that he'd designed as a getaway but now held the traces of violence and fear.

A tight knot settled in his gut, the edges pulling even tighter as a hard voice answered on the second ring. "This call better be to tell me how close you are."

"No, asshole. It's to tell you how this is going to go down."

The man hesitated only briefly before pushing forward. "Big words from a man who had his shot at me more than once and didn't have the balls to take it."

Max held back the emotion even as the tsunami of it threatened to flatten him. He focused on the job he'd agreed to do. "We all make poor choices. Don't think I'll make the same mistake again."

"Likewise."

"Where's Lange?"

"Busy."

"Then he can call me back. I don't negotiate with underlings."

The hard inhalation was more than evident, and Max filed away that bit of information. Sounded like someone didn't much like taking orders.

Interesting.

"He's expecting you here."

"Consider this notice of a change in plan."

Whatever Alex was about to say was cut off by an imperious tone in the background. "Give me the phone."

He could hear other voices, one clearly female, before

his grandfather's familiar baritone provided reassurance. Max's stomach clenched on a hard knot at the proof his grandfather was alive. Until that moment he hadn't realized how much he'd worried that it was too late.

"I'm waiting."

The harsh voice snapped him back to the conversation and the situation at hand. Max sent up a silent prayer his naturally gruff attitude and predilection for playing the rat bastard would work in their favor. "This is Baldwin. I want to speak to my grandfather."

"You don't give orders."

"I do today. I want to talk to my grandfather to ensure he's still alive and unharmed, and then we're going to negotiate."

"You should be on your way."

"That's why I'm calling. You're coming to us."

Rage—swift and strangely predictable—carried through the distance. Tripp Lange wasn't a man used to being disagreed with. "I made my request more than clear to Miss Richardson earlier."

"And I'm changing the deal. The rubies are here in Dallas, and that's where we turn them over. And in case you think you'll get somewhere playing hardball, listen up. If you so much as lay a finger on Diana, Josephine or Max Senior, you can kiss a deal goodbye."

"I *will* have the gems."

"Then you'd better ensure everyone remains unharmed. That includes roughing up by your man there."

Lange's voice was strangled when he finally spoke. "Neutral ground and a wide-open space."

"Put my grandfather on first."

"He's otherwise occupied."

"Then unoccupy him or the deal's off."

St. Germain waved at him from across the room, the

threats to call off the deal clearly not sitting well, but Max refused to back off. He'd see the avarice and greed first hand.

Lange wasn't going to allow anything to stand in the way of possessing what he most wanted.

Max heard minimal fumbling through the phone, and in moments his grandfather's voice came over the line. "Max?"

"Are you okay, Pops?"

"Fine. We're all fine. Jo and Diana, too."

Max ran through a mental layout of the dimensions of the house, the rooms he'd laid out and built by hand as familiar to him as his own palm. He'd called the landline and the only phone was in the kitchen, so Lange must have them all within the living room.

"Are you mobile?"

"We're—"

His grandfather's voice vanished, replaced with Lange. "He's fine."

"He'd better stay that way."

St. Germain had a recording device on the call, but it was his raised finger, spun in a circular motion, that confirmed what Max already knew. He was pressing his luck and he needed to wrap the call. He also sensed he was wearing Lange down, but it was a delicate balance between knocking him down and maintaining the subtle illusion of power so they could get what they wanted.

Whatever power Lange had or once had, the edges were fraying. And it only reinforced just how desperately they needed to get this over with.

"I'll meet you at Klyde Warren Park. Northwest corner. Dusk."

The park had been Violet's idea. A relatively recent addition to the Dallas cityscape, the park had been built over a major highway that ran through downtown. Open and airy, it left precious few spots to hide.

"You'd better make sure you have the gems and the women with you, Mr. Baldwin."

"The women stay behind." Max barked out the order, ignoring the dark stares that lit up the room.

"No, Mr. Baldwin, they won't. The women ensure you play fair. Miss Richardson and Miss Tate bring the gems, or those you care so much about won't make it out of the car. Understood?"

"They're innocents in this."

"Were innocents. But the moment they hid my gems in banks around town, they lost that innocence. Bring them."

Max fought the claustrophobia that threatened to muddle his senses. He needed his wits and every bit of leverage he could possibly divine out of the moment. "My grandfather, Reed's mother and Mrs. Beauregard remain unharmed. Or I pity what will happen to you."

At St. Germain's direction, Max disconnected the call. Unwilling to look at his still shaking fingers, Max allowed his gaze to drift over his comrades-in-arms positioned around the room. The old warehouse that he and Buck had turned into their office made a rather austere backdrop, but he couldn't deny it felt like home.

And as his gaze passed over each person—Tucker and Cassidy, Reed and Lilah, and then Violet—an amazing reality stared back at him.

He finally had a family. He just hoped like hell he could protect them all.

Violet let the hot water sluice over her and imagined them all later that night, Lange vanquished and their loved ones returned safely. In her vision, she could see

Max, seated beside her on her large sectional sofa, their hands entwined. Max Senior would hold hands with Mrs. B., and Reed and Lilah would have Diana tucked up close beside them.

They were safe. Unharmed.

And Tripp Lange and the evil minion who followed him like a shadow would be locked up, unable to pose a threat ever again.

Violet fought to hold on to that image, even when it shifted and morphed in her mind to one of Lange and Alex fleeing the scene, still lurking out in the shadows.

"You up for company?"

Violet saw Max's head in the doorway through the glass shower enclosure. The cold, cruel imaginings keeping her company vanished in the face of his smile. "Would you like an invitation?"

"Only if you want to make me one."

"Come on in, then."

He wasted no time in joining her, stripping as he crossed the small expanse of the bathroom. He stepped inside the shower, and she couldn't hold back the smile at his nearness and the reassurance of his large form.

And she reveled in how quickly he could lighten her mood.

"That was fast."

"Consider me a well-motivated individual."

He pressed his body against hers, the hard length of his erection solid against her belly. She gloried in the feel of him—the tension that roped his muscles and the slick rivulets of water that quickly coated his broad chest and arms. He caged her against the wall, and what should have felt like a prison simply felt like a welcome.

His mouth captured hers, the shower growing hotter as her body responded to his in the humid air. She clung to him, the events of the past few days, coupled with his confession earlier, turning her limbs languid.

She wanted him to know that she accepted him. All of him, including the parts he wanted to keep hidden from the world.

Max Baldwin didn't need to hide from her.

So she showed him with her body.

With her hands firm on his waist, she pulled him closer, rubbing against his erection with the press of her body. A hard moan escaped his lips, and she smiled against his mouth, satisfied at the effect she had on him.

Determined to have an even greater one, she slipped from his hold, turning him so his back pressed to the wall, then continued her movements. Sliding down his body, she took him in her mouth, gratified at the hard intake of breath that clenched the muscles of his stomach in hard planes.

"Violet—"

Her name vanished on the steam of the shower, and power flooded her veins at the simple, profound joy to be found in the giving of pleasure. And in the moments that followed, they surrendered to each other.

To what was a living, breathing need between them.

To love.

Max fought the swamping waves of pleasure, mad with his desire for this slip of a woman. Her generosity humbled him, and it was only as he felt himself nearly falling over the edge that he finally came back to himself. Gently pulling at her shoulders, he drew her to her feet.

"Violet."

Her name was a benediction, full of all the love and gratitude and need that he felt. He wanted her with a desperation that bordered the razor's edge of madness.

But even in that, Max knew it was something more. Something greater than himself.

He was better with her. More giving. And infinitely more complete.

The water continued to pound over them, and that steady beat that drove him on. He pressed his lips to her once more, his hands wrapping around her thighs until he lifted her against his body and buried himself within her. And as they moved as one, totally vulnerable, totally without barriers, Max knew.

He'd fallen so deeply in love that the life he'd lived up to now had simply crumbled and fallen away.

And in its place was a future he'd do anything to protect.

Knox paced the confines of his hotel suite, playing and replaying the expected drop in his mind. Lange had one of the rubies, and the women were off this afternoon to retrieve the other two stones.

The Renaissance Stones would be together again soon.

And then he'd have them, ensuring their return to their true and rightful owner.

After lunch at Dragon Designs, he'd driven to the park Violet had suggested for the drop. The wide-open space was a concern, but he'd make it work. He'd spent his life getting in and out of impossible situations, and he'd manage this one.

Failure was not an option.

Baldwin was a surprise. The man had been cool, making the call to Lange and setting up the drop. He'd played the perp like a fiddle, and Knox had been reluctantly impressed with the combination of grit and a deeper psychological understanding of the enemy.

Yep. Max Baldwin was a warrior. There was no doubt

about it. He did what needed to be done and didn't shirk what was hard. Knox had read the man's dossier, but a computer file couldn't truly give dimension to what a badass the man actually was.

But he now had an Achilles' heel in the form of Violet Richardson.

Knox had spent his life reading people, and Max Baldwin was so besotted it dripped off him. He and Violet had spent nearly forty-eight hours in forced proximity, under near-constant threat of violence, which would go a long way toward cementing feelings for each other, but Knox knew that wasn't the entire story.

There was something else there. Something that went deeper than either likely imagined.

The question was, could he use it to his advantage?

Baldwin was going to be focused on the protection of Violet before he worried much about the stones. If Knox managed that element correctly, he should be able to make the switch and get what he needed.

His mobile rang, and he snatched the satellite phone off the desk. "St. Germain."

"I trust you're close to closing this case?"

"In a matter of hours."

"Confidence. I like that in my officers."

"You won't be disappointed, sir."

"See that I'm not. And see that you update me once you've completed the work."

"Of course."

The connection winked off as quickly as it was made, and Knox imagined the man who sat at the other end. Large of stature and still relatively fit considering age, experience and the ongoing rot that had settled in the man's soul. For all the suggestion the man sat behind a desk and gave orders, Knox knew better.

Richard Moray was like the heartbeat at the very center of Britain's highest governmental organization. He had the ear of the Prime Minister and the Queen and used both with shocking acuity.

Which made what Knox had to do that much more challenging.

He had spent his life inside the British government. He knew how his higher-ups thought, which meant they knew how *he* thought.

Methodically.

Linearly.

By the book.

And nothing about this bloody situation was by the book.

He took the stiff-backed seat at his hotel desk and tapped in his password. Every action on his machine was logged and instantly reported back to headquarters, and he knew the data would be reviewed later, if not at that very moment. He could use that to his advantage.

Quite well, as a matter of fact.

He toggled back to a screen he'd studied earlier, reviewing the aerial maps of the park Violet had suggested for the drop. The park literally spanned the width of a major highway. He shook his head at the ingenuity—the Yanks had managed to build the park above a road—but it also meant all sides had exits. Which meant quick access to other places.

Ignoring the computer, he pulled up his personal phone and opened a web browser, retrieving the same website while he mentally calculated the distance between the expected drop at the park and what appeared to be the closest park entrance.

Fifty yards?

With that data in hand, he found a parking lot on his

phone and estimated about another two hundred yards from the edge of the park to his car.

It would work.

With a deft slam on the lid of his laptop, he accepted his plans were in place. His route was mapped out. And in about four hours, he would have three priceless rubies in his possession.

Moray's words filled his mind once more as he strode to the closet to retrieve the more casual clothing he'd wear on the op. A pair of khaki slacks and gray T-shirt Knox had mentally dubbed lazy American chic.

Confidence. I like that in my officers.

"You're not going to like it for long, old man. Not one bloody bit."

Chapter 17

Violet clutched her purse beneath her arm as she and Max walked out of the bank and straight into the late afternoon August heat. The ruby hadn't looked any different when she'd retrieved it from the safe-deposit box than when she'd placed it inside a little over a week prior, but it felt different somehow.

Weightier.

Whereas she'd been excited before—cautious, but excited all the same—now all she felt was a deep, penetrating dread. It lodged in her throat as if she'd swallowed the damn ruby instead of retrieving it. Even while inside the bank, a strange sort of menace had seemed to wink off the stone's many facets, and now it felt as if it pulsed from the very depths of her purse.

Had it been like that before? Or was something different?

At that thought, Violet had to acknowledge an even deeper truth. Perhaps it wasn't the ruby at all. Millions of years of the earth's pressure had formed and shaped a gem that was practically immovable.

Unlike her.

She'd spent years running from the sins of her parents—individuals who'd enjoyed meting out an odd scorecard of punishment to each other with their daughter as the prize.

And now...

Now she was with someone who made her see the true beauty and joy that came from mutual respect, caring and love.

Love.

She still toyed with the reality of that emotion. It had seemed so natural to consider those feelings for Max in the soft light of morning, after a night spent in each other's arms. But here? In the bright, vivid light of day, did she dare acknowledge it?

Or worse, admit it to him and risk him not feeling the same?

Max opened her car door, oblivious to her roller-coastering emotions as he kept his gaze firmly trained on the parking lot. He waited until she was seated before he closed the door and rounded the hood. Swift. Efficient. And most definitely in charge.

Tucker and Cassidy sat in an SUV on the other side of the parking lot, the gun Violet knew Tucker held out of sight on his lap. She and Max had acted similarly not even an hour before as Cassidy and Tucker had entered a different bank to retrieve her ruby.

Love and guns? What had happened to her life?

She was a wedding planner, for heaven's sake. She gave people their happily-ever-afters along with a kicky DJ, an open bar and a nicely plated dinner. And she did it with pride, damn it. She loved what she did. That moment when she saw the sheer happiness and excitement come over one of her bride's faces as she looked at herself in the mirror in her gown or as she posed for her wedding photo or when she shoved cake in her spouse's face in laughter.

That's what Violet did. It was who she was. She created forevers.

Or the illusion of them.

Yet here she was, her own illusions shattered into a million pieces. She'd believed herself immune to the gown and the cake and the photos.

And now she wanted them more than anyone she'd ever met. With a man who might or might not feel the same.

He enjoyed her company. Of that she had no doubt. And he liked her—their chemistry pretty much guaranteed that. But love her?

Could she possibly risk telling him how she felt, only to hear that he felt otherwise?

Even as a declaration of love stuck in her throat with a lump even greater than the imagined ruby, Violet wasn't completely bereft of the need to talk to him about the random ideas that wouldn't quite settle. She waited until Max had them back on the highway before she spoke. "Do you think we're doing the right thing? Taking the rubies out of the safe?"

"This has to end. Between all of us working together, a few of the good cops Reed's lined up to help and the assistance of St. Germain, we're going to end this. Tonight."

"I know." She hesitated, words she didn't even want to acknowledge hovering on her lips.

"Have you changed your mind?" Max asked.

"No."

He reached for her hand, entwining their fingers. "Then what is it?"

"What if the stories are true?"

When he didn't say anything, just kept his gaze on the road, she pressed on. "About the curse. What if we're doing damage by bringing all the stones back together?"

"There's no curse."

"But what if there is? And what if it gives Lange power?"

Violet knew she was being silly. Actually, she'd passed silly and had moved straight to ridiculous, ludicrous and downright absurd. Between her indecision about voicing her feelings and then using that indecision to bat the whole curse idea around, she'd definitely veered into the absurd.

But, what if?

She'd finally found something wonderful with Max. Their time together had been beyond anything she could have ever imagined. Even if he didn't love her, he liked her and enjoyed her.

And what if it was all about to go up in smoke? Or worse, what if he was killed helping her and her friends out of this whole mess?

"Those stones don't hold any power beyond their ability to make people see dollar signs."

"But they do hold power. Look at all that's happened. Kidnapping. Mrs. B.'s heart attack. Murder."

"That only reinforces *my* point, not yours."

"How so?"

Max stopped for a light and used the temporary lull to turn toward her. "Those stones lay in the floor of your shop for over half a century. If they had power, don't you think someone would have felt it? Don't you think Mrs. Beauregard's family would have felt it, too? Before she buried the stones with Pops?"

"She and your grandfather did break up."

"By mutual consent, I assume."

"Or because they were broken up by the power of the curse."

His laugh was unexpected, the tone at odds with the sudden seriousness that had filled the space between them. "I can't say I'm sorry for it. If they hadn't broken up, I wouldn't be here. And I have to say, I'm damn glad to be here."

He squeezed her hand before leaning over to press a hard kiss to her lips. "Especially after that thorough cleaning you recently gave me in the shower."

"Max!"

That husky laugh echoed through the car again as he moved forward on the green light. "Thought that might get you."

Violet sputtered a moment before coming back to herself. She never sputtered, damn it. She was a woman in control.

Even if heat was crawling up her cheeks at that very moment.

"Just because we had sex this afternoon and you are in a good mood does not mean the stones don't have a curse on them. Or that my concerns are silly."

"Sheesh, woman. Can't you give a man a few minutes to revel in some very sweet memories?"

"Revel later. Right now we have to discuss this."

He let out a long-suffering sigh as he turned onto the main thoroughfare through the Design District. Violet knew his reaction was for effect, but a small smile tilted her lips all the same.

"I'm not saying your concerns are silly. And despite teasing you, I'm scared out of my mind for Pops. It doesn't mean we should give the stones power they can't possibly possess."

"Why do you refuse to play 'what if?'"

"Why are you so insistent on it?"

Why *was* she so insistent? She certainly had never considered herself a fanciful woman when it came to things she couldn't see or touch. She's spent her life living with the belief that the proof was in the pudding and people acted as they chose.

So why the fanciful notions, layered in a panic she couldn't fully describe, even as she couldn't fully eliminate it? "You're awfully calm about this."

"Have you ever seen me calm?" Max pulled into one of the spaces in front of Dragon Designs. She had her hand on the door but he stopped her, reaching across her lap to still her hand.

When she turned to look at him, the depth of misery in his blue eyes would have buckled her legs had she been standing.

"I'm so afraid, Violet. So afraid I can barely see straight. What if we don't get there in time? Or what if he hurts Pops and Mrs. B. and Diana anyway?" Max leaned forward, his gaze never wavering as he traced a path down her cheek before cupping her jaw. "Or what if he hurts you?"

"He won't—"

Max covered her lips with his, the firm press of his mouth drowning her words. They stayed like that for long moments, their lips pressed to each other's in support and supplication, desperate to take as much from those stolen moments as they could.

A cool flow of air blew over them from the car's airconditioning, and the sounds of the city lumbered outside the windows, and still they stayed like that. Pressed together, summoning as much strength as they could from each other, as if each moment armed them with just a bit more of what they needed to face their enemy.

It's like a cocoon, she marveled as Max lifted his head, the sky blue of his eyes still focused on her. *A warm cocoon that keeps the world at bay.*

But soon they would have to emerge back into the world. Changed. And helpless to whatever it chose to throw at them.

Max listened with half an ear to Tucker, Reed and even St. Germain as they pointed out various points on a map of the park. Tucker had managed to snag a copy of the blueprints from a city database they had access to and had quickly drafted a section of the park in larger scale for them to work and plan against.

Standard op management 101.

So why was his head about a million miles away?

He'd fought the urge to call and check in with Lange, half to see if the bastard was still coming and half to check on Pops. He knew his grandfather was all right. And making the call could do more damage if Lange thought he was soft, but damn it.

It was Pops.

The old man was everything to him, and the idea of losing him turned his guts like thick cement inside a mixer. He knew he wouldn't have his grandfather forever, but he sure as hell didn't want to lose him like this.

To a madman with a streak of brutality a mile wide and the compassion of a sociopath.

"What are we missing?" Tucker spoke first, his question bringing Max back to the conversation.

"We've been over it and over it." Reed tapped the map. "We're as ready as we're going to be. I've got eyes at all four corners of the park, already there watching people come and go. They'll be ready to move in on my signal, but they won't interfere in advance."

"Lange's not showing up early." Max knew it with a certainty he couldn't describe but believed with every fiber of his being. "He wants the rubies, but he values comfort over everything else. There's no way he's sitting out in this heat, putting himself in play before he has to."

"Alex won't let him." Violet spoke up, her certainty equal to his. She'd stayed busy with Cassidy and Lilah, checking traffic cams on a web-based program Reed had provided, and Max had half believed she'd tuned out their preparation. Which was the wishful thinking of a man who wanted his woman out of harm's way, not the reality of Violet Richardson.

They all turned toward her, the certainty in her tone even more impactful than the observation, but it was St. Germain who spoke first. "Why do you think that?"

"Whatever abilities Lange has, they've either faded in time or were never all that hearty to begin with. Alex does his dirty work."

"Lange threatened Mrs. B. He's the reason she had her heart attack," Cassidy offered up. "We can't underestimate him."

"I'm not suggesting that. But we definitely can't underestimate Alex."

Max nodded, the truth of her statement borne out at every turn during their escape from Lange's compound. Alex had been the one to kidnap Violet from the hotel and then harm her once captured. And Alex had likely been the one to cut Reed's brake lines the week prior, putting him and Lilah in grave danger. And it was Alex who'd shot at Tucker on a chase through Cassidy's neighborhood shortly after the original break-in.

Lange might be dangerous, but he had help.

"But the whispers around town are all about The

Duke." Reed pointed toward a stack of files he'd brought with him from the precinct. "Everything I've been able to gather has my stepfather's chosen moniker written all over it. There's little to no mention of a henchman, just repeated references to The Duke."

"Yet we've seen the proof, and it suggests otherwise." Max moved around the table to lay a hand on Violet's shoulder. "You've got the most specific experience with him. Are we missing something?"

He deliberately kept his tone gentle and as soothing as possible—even as thoughts of Alex and the bruises he'd left behind on Violet's body were enough to drive Max to a murderous rage.

But he held it back and stayed calm for her.

"He's cold. His eyes are empty, and he takes a perverse satisfaction in meting out punishment. He's smart, too."

"How do you mean?" St. Germain moved close at Violet's statement. He still maintained a perimeter of distance, but no one could mistake the clear training. He might be the British equivalent of a Fed, but his stance was all cop.

Violet took a deep breath, her back rising beneath Max's palm. "Your first sense of him is that he's just a lackey. Sort of staying subserviently behind his master."

"But?" Max probed.

"But he's not. He's got an agenda. It's stamped in his eyes as clear as if he spoke the words. It's equally clear Lange trusts him. He keeps the man close and appears to include him in all his dealings. What he must know—" Violet broke off. "He's your key, Reed. Lange's not going to talk, but breaking Alex is the key to cracking open whatever life your stepfather has built."

St. Germain pulled out a small, sleek phone and swiped his finger across the curved face. He tapped in a few more commands, his focus absolute before he lifted his gaze from the slender device, his breath exhaling on a rush of air.

"I'll be damned."

Alex eyed the man beside him, his forehead pressed to the window as the highway grew increasingly heavier with traffic. They'd be back in Dallas in another half hour, but Lange had remained strangely quiet on their drive up from the Hill Country.

The old people and The Duke's wife had also remained quiet, but Alex had kept an eye on them throughout the drive to ensure their communication was minimal. The old lady had fallen asleep, but the old man had stubbornly remained awake.

Lange's wife spent the trip staring as sightlessly out the window as her husband.

Alex filed all of it away, even as he fantasized about killing each and every one of them. Although he'd never have recommended the meeting in Dallas as the way to resolve the situation, Lange's insistence on traveling for the jewels saved him a trip. He'd play the stoic, stalwart aid, making his move only at the very last moment.

After, of course, he'd removed the threat of discovery and the lingering noose that was Tripp Lange.

No, his time had come. Alex understood it now in a way he never had before. He'd seen himself as a loyal follower of the old ways, but the old ways were gone. Vanished as plainly as Lange's mind.

In their place was the opportunity to start fresh. He knew Lange's contacts, and it would be simple enough to set himself up as the new Duke, assuming the mantle as if bequeathed to him. He'd be far more benevolent in some ways, less forgiving in others. But unlike his predecessor, his sole interest was in assuming the core businesses—whores and numbers never went out of style, after all—and he'd avoid the rush to a public life.

He had no interest in being a pillar of society. Nor did he care one whit for a professional career.

Nope.

He wanted power. Control. And the respect that was a natural outgrowth of both.

It was not only his due. It was his birthright.

Whatever skills of subterfuge, deception and general craftiness Knox St. Germain possessed had fled as he tapped on his mobile phone. In their place was a shock Violet could only dub sincere.

"What is it? Did you find something on Lange?"

"No, his man Alex." St. Germain pointed toward the computer. "May I?"

Violet gave him her seat, standing behind him as he logged into a well-fortified database. But what filled the screen a few moments later had her gasping before Knox turned the computer to the broader team.

"He's a Nazi?" Max's question exploded in the room with all the finesse of a bomb. "You have got to be freaking kidding me."

Violet had scanned the page and seen it for herself. The file was more than clear on the lineage of one Alex Ebner.

"How the hell did anyone miss this?" Tucker stood behind Cassidy and took her hand when she lifted it to his. "And how did he end up here and working for Lange?"

Knox tapped the computer. "Radicals exist in every government in every country in the world. A quick scan of that article suggests he came from a family of devoted followers."

"Right. Of an ideology that was eradicated in 1945." Max stood to pace. "Aren't there people who monitor this? Isn't that what your fancy databases are for, Officer? To catch radicals and ensure they can't do damage."

Violet saw the battle brewing and knew Max's frustrations went far deeper. She'd seen the lingering effect of his own military experiences the day before—experiences steeped in a leadership rife with the intelligence necessary to make wartime decisions. So how had Alex and Lange flown so far off the radar?

"Is my stepfather a—" Reed broke off as he came to stand behind Lilah, the shock still painting his face in a ghostly white. "Is he a Nazi, too? Has my mother been living with that for the last two decades?"

"We've found nothing to suggest that," St. Germain said. "Lange might have taken Alex under his wing, but his focus was on a bigger game and one with more current stakes."

"Has Alex shown any other signs? Was he involved in hate crimes or any sort of organized push to advance his goals?" Violet asked the question, her own memories of his ready capability for violence shooting through her stomach in dark, greasy waves.

"No." Knox sighed. "The only reason we have this information is that his lineage flagged something in the government databases when he applied for a visa. He's got no record of any crime, and guilt by association isn't in anyone's jurisdiction."

"So are we going on the assumption he is or isn't a card-carrying member of a party dissolved seventy years ago?" Lilah asked. "I admit the whole concept gives me the creeps, but he's already proven himself to be a dangerous adversary, with or without Lange's implicit orders. Does his background matter all that much?"

"No. We're going on the assumption he's dangerous, and that's all that matters," Max said, the words falling from his lips like acid rain.

"You really don't care?" Violet wasn't sure why she suddenly did, but Max's complete disregard for the situation had her as confused as Lilah. "You don't think this is some clue?"

"Other than further reinforcement that Alex is a fellow psycho who has some power complex just like his boss?" Max shook his head. "I can't see it meaning much more."

"But it may explain how they got connected. And how my stepfather managed to garner such loyalty from the man." Reed moved toward the stack of folders about his stepfather. "If we find the connection, we may find a weak spot."

"Or we may simply end up with one more piece of this weird puzzle we can't solve." Violet didn't want to be the bearer of bad news, but for the first time since they'd developed their plan, she had to admit her fear of failure trumped her belief in their success.

What were they all walking into?

And was it disloyal to think they could very possibly be outmanned and outmaneuvered?

Even as she asked herself the question, Violet knew there was no way out. If they went to the meeting, they risked everything. And if they didn't go, Max Senior and Mrs. B. and Reed's mother were as good as dead.

Whether it was Lange or Alex pulling the strings really didn't matter. They wanted the rubies and had proven themselves more than willing to do whatever it took to possess them.

* * *

Max strapped a small side piece to his calf before standing to help Violet with her Kevlar. Had there been any other way, he'd have convinced her to stay home no matter how much she protested. Hell, he wasn't above tying her up to keep her safe, but Lange's expectations were clear.

Violet and Cassidy were to arrive with their stones.

As plans went, Max grudgingly had to give credit. The presence of the women, while risking their safety, only added to Lange's. But it made what they had to do that much more difficult.

He and Violet had garnered some small measure of privacy in a corner of the office, while Cassidy and Tucker took the corner opposite and Lilah, Reed and St. Germain still stood in conversation, heads bent over the park layout. Tucker held it together, but Max knew his friend, and he knew their trip to the park had Buck in knots.

Max ignored his own knots and focused on what he could control. The training he and Tucker had from their days in the corps made them well suited for what lay ahead.

No matter how many times he told himself that, his feelings for Violet had torn him in the opposite direction. How could he do what needed to be done when all he could think about was her? Her safety and well-being were foremost in his thoughts, but they weren't his only concern.

He'd seen the horrors of war. The evil people could do to each other. He'd give anything not to expose her to the same.

"Are you going to kill him?"

The question stilled his hands as he fitted his own vest, and Max simply stopped and stared. "Who?"

"Alex. Lange. They're almost interchangeable at this point."

"Not to me."

That green gaze was sharp, but confusion clouded the edges. "Why not?"

"Alex put marks on you. He beat you and, while you won't say it, I've no doubt he enjoyed it. For that, I'd give anything to kill him myself."

"Oh."

Max refocused on his vest, unwilling to look at the censure in her eyes. He already knew what he'd see: the horrified realization that he was a heathen at heart.

He'd tried to tell her. He'd shared what he'd done to the villagers while battling the terrorist cell, and she'd seemed oddly unfazed.

Perhaps now she'd finally understand what made him who he was. What made him wholly unsuitable for her.

"Max."

He tugged on the last strap, pulling his vest tight. "What?"

"Look at me. Please."

He'd look at her—he had far too much respect for her not to—even if he already knew the censure he'd find in her gaze. And the reality that they had no future.

He'd been deluding himself, thinking they could have a relationship.

But once this was over, he'd let her go back to her life. No matter what he believed about the two of them—or how deeply he felt about her—he had to let her go.

She deserved better.

On a hard breath, he lifted his gaze. "What, Violet?"

"I love you."

The breath never made it past his lips. Instead, it caught in his chest, stretching the Kevlar tight. "What?"

"I love you, Max." She moved up into his arms, her lips a whisper away even as she kept her hands at her sides. "I love all of you. Your loyalty. Your dedication. And I love how you make me feel."

"How's that?"

"Protected. Precious. Special." She pressed her lips to his, the warm welcome more than he'd ever deserve. "And sexy. We can't forget that one."

"Violet." Her name came out on a harsh moan as he dragged her into his arms. "You're all those things. And I'm putting you in danger. What does that make me?"

"Since we're both strapping on vests, I'd say we're both in danger."

"I know how to handle it."

"I've faced off with crazy brides. Don't underestimate my skills."

"I love you. I can't bear the idea that something might happen to you."

"Then let's trust in our plan and make sure it doesn't."

Max reached for her as she leaped into his arms. The move was immediate, as natural as breathing, and oh-so-right. Their lips met, and he was desperate to show her in the physical all he felt inside.

He wanted a future with her. And while he'd been on far too many missions to take her comment as anything but deeply naive, he found himself believing her anyway.

They had love on their side.

And now that they'd found each other, there was nothing he wouldn't do to keep her safe.

Chapter 18

The drive to Klyde Warren Park should have been a short one, but the early evening traffic was at a standstill. Reed crept, inch by inch, toward their destination, the snail's pace only raising the tensions in Lilah's delivery van to the point of breaking.

St. Germain had opted to drive alone. Violet wasn't sure how she felt about that, but she had to acknowledge it might be for the best their new friend was on his own. Or so she told herself. There was something about the agent that didn't settle right, and she couldn't define why.

She'd originally thought it was the fact that he was new to their small circle, but she discarded that idea when she acknowledged Tucker, Reed and Max were also quite new to their circle. And then she'd suspected it was Knox's natural British reserve, but even that didn't quite fit.

It really came down to one thing. Why was MI5 so interested in helping them?

She'd chewed on that since they'd returned home to

find Knox St. Germain in their kitchen, and she hadn't reached a satisfactory answer. In the end, Violet admitted, even if only to herself, if the problem went away and their loved ones were returned safe, did it really matter anyway?

With that foremost in her thoughts, she reached over and patted Cassidy's arm, the gesture a mirror to her friend's only a few days before. The drive home after her ordeal at Lange's hands seemed like it had happened in another lifetime.

And maybe it had.

Since returning, she'd made love to Max, accepted him into her life and fallen in love with him.

She was light-years different from the woman who'd stood outside a downtown hotel on Saturday night, contemplating her life and her future.

There was a time she'd have believed that transformation impossible. Yet when she'd finally given in—finally opened her eyes and *see* Max standing right before her—it had been so easy. And so very, very right.

Reed took the last turn for the park and pulled into a small parking lot in short walking distance. Although they'd argued about any number of getaway scenarios, they'd ultimately opted for basic parking, with the added benefit of backup from the cops Reed had already put into place.

"You're sure the cops are sound, Graystone?" Tension rode Tucker's words, the harsh tone so at odds with the normally laid-back man. Violet caught Cassidy's gaze, the quick roll of her eyes conveying exactly what they both needed to say.

Like her, Cassidy was strapped into Kevlar and carried a gun of her own. She'd also repeated their strategy and mapped out the plan to Tucker at least three times on the drive.

Despite the eye roll, Cassidy was gentle. "We're ready, baby. Please believe me."

"Promise me you won't take risks?"

"I promise."

Their conversation matched the one Lilah had had with Reed before they headed out, and again, Violet was struck by how much their world had changed in such a short time. She and her two best friends. All of them single, now all of them in love.

The ruby she'd protected since removing it from the safe-deposit box was hard in her grip, and she relaxed her hand, opening her palm to look at the stone. The fiery color that immediately identified the gem as a ruby winked at her in the dying light from outside the van window.

She'd been sincere in her questions to Max earlier. While the rational part of her didn't believe in curses, the question still lingered.

Did the stones hold some sort of power? And if they did, was there even greater power to be had in bringing them together?

While each of their relationships were unique, it was difficult to argue with the fact that a month ago, she, Cassidy and Lilah were all single.

And now, all three of them were desperately in love and planning their futures.

Did the stones have an impact?

"It's time."

Max interrupted her wayward thoughts, and Violet opted to keep them to herself. As far as she was concerned, it didn't matter how she'd found Max. What mattered was that she had found him. That truth lingered in her mind as he extended a hand to help her out of the van. And as she gazed into the crystal-clear blue of his eyes, she knew the truth.

How they got together mattered far less than all the reasons in the future they'd choose to stay together.

Alex pulled the zip tie into place around the old man's wrists before dragging him out of the large black SUV. He'd sensed a bit of fight in the old bear and braced himself for some sort of attack, but the man had remained surprisingly docile.

Which only set Alex's senses on high alert.

The old man had something up his sleeve. Of that he was sure.

With a nod toward the old woman he'd already tied, he pushed Pops toward her. "Hands out. Both of you."

The lingering fear he'd seen off and on in the woman's gaze flared to life, but the stubborn old man just stood still, staring him down.

Just like his grandson.

Alex fought the light shiver that raced down his spine at the blatant show of disrespect. Without thinking, he gave the man a hard shove into the side of the van. Baldwin's age coupled with the surprise attack had him stumbling, and the woman screamed out as he fell to the ground, unable to break his fall.

"You monster!" She screamed it over and over, her voice rising with increasing shrillness before he dragged out his gun.

"Shut up. Now."

The unease he'd felt at the selection of the park only grew. Even with the later hour, there were still people milling about, and he questioned again the wisdom of coming here.

"Alex. Leave them alone. Help the man up." Tripp stood by his side, his wife firmly in hand, her wrists already tied.

A wave of loathing nearly had his knees buckling, but Alex held it together. He reached down and dragged on the old man's hands, pulling him to a sitting position. He had to give the guy credit. He might be frail, but he was determined. Baldwin Senior dragged his hands away, rolling himself to a standing position as he shunned any further help.

"Max. Are you okay?" The old woman practically whimpered as she came to stand beside him.

"I'm fine, Jo. Let's get this over with."

Alex dragged one more zip tie out of his pocket and pulled at the two sets of bound hands. "You want to help each other so much. Why don't you work on standing upright."

Ignoring the feeble attempts to wrench their hands away, Alex managed to get them tied and stuck together before he moved behind them. With the old man's ability to run even more hobbled, he forced them to perp walk toward the northwest corner of the park.

As they'd arranged, Violet and Cassidy walked ahead of him and Tucker. Max fought the urge to move forward and cradle Violet beneath his arm and knew Tucker fought the same battle about Cassidy.

"How you want to play this, Buck?"

Tucker turned toward him. "Whoever has the cleanest opportunity gets them out of here as soon as the gems are passed. Whoever's left runs detail with Reed and his men."

"Men I'm still not fully convinced we can trust."

"I trust Reed. That's got to be enough."

Max knew the detective had done everything in his power to ensure the smoothness of the op and his mother's safety. Reed had spent quite a bit of time hand-selecting the men and women who were currently stationed around the park's perimeter. He'd also brought in Masterson again, and Max already knew the computer whiz to be a good guy.

But damn it, he didn't want to take any risks. None. Zero. Zilch.

"You know I want a shot at Alex." Max whispered the words, unwilling to have them catch on the light summer breeze that brushed through the park.

It wouldn't do to have Violet get wind of his plans. Literally.

"I know. And I'll give it to you if I can, but Cassidy and Violet come first."

"Of course."

Max understood what that meant now. Violet would always come first.

They found benches in the corner of the park, the late hour ensuring the area was empty. The support team Reed had brought in had also swept the area for their needs and had removed any unnecessary foot traffic.

They were exposed, but they weren't without help. He had to keep remembering that.

"Don't move."

The voice whispered behind them, and Max whirled, unsure of how any of them had missed Tripp Lange's entrance.

And then he was forced to reassess that. The man looked several decades older, his disheveled appearance at odds with the suave man-about-town he'd always been.

All except for the eyes.

That cool, reptilian gaze stared back at him, assessing Max, then moving on to Buck and further to Reed, Violet and Cassidy.

"You have the gems."

"Where's my mother?" Reed shifted on the balls of his feet, the only indication of just how close he was to leaping on his stepfather and beating the answer out of him.

"She's safe. For now."

"Why did you do it? She loved you. Cared about you. Why did you betray her? All of us?" Reed asked, the questions spilling forth with all the force of a geyser.

And then Max saw it. The gentle touch of both Violet and Cassidy, calming Reed as he stood before Lange.

The image he'd held before reformed in his mind, solidifying in that moment. Violet was a warrior. In the greatest tradition of the Greeks and Romans, she was a goddess—a woman who understood the real values in life. Friendship. Honor. Love.

The love he had for her welled up in him, seeming to spill outward even as it filled him to the point of bursting.

She was everything to him.

"Enough games, Mr. Lange. Where are Diana, Jo and Max Senior?"

"Safe."

"Get them. Now."

"Due time, Miss Richardson. Due time." Lange's eye were flat. Soulless.

"Are you hard of hearing?" Max tossed the insult, drawing Lange's attention off Violet. Curious as to what Lange might do next, Max was suddenly grateful St. Germain hadn't shown yet. The man would likely be giving him signals to wrap it up and minimize the jabs so as not to poke the bear in his den.

But Max was beyond caring. It was time to end this.

He kept his voice even and smooth, an effort not only

to control the situation but also to keep calm and order and minimize the roiling chaos that already gripped each of them with tight fists. "Why don't we move this off to those benches over there? I picked the northwest corner for a reason. This is between us, Lange. The rest of the park needs to remain unharmed. Call your man, have him bring your hostages over and we'll make a deal."

"Big words for a man who doesn't have a leg to stand on. I've got the people you care about, and if you don't quit screwing around and give me what I want, I'll start picking them off one by one."

The image of his grandfather dying at the hands of such a brutal criminal nearly stilled him, but Max chose that moment to go for broke and prayed Pops wouldn't be harmed for it.

"Then we walk. Let's go."

He risked his back, and it was only when he turned that he saw St. Germain in the distance, his casual form spread out on a park bench barely visible from their position.

"Don't toy with me, boy. You're not leaving without getting what you came for. Neither am I."

At St. Germain's subtle nod, Max turned around. "Fine. So how are we going to play this? You already have one ruby, and we could care less about the other two. So hand over the people who matter to us, and you can have what you came for."

The disheveled image that had greeted them seemed to shrink even further as he worked through the decision in his mind. Max shot a look at Reed, confusion stamping his friend's gaze. Whatever man had been part of Reed's life—even if he'd had a dual nature—was gone.

In his place was a worn old man trying desperately to hold on to a power he no longer possessed.

His hands trembling, he lifted his fingers and made a gesture to someone off in the distance. In moments, his grandfather, Reed's mother and Mrs. Beauregard appeared on the path, Alex following in their wake.

Max kept his gaze trained on Alex, the man's stance stiff as a soldier as he directed his charges. He knew he'd managed to nick the guy's knee in their shootout on the farm, but the stiff, even gait and focus on his task made him appear impervious to any lingering pain.

Was it possible?

Who could compartmentalize like that? The psychopath they'd feared in Lange had a clear counterpart in the soulless eyes of Alex Ebner.

"As you requested, Mr. Lange." Reed rushed toward his mother, but Alex shifted his stance to show off a handgun pointed squarely at Diana's back. "Let's wait, shall we?"

Reed stilled, his gaze locked on his mother's. Max left Violet to communicate silently with their landlady, and he focused on Pops.

A strange sense of unreality settled over Max as he stared at his grandfather across the small expanse of grass. Had it really come to this?

Was he at risk of losing the only father figure he'd ever known to a madman and his sidekick?

"They're fine." Lange moved forward, placing himself between Pops and Max. "Now I want what's mine."

Pops never moved, but he telegraphed his intentions with his eyes. And in that moment, Max sensed what they needed to do. Moving forward, Max faced Lange and placed his sole focus on the man.

"You've waited a long time for this." Max let his gaze drift toward Alex. "You, too. You both have a common heritage. A common background."

"I hire only the best." Lange practically preened with the answer, and Max left the hook baited while he slowly worked on Alex.

"Hiring those loyal to a cause. Any cause will do, when you come right down to it. But someone who believes in the old ways. Believes in their restoration. It's a powerful tool, isn't it, Alex?"

"I don't need tools. I know what I'm about."

"Restoration of a lost society and the power that comes from domination and fear?"

"I come from a society focused on being the best. The brightest. The strongest. It's in my blood. It's my heritage."

"Yet you chose to hook up with Lange." Max shook his head even as he dropped one hand behind his back, signaling Tucker into position on the opposite side of their little party.

"He was the best!"

Alex's shout—and the use of the past tense—gave Max all the answer he needed.

Was.

And then it all came together. The events of the past weeks had all centered on one core truth. Everything that had happened to Violet and her friends had come from connections. The setup for the initial break-in. The murder of Cassidy's former fiancé and Lilah's ex-husband. Even the placement of Reed on their case to help grease the information channels for Lange.

Everything had centered on the connections between the players.

There were no coincidences. And there sure as hell weren't any accidents.

But it was time to end it all.

With his attention back on Lange, Max moved up into

the man's personal space. "You show us your gem and we'll show you ours."

"Give them to me."

"Don't you want to see the three of them together? Feel the power of finally possessing all of them?"

"Yes."

That lone word was a whisper, and Max was careful to keep his gaze neutral as he looked over Lange's shoulder and into Pops's eyes.

They knew what needed to be done.

Lange reached into his pocket, and Cassidy and Violet did the same. All three extended their hands, the bloodred rubies like fire in each of their palms.

And then they made their move.

Pops pushed forward, his motions in step with Mrs. B., their combined force knocking Lange forward and making him unsteady on his feet as he stumbled. The ruby flew from his hand to land somewhere in the grass behind the line Max and his comrades had formed, and Lange let out a howl of pain as he rushed to find the gem.

Tucker surged forward in front of Cassidy and Violet, putting himself between them and Alex while Reed rushed for Alex's gun.

Max turned, ready to snatch Lange from behind when the man's body shook with an unnatural force. Lange screamed, his body trembling from the force of two bullets in rapid succession. It took only seconds, but they stretched on forever as he processed the scene before him.

"Gunfire! Everybody down!" Max shouted the order, scrambling to protect whoever was in easy reach. He had the Kevlar and placed himself over Pops and Mrs. B. as Tucker, Cassidy and Violet did the same for Reed's mother.

Reed added orders of his own, but it was all for naught

as a silent shot went whizzing through the air, centered square on Alex's forehead.

The strangest look of surprise painted the man's visage before his body went slack and he toppled to the ground.

"Who the hell!" Reed screamed the question as St. Germain ran toward them. "Knox! Down!"

"Stay down!" The officer screamed the order as he stared in the direction of the gunfire. "I don't have eyes on the shooter."

Max repositioned himself in protection over Pops but prepared to help the officer. The fact the shot was silent only added to the confusion rapidly descending over all of them.

Who fired the shot that took down Alex?

But it was when Knox stood that the real mystery became clear. Three rubies—each retrieved from where they'd fallen to the ground—were clutched in his hand.

"Thanks, mates. I couldn't have planned it any better myself. Do me a favor now, and don't come after me. You're free of this. See that you stay that way."

The officer ran off, weaving through the light of various park lamps, his form growing dimmer and dimmer as he headed for an exit.

Max wanted to race after him, but one look at Violet and he was rooted to the spot. She was okay. They were all okay. And Lange was dead, along with his henchman.

A glance toward Tripp and Alex's still forms only verified what he already knew.

Even as every fiber of his being hollered to stay put and not move, Max got to his feet. "We need to go after him."

"No, son. You need to stay right here. Where you're needed." Max turned to see Pops smiling up at him.

"You've done right by your duties. We all have. But it's time to let those stones go."

Max pulled out one of the various tools he had on his person and cut the zip ties on Pops and Mrs. B. before handing the tool to Reed. He gently freed his mother, then helped her to her feet. Diana had remained strangely quiet, her gaze locked on her dead husband until the removal of the zip tie seemed to free her.

She threw herself into her son's arms, hugging him tight. "You're okay."

"I could say the same about you."

"My baby. You're all right."

Violet crossed the small patch of grass that had seen so many revelations and such quick and deadly violence. If he'd expected her to shrink at that fact, she did the exact opposite.

She stood tall as she stepped into his arms.

Max reveled in the feel of her beneath his hands, relief a palpable force as his blood pumped through his veins. "You know what I was thinking before, when I had to stand there and watch you face off with Alex?"

"That no ruby is worth this?"

"That. But it was something more." He pressed his lips to her forehead. "You are a warrior and a goddess. A woman without comparison. And if you're willing, I want to make a life with you. A home. Maybe even a few really cute babies."

Violet lifted her head, an odd gleam in those green eyes. "*That's* what you were thinking as a bunch of goons had guns on us, held our loved ones hostage and threatened our lives. Oh, and if that weren't enough, our new British friend double-crossed us."

"Yeah. Sort of." He fumbled before catching the wink

of humor behind the smile she tried to hide. "Call me selfish, but yeah, that's exactly what I was thinking."

"Would you think less of me if I said, 'Me, too'?"

Max pulled her close for a kiss, the chaos of the past weeks fading away against their new reality.

"I'd say we're a matched pair."

"I'm stubborn and selfish and I like order. Are you sure you can live with that?"

Although he wanted to keep it light, Max knew the fears that lay beneath her words. So he answered her the only way he knew how.

With the truth.

"I'm grumpy and sullen and I still have days when my past seems more present than my future. But I love you. And I'd like to wake up every morning and see your face across the table."

"Coffee every morning? Together?"

"Together."

She wrapped herself around him and laid her head against his heart. "I can't wait to get started."

As he tucked her beneath his chin, his pulse finally beginning to slow to a dull roar in his chest, Max knew he felt the same.

He'd found his forever.

More precious than any gem, and full of the promise made in each and every heartbeat.

Because each and every beat was for her.

Epilogue

Knox clutched at the wound that gaped against his fingers and kept as much pressure on his shoulder as he could manage. He'd tried to feel around the wound as he ran for the car, but between juggling the stones in one hand and slowing his blood with the other, he hadn't managed a full assessment.

Richard?

Richard freaking Moray. The man hadn't been in London at all, but had stood at the edge of the park, watching and waiting for the drop.

Bastard.

He thought he'd cleared the scene but hadn't counted on what a damn good shot Moray was. His silent bullet had struck flesh as Knox was clearing the park. He managed a shot of his own, but the satisfaction was short-lived as fire ate a steady line from his shoulder toward his collarbone.

Knox dug the key from his pocket and unlocked the

rental. The white edges of the car blurred in his vision, and he was forced to wonder once more if the bullet was still in his shoulder.

Be a flesh wound. Simple. Easy. And in my wheel-house to fix.

A wash of pain blurred the edges of the car into even more indistinct lines of white and gray, and he pressed his shoulder once more. Ignoring the fuzzy edges of the sedan, he dragged the car door open and flung himself into the driver's seat. Pain radiated in spirals from the center of his shoulder toward his chest and stomach, and he fought the urge to gag.

Focus.

He could collapse later.

Where, however, was the question.

The hotel was out. There was no hiding a gunshot wound in a gray T-shirt. So was a dining establishment. Even if he got through the door, he'd never make it to the loo without someone noticing.

The button to start the engine felt hard beneath his index finger as he fumbled to punch it. The car made a hard sputtering noise and he pressed his foot once more to the brake, willing the engine to turn over as he stabbed the button again.

One glance out the rearview mirror and he saw Moray closing in. The shot he'd managed to the man's knee had slowed him, but he was still moving at a steady clip.

Riding a wave of adrenaline—likely his last for the evening, if past experience was any indication—Knox slammed the car into Drive and peeled out of the parking lot. The car shook beneath the hard turn onto the main road and the heavy push of his foot on the gas pedal, and he barely avoided missing a snazzy Jaguar.

Pushing onward, images of Moray right behind and

closing the gap, Knox took a hard left at the light for the Design District. He'd mapped several getaways earlier, including the several quick shots out of the city via one of the many highways that converged minutes from the park.

He needed the highways, yet he'd mapped a route to the Design District on a whim.

A whim he associated with one person—Gabriella Sanchez.

Knox knew damn well he could never see her again, but as the next light took him in her direction, he decided to go for broke.

He'd ditch the car a few blocks away and walk to her place. He'd charm her into giving him the time to stitch up and eat something, and then he'd be on his way.

It would work.

Besides, if he didn't stop soon, he'd pass out, and his efforts would be wasted.

The antiques shop he'd seen two blocks from Gabby's store was the perfect spot to leave the car, and he parked close to the grass in an effort to minimize the visibility of any blood on the ground. He staggered from the car, the woman who'd spent an inordinate amount of time in his thoughts in the last day filling his mind's eye.

Long curly hair. Warm brown eyes like the richest chocolate. And a body that was all long, lithe lines and soft curves.

Knox staggered past the antiques shop, a florist and a bakery before he saw the sign for Taste the Moment. Lights were visible through the window, and he hit the front door, counting off each step as if doing penance.

As he stumbled over the stoop, his body slammed into the front door's glass with a hard thud.

Had he come all this way for the store to be closed, the lights nothing but a mirage?

Knox pressed against the door once more, toying with simply shooting the lock off, when he heard a series of muttered curses through the glass.

"What the hell are you—"

The woman who'd occupied his thoughts for an interminably long twenty-four hours leaped toward the door, dragging it open.

It took every ounce of training—and a considerable layer of self-respect—for Knox to keep his feet. "Good evening."

"What is wrong with you?" Her eyes roamed over him, widening when she registered the blood pouring from his shoulder.

Just like the car, the edges of her delightful frame wavered as he tried to process her words around the increasing swoosh of his pulse in his ears.

And then his adrenaline simply gave out. He stumbled forward, pushing her backward with the force of his body. The last thing he remembered before the world went black was the hard press of her arms around his waist and the soft wash of hair that covered his cheek.

His last thought was that she smelled like home.

* * * * *

MILLS & BOON®
Christmas Collection!

Unwind with a festive romance this Christmas
with our breathtakingly passionate heroes.
Order all books today and receive a free gift!

FREE GIFT!

Order yours at
**www.millsandboon.co.uk
/christmas2015**

1015_MB515

MILLS & BOON®

Buy A Regency Collection today and receive FOUR BOOKS FREE!

4 BOOKS FREE!

Transport yourself to the seductive world of Regency with this magnificent twelve-book collection. Indulge in scandal and gossip with these 2-in-1 romances from top Historical authors

Order your complete collection today at
www.millsandboon.co.uk/regencycollection

0915_ST19

MILLS & BOON®

The Italians Collection!

2 BOOKS FREE!

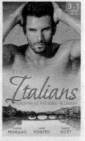

Irresistibly Hot Italians

You'll soon be dreaming of Italy with this scorching six-book collection. Each book is filled with three seductive stories full of sexy Italian men! Plus, if you order the collection today, you'll receive two books free!

This offer is just too good to miss!

Order your complete collection today at
www.millsandboon.co.uk/italians

0815_ST17

MILLS & BOON®

Why shop at millsandboon.co.uk?

Each year, thousands of romance readers find their perfect read at millsandboon.co.uk. That's because we're passionate about bringing you the very best romantic fiction. Here are some of the advantages of shopping at www.millsandboon.co.uk:

* **Get new books first**—you'll be able to buy your favourite books one month before they hit the shops

* **Get exclusive discounts**—you'll also be able to buy our specially created monthly collections, with up to 50% off the RRP

* **Find your favourite authors**—latest news, interviews and new releases for all your favourite authors and series on our website, plus ideas for what to try next

* **Join in**—once you've bought your favourite books, don't forget to register with us to rate, review and join in the discussions

Visit **www.millsandboon.co.uk**
for all this and more today!

MILLS & BOON®

INTRIGUE
Romantic Suspense

A SEDUCTIVE COMBINATION OF DANGER AND DESIRE

A sneak peek at next month's titles...

In stores from 16th October 2015:

- **Lone Wolf Lawman** – Delores Fossen *and*
  Scene of the Crime: The Deputy's Proof
  – Carla Cassidy
- **Secret Agent Santa** – Carol Ericson *and*
  Her Undercover Defender – Debra & Regan Webb
  Black
- **Clandestine Christmas** – Elle James *and*
  Hidden Witness – Beverly Long

Romantic Suspense

- **The Colton Bodyguard** – Carla Cassidy
- **Cowboy Christmas Rescue** – Beth Cornelison
  & Colleen Thompson

Available at WHSmith, Tesco, Asda, Eason, Amazon and Apple

Just can't wait?
Buy our books online a month before they hit the shops!
visit www.millsandboon.co.uk

These books are also available in eBook format!